Praise for Erin La Rosa

"*Plot Twist* is a love letter to the romance genre, to sisterhood, and to the strength of those in recovery—an absolute gem."
—Ashley Winstead, author of *The Boyfriend Candidate*

"Erin La Rosa delivers…. *Plot Twist* is a can't-miss romance that will leave readers swooning. I give it five stars—and five chili pepper emojis."
—Kate Spencer, author of *In a New York Minute*

"This sweet and spicy rom-com is a true treat! Witty and fun, yet firmly grounded in reality, *Plot Twist* is escapism at its best."
—Lacie Waldon, bestselling author of *The Layover*

"Spicy. Sexy. Swoony…. Rachel Lynn Solomon and Christina Lauren fans will love this story!"
—Suzanne Park, author of *So We Meet Again* and *The Do-Over*

"Utterly charming and fun! *Plot Twist* gives readers a steamy ride while also respectfully handling serious topics. A delight to read and sure to be a favorite."
—Mariah Ankenman, author of *The Firefighter's Dilemma*

"Sweet, deliciously steamy, and ripe with unexpected depth… *Plot Twist* will have readers pining along with the characters until the utterly satisfying happily ever after."
—Meredith Schorr, author of *As Seen on TV* and *Someone Just Like You*

"*Plot Twist* pulls at your heartstrings… If you decide to pick up a book this season, let it be La Rosa's enchanting novel."
—Silvana Reyes, writer at Book Riot and @thebookvoyagers

"An expertly-crafted contemporary romance."
—Becky Feldman, host of the *Too Stupid to Live* podcast

"Another sharp, sly, and very steamy rom-com from Erin La Rosa! La Rosa shines at genuinely funny and feminist romantic tales, and I'll read every single one of them."
—Amy Spalding, bestselling author of *For Her Consideration*

"This heartfelt and laugh-out-loud-funny romance had me rooting for Sophie and Dash until the very last page."
—Melissa Baron, author of *Twice in a Lifetime*

"*Plot Twist* is a sweet and spicy romance for everyone who loved Erin La Rosa's delightful debut."
—Elissa Sussman, bestselling author of *Funny You Should Ask*

Also by Erin La Rosa

For Butter or Worse
Womanskills
The Big Redhead Book

Look for Erin La Rosa's next novel
Change Your Tune
available soon from Canary Street Press.

PLOT TWIST

TWIST

ERIN LA ROSA

CANARY STREET PRESS

CANARY
STREET
PRESS™

Recycling programs
for this product may
not exist in your area.

ISBN-13: 978-1-335-45811-7

Plot Twist

Canary Street Press
22 Adelaide St. West, 41st Floor
Toronto, Ontario M5H 4E3, Canada
CanaryStPress.com

Printed in U.S.A.

For Lizzy and Shay, thank you for always being the first people to read my drafts (and for the pasta nights, obviously).

PLOT
TWIST

1

SOPHIE

Sophie Lyon was not in a good place.

More specifically, she'd had one (or three) too many the night before. So instead of falling asleep on her bed, she was lying on the couch with a paperback book as a makeshift pillow. Her legs were tucked up in the fetal position inside her billowy dress. And as she licked her lips, she tasted vodka and fried chicken, which she didn't remember drinking or eating.

She attempted to open her eyes, but her lashes stuck together from the makeup she'd forgotten to remove the night before. With the help of her index finger and thumb, she managed to peel one lid open. White-hot summer light poured in through the arched living-room window and her mint green walls, a color she'd specifically chosen for its soothing properties, were mockingly chipper.

But even more unsettling was the book on the coffee table directly in front of her, *Whisked Away*. Sophie's first published book. She closed her one good eye and wished she'd never opened it.

Her mom had always dreamed about Sophie filling an entire bookshelf with all her titles, the years of working multiple day jobs while tinkering on romance books finally worth the struggle. But, as it turned out, *Whisked Away* would be Sophie's one and only book. Had she known she'd be a one-hit wonder, she wouldn't have ordered the little placard for her writing desk: Ask Me about My Tropes.

The worst part was that she *had* sold a follow-up book—or, at least, a pitch plus the first three chapters—but she hadn't been able to finish *The Love Drought* (a title so tragically similar to her own personal problems that it made her cringe). She'd been given multiple extensions but missed all of them. And, per her contract, her publisher had the right to terminate their deal if those deadlines weren't met. But no matter how many drafts she started, Sophie couldn't find her way to the happily-ever-after that all romance books promised and that she loved.

The phone call with her agent started with *We need to talk…* and ended with *You have six weeks to finish this book or your contract, plus the advance, will be taken back.*

She'd spent most of that advance, though, along with the royalty checks that grew smaller and smaller as interest in her last book waned. She needed money from turning in the next book if she wanted to continue paying for things like food or a place to stay.

She should've seen the implosion coming. Her horoscope had warned that the entire month of June would be bad for important communication. But the damage was done: Sophie was a romance author with writer's block, and in six weeks' time, she'd lose her publishing deal.

So she'd done the only thing she knew would make her feel better: called Poppy. And her best friend had suggested a night out at their favorite downtown karaoke bar to drown away the loud whir of failure.

She cautiously sat up, then settled her feet into the woven jute rug. Her legs were as firm as Jell-O when she stood. Still, she managed to make it to the hallway mirror, where she saw that her normally side-swept curtain bangs had morphed into Medusa, snakelike tendrils across her forehead, and she had more flakes on her face than her pet goldfish had in his bowl.

She cringed. *Rain Boots.* Her goldfish was twelve years old and the longest relationship she'd ever had. She planted her hand on the wall for support and shuffled over to her bedroom, where a large glass fishbowl sat on her bedside table. Rain Boots swam in the exact middle and blinked at Sophie with large accusatory eyes.

"I'm sorry, honey," Sophie croaked out. "I know we have our bedtime routine, but Mommy got horribly drunk."

She tapped the glass with her index finger and waited for a response, but none came. Eventually the silence broke when her doorbell loudly ding-donged and caused her to jump in surprise. The next, and bigger, surprise came when she made her way to the front door and saw her landlord waiting on the porch.

Dash Montrose wasn't a tall man, but he had presence. Part of that was because he always seemed to be fidgeting—tapping his fingers, shifting his feet, or pacing slightly—but also, he had thick arms with swirling, inky-black tattoos.

It's not that Sophie had stared at those arms in prior instances but…well, yeah, she probably *had*.

Still, her first instinct was to hide behind the couch because what the hell was Dash doing there? She and Dash lived next door to each other, but they were not close. In fact, Dash hardly ever acknowledged her existence. He lived in the large house tucked behind her bungalow, but he was always walking away in some kind of a hurry. If she waved, he only ever nodded back. She didn't think he was intentionally being a jerk, but he clearly had no interest in interacting with her. They hadn't spoken actual words to each other in at least a few months. She Venmoed him the rent, and sometimes he left a thumbs-up in response. That was the extent of it.

But there he was, in jeans and a T-shirt. What could he want? Did he somehow know her funds were about to run out and he was preemptively evicting her? Sophie avoided confrontation at all costs, but she couldn't run away from him, not when his face was pressed against the window of her door and he was peering directly at her. She clutched her arms across her chest, extremely aware that she was still dressed in her clothes from the night before, as she made her way to him.

When she opened the door, she was hit not only with the heat from the high sun above but by the sight of Dash's wet hair slicked around his face. Water trickled down his neck and splotched his faded shirt, like he'd come straight over from a shower. Which meant a few minutes prior he'd been totally naked, covered in soap and water and...

"Hey, uh, whoa." His voice cut through Sophie's thoughts. When she glanced up, Dash gave her an uneasy expression, then gestured down the length of her. "What happened..."

She never left the house without a minimum of tinted sunscreen, but of course Dash came on the one day where she closely resembled a Madame Tussauds wax statue melting in the sun. Sophie gently swiped her index finger under her eye, and it came back coated in black liner. *Excellent.*

"Vodka happened," she muttered.

She rubbed the liner between her fingers. Something was wrong. Mercury must've been in retrograde. If thirteen-year-old Sophie had known that she would be renting a place from Dash Montrose—former teen heartthrob movie star turned still-hunky landlord—and he was seeing her hungover...she'd be even more embarrassed than she already was. And she'd probably also be delighted. Because Sophie had maaaybe had a photo of him from a magazine cover on her wall when she was growing up. His film *Happy Now?* was her all-time favorite movie.

She absolutely did *not* have a crush on adult Dash, though. Well, he was undeniably hot. No point in glossing over that thick, dirty-blond hair, the dimple in his chin, or any of the other tatted-up details. But he was Poppy's brother and so off-limits that Sophie had built a wall around Dash in her mind. Though bits of the wall appeared to crumble at the sight of his strong jaw and the dark circles under his eyes that made him all the more mysterious to her.

"Poppy asked me to come check on you. She said you weren't answering your phone." He glanced behind her, as if searching for a potential thief holding her cell hostage.

"My Poppy?" Sophie had worked at Poppy's spa, Glow, for years—one of the many day jobs she'd had before quitting to write full-time. Though, now that she had endless writer's block, she might have to beg for her old job back.

"She's my sister, so she's technically *our* Poppy." His hands landed in the pockets of his jeans.

Sophie looked behind her to where the phone usually was, and blessedly, while she'd been drunk enough to use a book as a pillow, she'd been just sober enough to plug in her phone. She rubbed at one of her throbbing temples and walked over to her desk, grabbed her phone, then held down the power button and watched the white icon flash back.

As she waited for the phone to boot up, she walked back toward Dash.

"Okay, she wants me to tell you that there's a video of you going viral?" Dash gestured to his phone, which made his forearm flex and Sophie's eyes widen in response.

She tried to process what he'd said. She needed an intense boost of caffeine—maybe a matcha—to be able to comprehend the words coming out of his mouth. "A video?"

"I don't know, she said you needed to see it. And that I needed to make sure you saw it." He shrugged, but the small motion lifted the edge of his shirt up just enough for Sophie to catch a glimpse of his boxers.

Sophie didn't want to be impolite—Dash was Poppy's

older brother, after all—but what was she supposed to do? She couldn't so much as look at a candle shop without rushing in to buy one. Dash was the male equivalent of fresh beeswax. She was definitely staring.

Just then, her phone erupted in a series of pings, vibrations, and what sounded like one deafening goose honk. If she owned pearls, she'd be clutching the hell out of them. The screen filled with notifications—emails, texts, missed calls, and push notifications from Instagram—but she pulled up Poppy's text conversation first.

Soph, are you up?

It's 10. You never sleep this late.

I'm at work, ARE YOU OK

I'm sending Dash over.

YOU'RE NOT DEAD! YIPPEE!

OK, here's the vid. Don't freak out!!

Dash's phone pinged, too, he looked down, then sighed. "Did you get it?" He sounded a little irritated.

Sophie frowned at the blurry thumbnail of a woman, but clicked the link, which sent her to the TikTok app. Then, almost immediately, she saw herself reflected on the screen. The video was taken at the karaoke bar, and Sophie was the main event. She stood onstage as the undeniable background music to Elton John's "Tiny Dancer" played. She had requested that song, hadn't she? The small pieces of her lost-memory puzzle began to click into place.

Only, in the video, she was sobbing, with tears running

down her cheeks, as she gazed wild-eyed into the crowd. Poppy ran onto the stage and attempted to coax Sophie off, but Sophie grabbed the mic and shouted, "I've never been in love, okay?!" Her voice was so angry and vehement that she appeared to be deranged. The person holding the phone zoomed in at that exact moment to capture Sophie's grimace as she shrieked out, "Love isn't real!" Then Poppy yanked the mic out of Sophie's hand and dropped it for her. End of video.

"Stop, stop, stop!" The words screeched out of her as she furiously poked the screen to try to delete the video. Then she remembered this was not *her* video—someone else had uploaded it. Eventually, her eyes drifted down to the caption, which read Relatable! The video had over two hundred thousand views and thirty thousand likes.

"Oh, my holy hot hell." She was a writer but could not think of any other words in that moment. Her mind raced at the thought of hundreds of thousands of people watching her have a public meltdown and *liking* it.

Normally, Sophie was an optimist, but after the last twenty-four hours, she was beginning to understand the appeal of pessimism. Her hand instinctively went to her chest and her fingers tap-tap-tapped at her pacemaker—something she always did to steady herself—as she scrolled through the comments and saw that not one but multiple people had recognized her.

Sophie Lyon is FUN

Sophie Lyon is secretly unhinged and it's sending me 👏

I hated her book, but I like this?

"Just breathe." Then Dash's hand was on her back, steady and warm, which momentarily distracted her, but not for long. The heat outside had intensified to Palm Springs–level boiling and caused Sophie to break out in either hives or a rash. She furiously clawed at her throat with her free hand. She walked away from Dash and down the porch steps. Her bare feet hit the cool blades of grass in her yard, and when she looked up, the iconic Hollywood sign perched in the Santa Monica Mountains shined pearly white in the distance. Seeing those letters from her yard every morning used to make her feel closer to the success she so deeply craved, but now she felt buried under the weight of its implied expectations.

She stumbled, and Dash was next to her within seconds, holding her steady. He grabbed her elbow with one hand, and the other wrapped around her waist to cup her hip. His skin was warm against her, even through her dress. Her stomach flipped, probably from the lingering alcohol. "Sophie, you really need to sit. You look like you're about to faint—"

The sound of her phone pinging cut him off. And when she looked down, a familiar name flashed across the screen. *Carla.* Sophie stopped scratching her throat. Her ex. The woman who she'd dated for close to a year. A year in which Sophie could feel herself beginning to fall head over heels, and then... Carla had ended it and dragged their relationship to the trash. Sophie stared at Carla's name, and the text underneath, which read Saw the video... As in her ex had seen the video of Sophie having a full-on meltdown.

It was at this moment that she tilted her head back, let the punishing sun burn her eyes, and shouted as loudly as she physically could. When she eventually stopped screaming, her head felt light. The edges of her vision blurred with the realization that she had nothing left, her life was over, and she was completely mortified.

"Seriously, Sophie? My ears are ringing."

Sophie was so focused on her own humiliation that she must've forgotten that Dash was *right there.*

"Are you *on* something?" Dash asked.

Sophie frowned. No, she was not *on something*. She may have been braless, hungover, and hanging by a thread emotionally, but what kind of an accusation was that?

And even if she were on ayahuasca and beginning to see rainbow caticorns encircling her feet—which sounded great, actually—what she did with her body was absolutely none of his business. She paid her rent on time. This was her place. He was the one who'd come bounding over, all wet and wearing a too-tight shirt, and now he had the nerve to suggest she was the one out of line?

She would tell Dash that he needed to leave. But when she opened her mouth to say as much, she felt the bile rise in her throat. Her eyes bulged wide as she closed her mouth and held back something akin to a burp. Dash clocked her panic, and his eyes narrowed. She shook her head, but there was no use. She was definitely going to hurl all over her high-school celebrity crush. And without even being able to call out a warning, she projectile-vomited all over Dash.

2

DASH

Dash growled at the vomit on his shoes.

The thing was, he'd *just* showered. Like, he'd been in the shower and enjoying a post-workout scrub and tug, to be honest. He'd soaped up his hands, grabbed his dick, and thought about his head between a woman's thighs, licking his way up while being watched. He was all about eyes. Give him eyes that sizzled like hot pavement in the dead of summer. Eyes that crinkled at the edges with mischief. A woman who could give him a single look and make him hers. He hadn't had sex in eighteen months, and while he didn't have much sexual tension with anything these days, beating out any lingering needs never hurt.

But then he'd heard his phone ping, then ring, and when he looked at the caller ID he was nervous because Poppy only called when it was an emergency. So he'd turned off the water, quickly towel-dried, and answered.

He hadn't intended to be gone for more than a few minutes to check on Sophie, but now he was still holding her elbow to make sure she didn't crumple to the ground like a slinky. And then, of course, there was the vomit. Which was just…not great!

Sophie's head lifted, and her dry, bloodshot eyes met his. "I'm so, so sorry." Her painted nails flashed like bright red warning signs as she wiped at the corners of her mouth.

Even though he didn't want to spend another minute in this situation, he couldn't just leave her there. He was going to have to help her back inside because, with her shaky legs, she looked about as stable as a Chihuahua in a wind tunnel.

"Do you think you can walk?"

She shook her head no. "I just need to stop moving for a minute, if that makes sense?"

He let out a resigned sigh. "Sit here. I'll get you some water."

"Can you make it a coconut water, please?" She looked up at him. "Extra electrolytes. Thank you!"

She'd clearly been spending way too much time with his health-nut sister. He cocked his head in an intentionally mocking way. Then he quickly moved up the steps, through the open front door, and into her place.

Well, his place, legally speaking. But as he eyed the potted ponytail palm, the framed photos of clementines over the gas fireplace, and the honey-lemon couch in the center of the room, he realized this wasn't really his anymore. The guesthouse was sunshine—unrecognizable from when he'd first rented the plain one-bedroom to her. He couldn't say he appreciated all of Sophie's choices—he was pretty sure an IKEA kitchen table was threatening to disintegrate from the weight of a stack of notebooks—but this wasn't his space to decorate.

And he couldn't linger for too long, as Sophie was waiting. So he walked to the kitchen, went to the sink, and cleaned up with paper towels. His shirt was another matter, so he decided to just take it off. Dash carefully peeled the shirt over his head, crumpled it into a ball, and threw it in the trash.

In the kitchen, she'd installed a twee, retro-looking fridge, but the only food inside was a half-eaten wheel of Manchego cheese. There was, however, an abundance of water options—sparkling, mineral, and coconut, which he grabbed a bottle of.

As he walked toward the door again, she was not sitting in the grass, as he'd instructed. Instead, she stood at the top of the steps with her body pressed against the pillar for support. Apparently, she hadn't listened to him at all.

"Dash…what happened to your shirt?" She smiled, a cocked little thing that raised one side of her mouth and revealed a very pronounced canine tooth, like a demented hungover vampire. He'd occasionally found that smile charming, but today? Not as much.

"Someone puked on it." He gave her a tight nonsmile back.

A hot wind whipped across the porch and her dress opened slightly to reveal a sliver of freckles that trailed between her breasts.

He coughed and looked away. Part of the problem was that Dash had always found Sophie attractive. Before renting to her, he'd met Sophie through Poppy a handful of times, and every time, he inevitably noticed something kind of tempting about her. Like, when she genuinely laughed, it was loud and uncontrolled and caused people to turn and stare. And perhaps it was a little weird, but he liked the scar on her chest and always wanted to ask her how she got it—he knew there was a story there. Not to mention that she wore these light, flowing dresses that clung to her whenever there was so much as a slight breeze…

But despite all those little details he continued to notice, he knew that he had to keep his distance from Sophie Lyon. Because not only was she his tenant but also his sister's very best friend in the whole world. And his sister didn't have a lot of close friends. None of the Montrose children did, because of who their family was. And he wasn't about to mess up the one true connection Poppy had just because he thought Sophie was kind of cute.

"You're dehydrated," he quickly said, clearing away any lingering thoughts. "Here's your papaya water."

"Coconut water," she corrected. "But thank you." She reached for the bottle, and their hands met. Despite the heat outside, her fingers were icy cold.

"Don't take this the wrong way, but you're not usually this… messy." He couldn't think of a better word for what she was in that moment, but he still winced as he said it. "What happened?"

She let out a pitiful little laugh, then unscrewed the cap and took a small sip. "Well, my life is over. Like, I will probably never work again, and I'm totally embarrassed, and I can no longer go to karaoke bars. And I *love* karaoke, so it's kind of tragic… Did you *see* the video of me?"

"I did." He'd watched it over Sophie's shoulder right before she let out the scream of an angry banshee. Not that he blamed her. She'd gone viral while drunk and shouting that love wasn't real. How many times had he been wasted and done things he couldn't remember?

"Are you going to make a response video or something?" Dash tried to be helpful, as TikTok was something he actually knew a bit about. "People would eat that up."

"A response video?" She swallowed loudly. "Maybe I'm just really hungover, but I feel like you're not using words correctly." She rubbed the back of her hand across her forehead.

Why had he said anything? He didn't need to be doling out advice, but he couldn't seem to help himself. "Just tell people your side of the story. And make sure to add hashtags. Those are important."

Sophie frowned. "The thing is, I don't really have my own side of the story. What I said is true—I've never been in love."

"So I heard," he said jokingly, but she just carried on talking.

"And I can't seem to finish my next book because I can't figure out how to give my characters a happily-ever-after." She blew air through her lips. "Sorry, I know I talk a lot."

She talked a lot *and* kind of quickly. But Dash wasn't comfortable with people who just unzipped their issues and spilled their feelings all over the place. He found that a lot of actors had this quality. Being on camera meant you were required to be able to tap into a range of emotions at the word *Action!* But he'd never gotten used to the immediate openness of his former job. Dash was more of a tin can when it came to feelings: tightly sealed, hard around the edges, and not worth the effort.

So he did what any person would when wanting to avoid emotions and pivoted the conversation. "I'll carry you to the couch," he said.

"You will not carry me," she said. "Dash, that's absurd."

"I don't have all day." He checked the time on his phone, as if he had somewhere to be when, really, he had an entire day of *nothing* ahead of him. "If you fall here, it's much more serious than falling in the grass. And besides, I can bench-press at least five of you."

Her gaze flitted to his bare chest, and he decided to flex his pecs, just for fun. She awkwardly coughed at that, but eventually looked back up.

"Come on." He came next to her. "Wrap your arms around my neck and I'll scoop you up." He planned to put his hands underneath her knees and lift once she'd latched on to him.

"I want to die," she said. But she wrapped one, then both hands around his neck.

"If you do, Poppy will kill me, too." He wrapped an arm around Sophie's waist and another behind her knees. Her head was tucked under his chin, and her soft hair grazed his Adam's apple.

"Okay, one, two, three." He picked her up so her body pressed into him and her arms tightened around his neck. The soft fabric of her dress brushed against his skin and gave him goose bumps despite the heat outside.

"I'm not sure if *this* or the vomit is more embarrassing." Her breath came out hot against his chest as she spoke.

"The vomit." *Definitely the vomit.* He took careful steps toward the front door and into the living room, then quickly deposited Sophie on the couch.

"Need anything before I head out?" He was desperate to get home. A headache loomed just behind his eyelids, and he pinched the bridge of his nose with his fingers. Surprises were not his idea of fun, in general.

"No." Sophie undid her messy bun, and wavy honey hair spilled around her face. Then she looked up at him. "Thank you. I feel like I owe you rent and a half now."

But she didn't owe him anything, seeing as he didn't have plans or anywhere to be. Not unusual for him. More like the usual, really. He had hobbies—a collection of things he'd slowly built up to fill the hours. He could tend to his basil plants and pick some for a pasta later. There were always more episodes of his favorite reality show, *Dating Roulette*, and he could start a new crafting project while he watched. Or he could see if there were any ripe avocados on his tree to pluck off.

But he was mostly trying to keep to himself. Because his job—which his sister, and the rest of his family, didn't know about—was to stay sober, one day at a time.

"You don't owe me anything," he finally said. He hadn't meant to look at Sophie, but he did. And she gave him what seemed to be a genuinely appreciative smile. He almost smiled back but then remembered the morning he'd had.

Instead, he looked away and broke their eye contact, then

grunted in response, and turned to walk out—making a point not to look back.

When he opened his heavy dark-wood front door and closed it behind him, he took a deep breath in then out. His entryway smelled like wet grass and lemon from the homemade candle he'd lit earlier. He walked across the plush charcoal entry rug, and the tension he'd been holding in his shoulders eased. He was home, in his safe place.

He padded along the terra-cotta floor toward the hallway, then headed into his living room, where he lay on his modern leather couch. He wanted to decompress, so he grabbed his phone and opened TikTok. He had about fifty new notifications from people liking his latest CraftTok video, where he'd made a speckled vase. His account, @tokcrafty2me, was anonymous. He never showed his face or used his name. Not only because his parents would eviscerate him for making social-media videos instead of what they considered real films, but as he was trying to figure out what to do with himself he really didn't want any extra attention.

He'd been in a few indie movies with cult followings over the years, then stopped acting altogether when he decided to get sober. But sometimes he still got recognized, and that wasn't what his TikTok was for. His account gave him something that was solely his own. He'd spent his whole life growing up in his dad's shadow, then his older brother's—Reece had become even more famous than their dad. When Dash went into acting, his family assumed he'd happily follow down the same yellow brick road. And he'd tried to be as successful as they were because he knew that's what they'd wanted for him. But then he never really landed the roles his mom hoped he would. And drinking became the only way he could cope with the pressure from his family and being on set. And suddenly, the clear path that had been presented to him was so fuzzy he couldn't see a way out.

Dash shook the memories out of his head. He was staying focused on building a new life without drinking, and crafting had given him an unexpected outlet. He went into his mentions and scrolled through the likes, giving a few comments a heart back. His account had a little over fifty thousand followers, which was strong, considering he only uploaded two videos a week. Compared to some of the other crafters he followed, who posted daily, he was lagging. Then he tapped into his DMs and saw a message from Cindy, a crafter he was friendly with.

@craftycindy your speckled vase is showing

Well, maybe *more* than friendly. Their DMs often bordered on flirty or were just straight-up innuendo. Which Dash didn't mind at all, seeing as he had no other sexual outlet to speak of.

@tokcrafty2me I showed you mine, show me yours? he typed back.

Dash exited out of the app and went to his texts. Can you talk? he texted Chris, the man he'd met at an AA meeting and was now his sponsor and best (and maybe only) friend.

To his surprise, his phone buzzed, and Chris was FaceTime calling. Dash took in a big breath as he tapped *Accept*. "You know, most people consider phone calls to be rude these days."

"Most people don't have a four-month-old asleep on their chest." Chris's eyes were puffy, and even his hair seemed to flop into his face from exhaustion. He panned the phone so Dash could see a sleeping Luna and the back of her dark curls.

"Are we going to wake her up?" Dash asked.

"Nah," Chris responded. "This one sleeps like she got hit by a two-by-four. I've been rewatching *The Takeover* and not even the title sequence wakes her—Mira made those drumbeats loud."

Mira, Chris's wife, was a composer, and her latest theme

music for an HBO family drama had earned her an Emmy nomination.

"How is Mira?" Dash poked. "She doing okay?"

"She's exhausted." Chris wiped a hand down his face. "We're both barely sleeping."

"I'll come by this week." He reached for the remote on the coffee table. Maybe he could try watching *The Takeover* instead of *Dating Roulette*...though, probably not. "You and Mira can sleep. Luna and I will hang. I'll take a day off," Dash said as a joke.

Every day was his day off, really. Plus he liked kids. He'd always wanted a big family of his own, but he knew that would never happen—he couldn't put a child through the possibility of him relapsing. But if he was lucky, he'd have the kind of marriage Chris and Mira had someday, when he was solid in his sobriety. Just not now, while he was still learning who his sober self was.

"Okay, I'll take you up on that, but only because I can't remember my own name anymore." Chris blinked hard. "What did you want to talk about anyway?"

"I was feeling a little..." Dash did not finish the sentence with the words that immediately rang true: anxious, wound-up, restless. Instead, he cut to the chase. "Long story, but my hungover tenant needed help."

"Right." Chris scratched at his beard. "Do you need a meeting?"

"Maybe." Dash pursed his lips.

"Make time for one." Luna fussed slightly on Chris's arm. Chris eyed her, then looked back at the phone. "I better go."

"See ya," Dash said, then hung up.

He stared at the blank screen for a beat, then pocketed his phone. He got off the couch and went to the window that looked out at the lawn and Sophie's bungalow. Her door was closed.

He didn't see her outside. She was likely fine. Still, his gaze lingered on the arched window next to her door—identical to his own—and he wondered what she was doing.

SOPHIE'S TIKTOK
Name: Sophie Lyon
Occupation: Writer (???)
Weeks until next book is due: 6

"I've never been in love, okay?! Love isn't real!" Sophie had queued up the clip from her unintentionally viral video, then it cut to her in the living room, where she sat on the couch. A response video, just as Dash had suggested.

She fixed the curtain bangs around her face and took a deep breath in. "Well, *that* was me, and it's pretty embarrassing. But yeah, I've never been in love. Which is maybe a little weird, considering I'm a romance author. And as you can see, I'm not afraid to spill my emotions after a few drinks, but I've never experienced the feeling of actually falling for someone so…"

Sophie cleared her throat. "Anyway, a friend of mine told me I should explain my side of the story. And I think he's right."

She leaned closer to the camera. "We've all had a bad day. And that—that video—was one of my very worst days. I'm going to be totally honest with you: I am on the verge of losing just about everything I've worked for. I have writer's block, and my next book is due in six weeks. It's been two long years, and I can't figure out the ending. I'm a total fraud, and once my contract is up I will have to accept the fact that maybe I'm not a writer, after all."

Her lower lip wobbled at the sad realization that she'd been so close to achieving her dreams but hadn't been able to keep the momentum of being a full-time writer going. She eyed the ceiling, blinked away the impending tears, then looked back to camera. "But I'm still a hopeless romantic. Like, I *believe* there's someone out there for me. And there have been relationships in my life where I really, really thought I was going to fall in love. But something keeps me from saying the words. So what's my problem? I don't know. But I want to find my person, and maybe the answer is that *I'm* the problem, not my exes."

Her knee started to nervously bounce, and she placed a hand on top to still it. "Would it be weird to go back and ask my exes what went wrong? I mean, there could be something they noticed that I never did. And maybe if I figure out why I can't say those three magical words, I'll find a way back to writing a happily-ever-after for my characters." Sophie's tone lifted as the words began to feel true. Maybe this whole thing *could* work. Perhaps all she needed was a little self-exploration to get to the root of her issue. "Tell me what you think in the Comments."

She stopped the recording, then hit Next, chose a thumbnail, wrote a caption—I'm the romance author who's never been in love ☺—added some writerly hashtags, per Dash's suggestion, and hit Publish. The video had an option to post to her Instagram page, and if she was going to put herself out there, she might as well go all in—so she published it there, too.

She fell back into the plush couch cushions, tapped her phone against her thigh, and wondered, not for the first time, if she was doing the right thing.

3

SOPHIE

"Hey, you okay?"

Sophie almost didn't register her sister's concerned voice over the loud hum of paparazzi shouting at them, but she still managed to mouth a *yes*.

"Nina, one more photo!"

"Nina, where's Leo? Trouble in paradise?"

"Nina, any details on the final episode of *Second Chance Kitchen?*"

Sophie kept her eyes trained on the entrance to Craig's as they walked. She was keenly aware that the photographers didn't want a photo of her, and after her brush with TikTok fame, she'd had her fill of being a news item. But Nina stopped and gave a quick smile for the cameras. Her sister had, of course, planned this breakfast excursion. Craig's was strategically frequented by celebs who wanted to have a photo opportunity with the line of paparazzi who waited outside and then enjoy a meal at the discreet and private restaurant. Nina was a celebrity chef, and the season-two finale of her latest cooking show,

Second Chance Kitchen, was about to air. As Nina liked to say, the more press the better.

Sophie got to the door and pulled it open just as a paparazzo's voice sailed over the crowd.

"Nina, is that a baby bump?"

Sophie's eyes darted to Nina, whose jaw went tight. She didn't wish bad things to happen to other people very often, but whatever jerk had called that out deserved to be pooped on by a bird in one of the overhead palm trees.

"The only baby you'll see on me is a food baby," Nina called out. Then she plastered on a megawatt smile and calmly walked past Sophie and into the restaurant. Once the massive door shut behind them, though, Nina's fists balled at her sides.

"They never ask Leo about having kids," Nina quickly said.

Sophie sensed her sister needed to rage, so she joined in. "I bet this restaurant has very heavy pots. Want me to throw one at that guy's head?"

Nina sniffled. "Yeah, would you?"

Sophie rubbed Nina's back, and they stood close together for a beat. Nina and her husband, Leo, had decided early on that because of their busy careers, they weren't ready to have kids and maybe never would. Still, Nina had gotten her eggs frozen, just in case they changed their minds. Sophie knew her sister was okay with their decision, but she had a right to be annoyed that she was the only one ever asked about it.

"What did I miss?" Poppy's long blond hair was tied up in a high ponytail and swished as she walked toward them. She wore flowing black pants and a matching top, looking equal parts resort chic and like a CEO in uniform. She removed her designer sunglasses and slid them into a pocket on her shirt. "Why are you both sad? Did they run out of that really tasty pita bread? I miss everything by going in the back way."

As a habit, Poppy avoided anything to do with celebrity,

which wasn't easy considering she lived in Los Angeles and happened to have a very famous family.

"Oh, just the patriarchy at it again." Sophie readjusted the sleeves of her lime green caftan. She owned pants but never cared to wear them.

Poppy crossed her arms solemnly. "I know those dummies well."

The outdoor patio had a high fence covered in climbing vines and an overhead canopy of dangling plants and cream shade sails to block the sun. Their table in the corner was private enough that they could have a conversation and not be overheard, which was why Sophie supposed Poppy immediately launched in after they'd placed their food orders.

"This is a safe space. We were best friends in our past lives, too. You know that, right?" Poppy's fingers slid toward Sophie's hand and gave her a sincere squeeze. Sophie *did* know that because Poppy had told her as much after her recent hypnosis session.

"How are you feeling?" Nina crossed her arms and studied her. She was the older sister and had practically raised Sophie. Ever since their mom passed, she'd become the de facto parent.

"Not great. I have six weeks to deliver a book I can't finish, and a video of me drunk-sobbing to Elton John went viral. I can move into your place when I run out of money, right?" Sophie's voice went up at the end, as a chunk of her pride chipped off.

"I'm usually the cynic. It's weird to see you so down." Nina's brows pinched together. "The viral video thing sucks, I'll give you that. But you're a writer, and you'll write another book."

Sophie didn't want to whine or complain, but… Nina's career was completely different from hers. Nina had known from a young age that she was going to be a chef, and she'd worked every day of her life to make that happen. Whereas Sophie had always wanted to be a writer but had never had the same courage to fully commit. She'd tried out every single job other than writing to find something else she could do: a practical, reliable gig with a steady paycheck. She wasn't brave and fearless, the way Nina was. She wanted a job that would bring her the security they'd never had growing up. Unfortunately, her passion just happened to be writing—one of the most unstable and least lucrative of all the creative pursuits.

Their waiter set down their food—crab omelet for Nina, avocado toast for Poppy, and a burrata plate for Sophie—which was a great excuse to not talk.

Once the waiter left, though, Nina continued, "I don't want to go all Hollywood-PR-machine on you, but your video going viral is an opportunity. You can build a brand-new audience so that when you do finish this book, you'll get on that bestseller list, like you've always wanted. BookTok is one major way books blow up, and fans of your first book tagged you in the video. Now they know you're a romance author who's never been in love, which sounds like the plot of a rom-com, if I've ever heard one. So give your fans *that* story."

"That story? You mean, my story?" What exactly was her sister suggesting? Sophie wasn't a character in her own book, she was the author.

"Soph, you work well when you have a roadmap. For *Whisked Away*, you used Leo and me as inspiration." Nina shrugged. "Why not use yourself?"

Sophie had based *Whisked Away* loosely—very loosely, as she'd mentioned in interviews—on her sister's real-life romance with Leo. She'd turned both love interests into bakers and utilized the secret-billionaire trope. But Nina was right: Sophie had been able to finish the book because she knew how it ended. She'd had their relationship as a kind of outline.

"But your answer here is that I do the very simple, quick, and easy thing of falling in love in order to solve all my problems?" Sophie wanted her question to hang for a beat so Nina would feel, even just momentarily, a bit silly. But that was not who Nina was, and so she launched back in with solutions.

"Just take control of the narrative." Nina cut into her omelet. "People paying attention is an opportunity, and you should see the comments—they're rooting for you."

Sophie remembered some of the comments.

My new Tinder bio.

You and me both, sister.

mood.

"Don't just roll over and never write another word again. Writing is your dream. So do whatever it takes to make it come true." Nina leaned across the table, then added, "Mom wouldn't have wanted you to give up."

Well, Nina definitely knew how to punch Sophie right in the feels. Their mom had been so encouraging of Sophie's writing and always knew she'd be a published author. What *would* she say about this situation if she was still around?

"How many views does your new video have?" Poppy cut off a piece of avocado toast and popped it into her mouth.

"Six thousand." Sophie held the phone up, as if it were evidence in the trial of *The People of TikTok vs. Drunk Sad Lady.*

"I'd raise my eyebrows, but I just had some Botox." Poppy pointed to her forehead, which didn't move. "Trust that I'm impressed."

When *Whisked Away* came out, Sophie's publicist, editor, and agent had all encouraged her to build up her social-media presence. The more followers she had, the more book sales they could bring in. Which meant she had to try her best to curate an exciting and bookish life, like an author you might want to be friends with. Even though she was squarely an introvert, part of the game was putting herself on display. So she'd posted selfies wearing bright pink lipstick in bookshops, lined up her to-be-read list in her apartment, written quippy captions, and done Ask Me Anythings on her Instagram stories. She wasn't famous, like Nina, but she had fans.

Still, she had a sinking suspicion this was not what her team had in mind when they suggested she try to grow her social following.

"Are you really going to meet up with your exes?" Nina sipped from her cappuccino. "As someone who made the mistake of meeting up with an ex to hash things out, it doesn't always end well."

"I don't want to see them either, really, but maybe I'll learn something about myself. I mean, it's weird that I've had a few long-term relationships but never said *I love you*. And I do want to find someone." Sophie fanned herself, feeling intensely warm from the overhead sun plus all the attention.

Poppy suddenly gasped and covered her mouth with both hands. Still, she managed to talk through the hand wall. "Carla. Heart doctor slash heartbreaker. You won't see her, right?"

Sophie stabbed a piece of burrata with her fork and took a bite before answering. "Carla did text me."

Poppy gripped the sides of the table dramatically. "No! That gorgeous temptress. What does she want?"

When it came to Sophie's relationship with Carla, her ex had the upper hand in several ways. For example, Sophie still followed Carla on Instagram, but Carla didn't follow her back. And Sophie had, on a handful of occasions, reached out to try to reconcile. She'd sent Carla a *Happy Birthday* text, then tried calling her after she'd had a gummy-bear edible and was feeling sad. Carla never responded—another move that gave her the prime position of the ex who was better off. So to see Carla finally reach out after something completely humiliating had happened was an unfortunate plot twist in the novel of Sophie's life.

"Carla said she saw the video." Sophie dabbed her lip with a napkin.

"Ugh." Poppy's beaded bracelets had ridden up her arm, and she smoothed them back down toward her hands. "Of course she did. I think all exes have radar that beeps anytime we fuck up. Not that you fucked up. Just, ya know, had a moment. You know what I mean."

"I do." Though, Sophie was sure an embarrassed flush crept across her cheeks.

"Do you still have feelings for her?" Nina asked.

Sophie pursed her lips. "I mean, I don't know? Carla has always been my catnip."

"Yes." Poppy raised her glass of celery juice in acknowledgment.

"Or kryptonite? I never really read comic books, but she always makes me—"

"Not yourself," Poppy cut her off.

"Right." Sophie did know that Carla brought out a different side of her—some of that great, and some of it less so. But still, she'd almost loved Carla. They had history, and Sophie thought she'd be a good ex to talk to, especially if there was still a connection between them. She wouldn't know for sure until they saw each other again.

Sophie put the phone back in her dress pocket and exhaled sharply. She knew what she had to do.

Nina was right: there would be another book. Sophie would make their mom proud. She wouldn't be a one-hit wonder, and she wasn't going to let her writer's block get the best of her. She was a fighter, and self-sufficient, the way their mother had taught them to be. She'd worked hard to get to where she was, so she was going to do everything she could to save her career and find a happily-ever-after she could write about, even if it meant putting herself out there way more than she liked.

"I'll be right back." Sophie pushed her chair out and stood from the table.

She walked through the restaurant and wove around the tables. She overheard hints of conversations—"She's a Pisces rising with a Capricorn moon? You better run"—and took a moment to eye a massive, framed painting of bananas covered in the Louis Vuitton logo. Eventually she found the bathrooms and locked herself in a stall.

She leaned a shoulder against the wall and took out her phone. Loud background music played through the speakers as she went into her texts and typed in Carla's name. She stared at the message from her: Saw the video... Sophie squeezed her eyes shut. She'd never been given closure with Carla. So maybe talking to her could finally help Sophie understand what had happened with their relationship. And, whatever—Carla had already seen her at her lowest because she'd watched the viral video—there wasn't much else to lose.

Sophie shook the lingering apprehension out of her shoulders, then typed back, Yeah, about that video... Can we talk? and hit Send.

So what if Carla never responded? At least Sophie would know that she'd tried. And if Carla did want to talk, then maybe Sophie could turn it into a new book idea, or something.

Sophie unlocked the bathroom door and pushed it open just as her phone pinged with a text. When she glanced down at the screen, she stopped abruptly in her tracks.

Carla: That would be good.

★ ★ ★

When Nina dropped her back off at home, Sophie felt motivated for the first time in a long time. She had a mission, a potential way out of her writer's-block fog, and she also had a bag filled to the brim with cinnamon-sugar bagels—Dash's favorite treat, according to Poppy. She wanted to properly apologize for the previous morning's...disaster. Vomit fest? Whatever, she planned to make things right.

Sophie avoided the fallen purple petals from the overhead jacaranda trees as she walked across the pavers of her lawn that led to Dash's 1920s Spanish-style house. When she got to his door, she rolled back her shoulders and rang the bell. For some reason, a little jitter of nerves fluttered through her at the idea of seeing him again. Or maybe she'd had one too many coffee refills at breakfast. So she took a breath in, put on a smile, and told herself to relax.

And she did relax, sort of, because Dash didn't immediately answer. She waited, and waited some more. She stood outside for what seemed like a few solid minutes, then checked her phone. It was noon, practically lunchtime. The sun had fully come out, and the air had turned into the dry desert heat she actively avoided by staying inside. But maybe Dash wasn't home, though his car was in the driveway...

As she bent down to leave the bagels on his welcome mat, she heard the unmistakable sound of his front door creaking open.

She looked up, and Dash stood there in nothing but boxers, rubbing at an eye with the palm of his hand. He ran fingers through his thick dirty-blond hair, and a strand fell across his forehead as he took her in. His hands landed on his hips, drawing her attention to the thick black outlines of a tattoo that traveled down and into his boxers.

"Shit," she muttered. But what she meant was *I cannot think about Poppy's brother's dick.* Sophie was doing everything she could not to stare at his junk, but honestly, it was just there, filling out those boxers and practically winking at her.

"Are you telling me that's what's in the bag that you just left on my doorstep?" An amused look crossed his face, and his muscled thighs flexed as he shifted from one foot to the next.

"Uh, no." She stood and brought the bag up with her. She held it out directly in front of Dash's boxers so she'd have something physically blocking her view of the…elephant in the doorway. "This is not a bag of shit."

He raised an eyebrow. "Good to hear."

"I hope I didn't wake you?" She waited for him to respond, but all he did was cross his arms over his chest so, yes, she'd guessed she *had*. She internally cringed for ruining not one but two mornings in a row for him. So much for making things right between them. "I don't know if I'm Sorry Bagels are actually a thing, but I am sorry about yesterday. I still owe you, but food tends to make everything better, in my experience."

Dash cautiously took the bag from Sophie and opened the top. He grunted back—a sound so low and deep it made the hair on her arms stand up.

"Poppy said you like cinnamon-sugar bagels?" Sophie really, *really* hoped he did, because if he didn't, then she was officially the worst tenant ever.

"I don't like them," he said.

Her breath caught at the realization that she'd made a huge miscalculation.

"I'm obsessed with them." He rubbed a hand across his chin as he eyed her. He had just the shadow of a beard. "Consider us even, Soph."

She'd never heard him shorten her name to Soph before. She couldn't help the small smile that crossed her lips. He held her gaze; she'd forgotten how deeply blue and piercing his eyes were.

She almost leaned toward him, but the sound of Dash's phone

pinging startled her. Dash flipped the phone over and read the screen. His expression went dark.

"Gah," he muttered to himself.

But Sophie had always been a bit nosy. "What is it?"

He looked up and glared back at her, like he'd forgotten she was there. "You don't want to know."

4

DASH

FROM: KittyAssistant@KittyMontroseAgency.com
CC: Kitty@KittyMontroseAgency.com
TO: DashMontrose@smail.com

SUBJECT: URGENT / TIMELY REQUEST / RESPOND IMMEDIATELY

Dash, Kitty has requested to see a copy of the speech for William within the next few weeks. Please respond immediately with your thoughts.

Something about the email from his mom—well, his mom's assistant—and the reminder of his mom's expectations had his heart thudding harder than he liked. The same way it always did whenever he was dragged back into the family business.

Sophie's earnest voice came through, though. "Maybe I can help?"

"It's nothing." He cracked his neck and intended to end the conversation and head back inside to deal with the email. He shouldn't have even opened the door, but something had propelled him out of bed. And when he'd seen Sophie standing there, he couldn't help but feel relief. He'd spent half the night wondering whether or not she was okay, but now he knew she was. He should've gone back into the house, but to his surprise, he continued, "I just got this email from my mom that kind of stressed me out. My dad is getting a star on the Walk of Fame, and she wants me to present it to him."

"Wow, that sounds…" If he had to guess from the excited expression on her face, Sophie was probably about to finish her sentence with *amazing!* or *fun!* but then seemed to assess his demeanor and thought better of it. "But you don't want to?"

"It's complicated. I'd have to write a speech for him, but I don't even know how to start something like that. I've never been great with words." Dash fussed with his hair briefly. What he wouldn't give for a long and intense workout to burn off some of the anxiety that filled him.

"Not to brag, but when I was in the fourth grade I won my class speech contest. So speeches are kind of my thing." Sophie waggled her fingers in a razzle-dazzle gesture that made him chuckle, to his chagrin. "I could help write yours if you want. I do owe you."

He was admittedly more than a little amused by the notion of her elementary-school speech qualifying her for this. "What did you write about?"

"Tractors. I made the argument that everyone should drive one." Sophie absent-mindedly pushed a cuticle on her thumb back. "What? We grew up around a lot of farms, and they are honestly very cool."

He tried his best to hold back a laugh, but a little one tumbled out as he said, "So just to be clear, you think writing about tractors would be the same as writing for the Hollywood elite?"

"That's correct." She cracked her knuckles in an intentional I-mean-business kind of way. "Did I mention they gave me a gift certificate to In-N-Out as a prize? Let's just say I'm a big deal."

He bit his lower lip. He didn't want Sophie to feel like she owed him anything—she didn't. So he'd change the subject, which was something he was quite good at. "Speaking of big deals, I saw your latest TikTok video. Are you going to document each meetup you have with your exes?"

"Do you think I should?" Her mouth stayed open just enough that her canine tooth poked out of the side. He hesitated, momentarily distracted.

"It would be pretty interesting. Ya know, you could kind of do an intro for each ex you're about to see, then do an update after the meeting. You'd get a lot of video content and be able to create a narrative."

She tapped an index finger against her downturned lower lip, which drew his attention to her mouth. He didn't want to stare, so he asked a question. "Do you think it will help with your writing?"

She stopped the tapping and shrugged. The upward slope of her nose seemed like it would be an interesting shape to mimic for one of his craft projects. "It can't hurt, since nothing else has worked and I'm kind of scrambling at this point. Did you like the video?"

"It was a solid response." He leaned against the door frame and crossed his arms. "And TikTok loves authenticity," Dash said. "That's why your first video went viral. If you want to grow an audience, just be yourself. That's what I do."

He recognized his fatal error almost immediately. *That's what I do.* As in, that's what he does when he makes his own TikTok videos. He frowned. Maybe Sophie hadn't noticed…

"Dash." She cautiously said his name, and it came out breathy. Why did he like the sound of it so much? "When you say, 'That's what I do,' do you mean that you make TikTok videos?"

"I did not say that." He shook his head no, but a sly expression crossed her face.

"And, like, you have some account where you do what, exactly?" Now Sophie sounded almost amused, which he didn't like at all. "Is your username just @DashMontrose? Does Poppy know?" Sophie took a phone out of her dress pocket, but Dash stopped her before she could open the app. Not that she'd ever find him.

"No, I just meant that I always try to be myself when I'm in front of the cameras. Like, in my past films, or whatever."

Sophie looked up and just blinked for a few moments. "So you were trying to be yourself in that movie where you played a psychopath in a rabbit costume?"

"Especially for that role, yes."

"Whatever you say." Sophie quirked up her lip, as if about to push him more, but he didn't want to explain himself.

His whole body felt warm from the very real threat of his anonymous account being discovered. If his parents knew how he was spending his days, they'd find a way to shut his TikTok down. He'd never let a slip like this happen before. What was wrong with him?

"Look, could you just not mention this to Poppy, please?" She quickly nodded. "Okay, I won't."

"Good." Dash straightened. Well, this was turning out to be a total mess. Not only had he managed to spill to Sophie that he was having trouble writing a speech for his dad, but now she knew he had a TikTok account. He really needed to stop answering his door.

"This might sound a little weird, but I need this TikTok thing to work." Sophie pocketed her phone, perhaps as a show of good faith. "It's kind of my last-ditch *all is lost and I need to turn my career around* moment. And it sounds like you know how to be successful on TikTok. You...may or may not have some account that I'll never have the pleasure of seeing. But

I would love your help to build mine into something meaningful. If I can use this awful viral video to help me get a big following and, who knows, get some creative juices flowing again, then that will change my life. So, like, maybe we can help each other here. I can write this speech for your dad, and you can give me video advice."

He planned to solve his speech problem the good old-fashioned way by simply avoiding working on it. So he waved her suggestion off and grabbed the door frame to show he was ready to end the conversation. "You don't need my help."

"Social media really isn't my thing." Sophie took a step forward, and he was surprised that he didn't mind having her close. "But I'm willing to get good at it if it means another book. And not to be dramatic, but if this doesn't work, my life is over. So, like, please help me be better at TikTok."

She clasped her hands in front of her chest, very much begging for help. "If I say *please* again, does that sweeten the deal?"

He wasn't sure what to say. Her kind, almond-shaped eyes pleaded with him, and for whatever reason, he was inexplicably lingering when he should've simply closed the door. Why was he so stuck in place just from looking at her? Had he avoided other people for so long that now, when faced with one, he was at a loss for how to act?

"Okay, fine, I'll help." The words tumbled out of him before he could think through what agreeing to working with Sophie would really mean.

But they *had* come out, and he realized that he couldn't easily take them back. Sophie's whole face lit up with pure relief, and she clapped with all the enthusiasm she had.

Dash was close enough to cover her hands with his. "No clapping, though."

She stared at their hands for a beat, and he realized how warm his were when compared to the coolness of her skin.

"You got it, boss." Sophie took her hands back from his, and she glanced at her palms before meeting his gaze again.

"Don't call me *boss*," he added. "That's weird." *Weird* in that his dick seemed to kind of like it. Which was when he remembered that he was still only wearing boxers. He readjusted his stance and put the bag of bagels in front of him for an added buffer.

Sophie tightly smiled and, perhaps sensing that Dash might change his mind, turned away from him with a nod. He was relieved as he watched her pad back toward her house. What the hell was he thinking? His whole world was meant to be routine, boring, and singularly focused on staying the course. But now, not only had he agreed to help Sophie, he was going to have to rely on her as well.

Dash's thoughts spun like unwieldy clay on a pottery wheel as he drove his cherry-red Volvo P1800 to Chris's house. The car was a birthday gift his dad had bought him—gifts were his dad's only real way of showing affection—because Roger Moore had driven one in a *James Bond* movie. The car was more his dad's flashy, old-Hollywood style than Dash's. But still… even he couldn't deny how gorgeous she was as he removed the tarp. She was all shiny and round with smooth edges. And he'd lovingly cared for his car since the day he got her eighteen years ago.

Chris only lived a few blocks away, but with the windows down, the wind from the short drive slapped Dash across the face in a necessary and helpful way. So by the time he parked, his jitters had faded and he felt refreshed.

When he rang the doorbell, Chris answered with Luna on his hip. The baby seemed to assess Dash, her gaze more than a little skeptical. "Is she mad at me?" Dash asked.

"Don't take it personally. Mira calls her *discerning*." Chris opened the door wide, and Dash stepped in. Their house pre-newborn had always been a little messy, and now it was the same level of mess, plus a bonus smattering of toys.

Dash nodded to Chris. "The FaceTime calls didn't do that beard justice, man."

"I have a beard?" Chris, who was usually clean-shaven, now had thick and scraggly facial hair.

Dash held out his hands to take Luna. She glared back but didn't protest when Dash lifted her.

Chris shook out his arms. "She's twelve pounds. It shouldn't hurt this much."

"I work out for an hour and get sore. You're lifting all day." Dash spoke to Chris but kept his eyes on Luna. Her little fingers found the collar of his cotton shirt and tugged.

Chris patted Dash on the back and grabbed a baby carrier from the bar stool at the kitchen island. "You're going to a meeting."

Dash frowned, both at Luna's Hulkish grip on his shirt and Chris's words. "I came over to help—"

"She naps like a pro in this thing." He strapped the carrier on Dash and nestled Luna inside of it, all before Dash could get out another word of protest. "If she wakes up, I've got diapers, a bottle, and formula in here. And you have my cell. Just call if you need me." Chris picked up a bag from the counter and eased it onto Dash's back.

Dash had been in the door for less than five minutes, but he had an infant strapped to his front, a backpack on, and he was, apparently, about to head out to a meeting. What the hell was happening?

"I can't bring a baby to AA." Though, Dash already had a hand on Luna's back and was lightly bouncing on instinct to try to soothe her.

"Of course you can." Chris opened a bag of avocados and gave one a squeeze to test if it was ripe. "It's just down the block.

Now go, because I have big plans to put this bad boy on some focaccia, then crash."

Dash wanted to protest, but one flicker of Chris's appreciative smile stopped him. And then, when he looked down to Luna, she'd already fallen asleep against his chest. He wasn't about to wake the sleeping baby.

So he left and started to walk toward the AA meeting. This was the same spot where he'd met Chris, and where they'd gone every Tuesday. He hadn't been to a meeting in six months because he felt secure without one. And not needing to go into that building had felt like an accomplishment. Because if he didn't need a roomful of people to be accountable to, then maybe he could stay sober on his own.

So when he got to the building, instead of slowing down he just kept walking. He thought he'd circle the block, then come back. But he continued straight down Melrose.

Luna shifted slightly against him, and he gently rubbed his hand along her back through the fabric of the carrier. They'd been on a walk for almost an hour: past the designer-clothing shops, trendy bars, and late-afternoon traffic. They'd strolled right by the iconic pink wall where tourists came to pose for photos, and the enormous blue, green, and red Legolike exterior of the Pacific Design Center. He realized he should turn around and head back before Luna got restless, but when he did, he nearly collided with a person in front of him.

"Sorry. Excuse me," Dash said.

He looked up and saw two fortysomething women, one with long, dark hair and a phone in her hand, the other holding a purse that contained a tiny dog.

"You were in that movie, right?" The phone was eye-level with him, and she was clearly filming.

He didn't respond, but he put a protective hand against Luna's back. He sometimes *did* get recognized, and he didn't mind when people remembered him, necessarily. He just didn't love when they started filming without his consent.

"This guy was in a movie?" the one with the dog asked.

"Yeah, the sad one where they go to Coachella and fall off the Ferris wheel?"

"Oh, I hated that one." Even the dog barked, almost as if in agreement.

Dash had been nominated for an Independent Spirit Award for Best Actor for that film, *We All Fall Down*, but he'd keep that little nugget of trivia to himself.

"And his brother is—"

"Sorry." He sidestepped away from them. His older brother was, by all accounts, an actual celebrity. Whereas Dash had mostly performed in indie movies, Reece had blockbusters to his IMDb credits.

"Why are you so short?" the one with the dog asked loudly.

"Angel*uhh*." The other woman extended her friend's name and laughed.

Yes, he *was* kind of short, but he wasn't altogether in the mood for discussing biology, and genetics, and how those things worked to determine a person's height. This was why he didn't love going out. Whether people recognized him or his famous family didn't really matter. They always seemed to have an opinion and weren't afraid to share what they had to say because, to them, he wasn't a person with feelings, he was an object for public consumption.

He was just trying to get Luna back to Chris, really. So Dash turned, put a finger up to his lips, and pointed to the baby, hoping this would squash the rest of their conversation.

But the women continued to follow him as he walked down the sidewalk.

"What are the tats of? Is that one a horse?" one of them called out behind him.

"It's actually just the words *Mind your own damn business*." He shouldn't have responded—he realized that too late—because there was a very real chance these women could upload the video to social, and then his mom would have a lot of questions he didn't want to answer.

Their jaws dropped in unison, and they stopped walking, so Dash took the opportunity to pick up the pace, keeping a hand on Luna's back as he walk-jogged down the street and out of their sight.

He was more than aware (and a little annoyed) that if he *had* gone to AA, none of this would've happened in the first place. As if the universe was reminding him that he'd broken a promise to Chris. Still, he hadn't gone, and maybe he did deserve a bit of skewering as a result.

"You look like you've been through the wringer." Chris reached for Luna as he opened the door. "Was it a rough meeting or something?"

Dash shook his head as he took off the backpack and placed it on the table in the entryway. He couldn't meet Chris's eyes and lie to him about not attending the meeting. So he changed the subject. "My tenant—"

"The drunk one?"

"Well." Dash licked his lips, because Sophie wasn't just *the drunk one*, and now he was regretting telling Chris that fact in the first place. "Yes, but she's also a successful writer. She wants to help write the speech for my dad, actually."

"Oh, I assume you told her *no*?" Chris, who had acquired the power to multitask now that he had a kid, had prepped a bottle and was already seated in a rocker with Luna. Her hands wrapped around the bottle as she drank.

"Not exactly. I mean, she seemed excited about it." Dash traced a finger along the outline of his jaw. "And I need someone to be excited. My mom thinks the speech will put me back in the public eye and into acting again. But I don't know how to tell her that I'm not interested in acting anymore."

"A job can be fluid, and you're allowed to change your mind." Chris was a former pro baseball player turned stay-at-home dad, so it was hard to argue with him there. "Surely even Kitty understands that."

Dash was fairly certain that Kitty did *not* understand that, though. She'd pitted Dash and Reece against each other their entire lives to see who would become America's Next Top Leading Man. And while Reece had been more than up for the challenge, Dash had never risen to the occasion, much to his mom's dismay.

"Have you thought about a timeline for telling them yet?" Chris asked.

"Not really. I'm just trying to get through this speech."

Dash wandered toward the kitchen and away from the living room where Chris sat with Luna. He really didn't want to have this discussion.

"Maybe this speech will open a floodgate for you. Once you get through it, you'll see some of that inner strength I know you have. And I'm telling you, when and if you share your recovery journey, you never know who you might inspire."

Dash did not respond. It was taking a lot of his inner strength to not tell Chris to back off. And Chris, to his credit, must've realized Dash wasn't going to take the bait.

"I'm just saying that it's been a long time since you've said yes to anything," Chris said. "If you keep shutting everything down, you're going to miss out on your life."

"Jesus, Chris, the guy just came in the door." Mira padded into the room in slippers and sweats. Her hair was wet but fell in loose curls across her shoulders.

"He's going to become one of those reclusive types with a million cats…"

Mira rolled her eyes at Chris. She took Luna from him, and the baby instantly burped. "First of all, cats are a gift to this world. He should be so lucky to have a million."

"Mira is a bit of a hoarder," Chris whispered to Dash.

Mira knocked Chris with her hip. "Thank you for watching Luna, Dash. I came home from work and finally got to shower. You're a good friend. That's what you should've said, FYI."

"Okay, fine, you're right." Chris gave Mira a knowing look, and she smirked back.

Dash turned away from their moment. He needed coffee, so he found a mug in their cabinet and intended to fill it all the way to the top. But the words Chris had said bubbled up to the surface of his thoughts. *If you keep shutting everything down, you're going to miss out on your life.* Dash didn't shut everything down. He'd had to scrape away so much of his old life just to be secure in his sobriety, but that didn't mean he wasn't living...

When he turned back to tell his friend as much, he saw Chris and Mira sitting on the couch. Luna's head rested against Mira's chest, as she gripped Chris's index fingers with her hands.

He'd always thought he'd be a dad, but he now knew he wouldn't be able to have a family. What if he relapsed at some point? He couldn't imagine having a baby, a little Luna of his own, and then putting them through a life where he may or may not be drinking.

Chris had been sober for five years before even considering the idea of a family. He'd met Mira, and eventually they had Luna. He should've been able to see Chris as a role model, but Dash wasn't like Chris. And he realized, in that moment, that he was an outsider looking in on what he would never have.

SOPHIE'S TIKTOK
Ex number one
Name: Serenity
Occupation: Yoga instructor
Length of relationship: Four months
Reason for breakup:
Serenity wanted an open relationship
Weeks until book is due: 5.5

"I should be writing. I'm sitting at my writing desk, surrounded by the books I love most, and this would be a perfect time to finish my second book. But I still have writer's block." Sophie was flanked by bookshelves—her happy place. She'd organized the books by romance trope—fake-dating and second-chance on one row, slow-burn and Regency on another, billionaire, forced-proximity, and friends-to-lovers all in a line. Her enemies-to-lovers book collection took up two full and glorious rows—by far her favorite.

Sophie clocked the framed photo of her and her mom on the desk and had a twinge of guilt. She sighed deeply, then continued, "So instead of writing, I'm meeting up with one of my exes to see if they can help me figure out why I've never fallen in love. Because yes, I know I need help, and I'm not afraid to ask for it. But before I tell you about the first one I decided to reach out to, who I will call Serenity for privacy reasons, I wanted to lay out the rules for who I'll be meeting up with.

"One, we must have dated for more than three months, which is the threshold for whether a relationship is a relationship, in my opinion. Two, I must ask the question *Why didn't we fall in love?* And three, I need to ask if they'd ever be open to dating me again. After all, I write romance, and second-chance romance is a big and beautiful trope in my world. I'd be missing out if I didn't at least explore that option, right?

"Serenity is spiritual, and thoughtful, and all around a much better person than me. I'm sure they'll have some great insights into why we didn't work out. So let's all do a little sun salutation and hope that I don't say anything too humiliating and that this experiment helps me to learn more about why I can't say those three very special words."

COMMENTS

@JessErrera you got this!!

@EditorLynnHere Friends-to-lovers is my favorite trope, for the record. ☺

@Lizzy4Cats Yoga instructor thirst traps. Look them up.

@NoelleLovesBooks You know what they say about yoga instructors...

>   **@FloWithMe** no, what?

>   **@NoelleLovesBooks** they're heavily meditated

>   **@FloWithMe** ☺

>   **@tokcrafty2me** good vibes only

5

SOPHIE

Cardio was not Sophie's *thing*. But she wasn't sure if carrying a yoga mat while speed-walking counted, exactly. Still, the overhead afternoon sun made her sweat through her sports bra and caused her thighs to rub together in a deeply unpleasant way. So yeah, it counted as cardio.

The first ex she was meeting up with was Jewel—aka Serenity—who led a weekly Vinyasa yoga class in a nearby park. Jewel was decidedly not a dramatic person—not just because their entire life was devoted to finding inner peace but because they'd made a point of ending the relationship on good terms. Well, *relationship* wasn't a word Jewel would've used, so much as *coupling*. But still, after four months they'd *uncoupled*, and Jewel had told Sophie she would always be welcome in class despite their mind-body-soul separation.

When Sophie arrived, there were two rows of people on their mats, seated in Lotus pose, with their eyes closed. Gregorian chants played softly in the background, and there, in bicycle shorts and a fitted tank top, was Jewel. Their hair was buzzed, drawing more attention to their thick, dark brows and strong jaw.

Sophie hoped to go unnoticed until the end of class and took a seat behind a woman and her Pomeranian, both of whom had matching pink hair. She was late, and the class had already started. She laid out her mat and moved into Downward Dog, as Jewel instructed. As Sophie's eyes closed and she exhaled, she felt something poke her big toe. Her head whipped around, but there was nothing on the mat. She readjusted herself, closed her eyes and...poke, poke, poke. Yes, there was something pointy repeatedly nudging her foot. She jumped off the mat with a squeal, no longer caring if Jewel saw, because what the hell was underneath her?

She moved the mat, and there was the unmistakable furry, buck-toothed grin of a little mole digging out a hole. Sophie clutched both hands to her chest as she watched the mole pop its head out before diving back down and into the earth. She let out a yelp of fear because, really, moles had aggressive-looking teeth.

Sophie turned her attention back to the class and found her fellow students were all on their mats and looking directly at her, but she locked eyes with Jewel, who stared back. "I'm..." she started to say. "There was a mole, I swear!"

The class ended with an abrupt *Savasana* from Jewel, and though Sophie couldn't be entirely sure, even the Pomeranian seemed to glare at her.

Sophie sheepishly walked up to where Jewel was at the front of the group and shrugged an apology.

"You always knew how to make class fun." Jewel stood with their hands on their hips and smirked at Sophie. "Remember when you fell asleep and snored so loudly I had to wake you up?"

"Child's Pose is very serene," Sophie said. "Unfortunately, I seem to have a history of animals trying to court me. There was an incident with a peacock in a garden…" It was hard to forget Reginald, the peacock who'd tried to mate with her.

"You're lucky, you know. Peacocks can symbolize new growth." Jewel rolled up their mat. "Maybe the universe was sending a message."

"And what message do you think the universe is sending with a mole?" Sophie laughed.

"Hmm…that one I'm far less familiar with." Jewel tucked the mat under their arm.

"Do you have some time to talk before your next class?" Sophie asked, grateful when Jewel nodded.

There was a bench under a nearby oak tree with many branches and much-needed shade. They parked themselves there, and as Sophie sat, she gave Jewel a hopeful look. Hopeful that they could talk and she would find some answers.

"I'm surprised to see you." Jewel put their hand on the back of the bench.

"A good surprise, I hope," she said.

"Always good." They gently brushed a thumb across Sophie's shoulder to reassure her.

Because Jewel wasn't on social media, Sophie had no idea what they'd been up to, so she asked. Jewel was single, had recently gone on a meditation retreat in Costa Rica, and adopted two cats: Warrior One and Warrior Two.

When Jewel asked how Sophie had been doing and what was new, she felt comfortable giving them the highlights about her book, new bungalow apartment, and how she was trying (and failing) at writing a second book.

"You'd be amazed at what meditation can do for the creative soul." Jewel sipped from the copper water bottle at their side.

"Trust me, I love finding my third eye." She smiled at Jewel. "I think my writer's block might require more than meditation, though. I'm going on a bit of a journey to understand why I've never fallen in love. And I wanted to ask, why do you think we never did?"

Their breakup had been a series of conversations where it became clear that while Jewel was happy in their coupling, Jewel might *also* be happy exploring other people while they were still together. But Sophie had not been interested in sharing.

"You know I don't dwell on the past. I live in the moment." Jewel glanced off and admired the urban nature around them, as if to prove their point.

"Right." But Sophie wanted Jewel to dwell in the past, if only for a few minutes, so she pushed. "But did you feel like we weren't working for any particular reason?"

Jewel shifted on the bench to face her before saying, "Maybe it's best for you to see who you are *now* instead of digging into what went wrong *then*. We can't change the past. We can only shape our future. Who are you, Sophie?"

Sophie's head fell back as she let a big breath out. "I'm not sure I know how to answer that."

"I've meditated in this very spot before when searching for answers." Jewel stood, and so did Sophie.

"Uh-oh, you just brought up something you did in the past." Sophie pointed a finger at Jewel accusingly.

Jewel's eyes narrowed at Sophie, the way they used to when she needed extra help with a yoga pose in class. "Focus on Future Sophie and you won't miss the past one." They hugged, and Sophie let their firm yoga arms wrap her in a very tight embrace. She *had* missed that.

As Jewel began to walk away, Sophie remembered the question she still had to ask, even if it was deeply uncomfortable. "Wait, would you ever consider dating me again?"

Jewel considered, then said, "I only look forward, remember?"

Jewel left, but Sophie plunked back down on the bench in frustration. She was more than a little annoyed that her ex wouldn't so much as budge or give her anything in return. How could Sophie plan for the future without resolving her issues from the past? She took a deep breath in, then out, and eventually closed her eyes. She might as well try to meditate, like Jewel said, because her ex hadn't exactly been helpful when it came to finding answers.

Focus on Future Sophie. Okay, future her would publish more books. Future her would be able to wake up in the morning and not feel like a total failure. Future her would have a relationship that was happy and healthy and included the words *I*, *love*, and *you*. Those all felt like the goals she'd had in her mind since, well, forever.

Who are you now, Sophie? Ugh, she kind of hated this question. Who was she? Oh, she was many things: almost unemployed, aimless, feeling like a total fraud. Not actually all that far from the person Jewel had dated.

When she had been *with* Jewel, Sophie was newly out as pansexual. And, in an attempt to make their relationship work, she'd started doing yoga almost daily and taken on their vegan diet, even though she didn't much care for either of those things. Sophie had been searching for who she was then—still working as a massage therapist and tinkering on a book—was it possible she was still searching for herself now, even after all this time?

Her cell buzzed in her pocket with a new text. She snapped out of her thoughts and pulled her phone out.

Carla: When do I get to see you?

Sophie should've been ecstatic: this was the moment where she could inch her foot into the door and prop it open to see if she and Carla could revisit their relationship. She'd fantasized about them reconciling for months after their breakup, and there was a possibility that it could happen. Maybe this was the love story she needed to fix her book.

But she was drained from yoga and trying to find meaning from Jewel's words. So instead, she opened TikTok. She had writer's block when it came to her book, but not when it came to recording a video.

"I live in LA, so of course I dated a yoga teacher." She rolled her eyes to the camera. "I saw them today, and it was surprisingly nice to catch up."

Sophie licked her lips before saying, "I asked why we didn't work out, and they wouldn't tell me. Instead, they told me to focus on who I am now."

Sophie took a breath in. "But I don't know who I am yet. And maybe that's a bigger problem than I even understand."

She bit her lip as she thought about her next words. "Maybe seeing these exes is helping. What do you all think, time for another ex meetup?"

She posted the video, exhaled sharply, and went into her inbox. She had a long line of new followers and likes to scroll through. But she stopped and her breath caught when she saw a new comment on her original response video.

@Ned967 Weird, since you told me you loved me.

She clicked into the profile and saw the unmistakable face of the first person she'd ever dated looking back at her.

6

DASH

Nothing changes if nothing changes, Dash posted in the comments on Sophie's latest TikTok video. The video had five thousand views—not viral, but not nothing either—and she'd stuck to her goals and been brave enough to revisit a past relationship. He was proud of her, really.

Which was more than he could say for himself. He hadn't made any progress on the one job he'd been given. Instead, he was parked in the driveway of his parents' house, delaying the inevitable: the Montrose Sunday Roast, a weekly dinner he and his siblings *had* to attend unless there was work to be done on a film set.

Dash no longer had a career to spare him, though, so he hadn't missed a family dinner in a very long time. He switched over to his DMs and found a new one from Cindy.

@craftycindy you haven't posted this week. What's up?

@tokcrafty2me just dealing with some family stuff.

@craftycindy Drama? Did they find out about the sober thing? Or the rehab?

@tokcrafty2me No, haven't told them yet.

@craftycindy if you ever need to talk (or tok), I'm here ☺

Through their months of messaging, Dash had revealed to his TikTok friend that he'd gone through rehab and was newly sober. Telling an anonymous person on the platform felt safe, and he'd needed someone other than Chris to talk to. She didn't know who he was and never would, so giving her a glimpse into his life didn't feel like a risk. Still, he didn't love when she brought it up, even if she was just checking in on him. He gave the message a like, then closed the app entirely.

His sister's car was in the driveway, but his older brother's was missing. Dash sighed. He was the middle child, even when it came to arriving for dinner. He killed the engine and got out of the car.

His parents' house in Bel Air was what *Architectural Digest* had more aptly called a *villa*, perched at the top of a hill and overlooking the city, with views that stretched to the ocean. His shoes crunched along the white-pebbled driveway, past the Italian cyprus trees that lined the path. Two tall columns flanked the oak and iron front door, and Dash stood between them as he rang the bell.

His mom answered, wearing a cotton wrap dress and high heels. He rarely saw her in flats, even though she was taller than some NBA players and didn't strictly need the additional height.

"How was the drive, then?" she asked as she hugged him. Her thick Irish accent made all the words lilt together like a nursery rhyme. "Did ya give the fuckers hell?"

He laughed. His mom was possibly the worst driver in all of California, and she had the traffic tickets to prove it. "I thought about running a red light, but then remembered that I like *not* being in car accidents."

She raised a brow. "Your father is grilling. Something about the warm weather makes him feel very American, I guess."

They walked through the entryway and into the living room, which had soaring eleven-foot iron and glass doors that looked out to the backyard. Their home had never been simply for living—it was an entertaining space for guests, with multiple brown mohair-velvet sofas, blue silk armchairs, and a massive cowhide-patterned carpet. Dash hadn't been allowed to eat or drink in the living room as a child, yet his mom had held elaborate viewing parties of his father's films there with live music, servers with trays of food, and multiple bartenders. Every event was a business opportunity, as she liked to say.

They walked through the open doors to the terra-cotta terrace and looked out. His dad was set up at the built-in outdoor grill next to the pool, and Poppy stood beside him. She looked up and grinned, raising the beer in her hand.

Dash leaned over the railing as he asked, "Need any help?"

Then Dash's dad turned to him, metal spatula in hand. Like Dash, William was quite a bit shorter than Kitty and Poppy, but had a presence that filled up the room. His thick salt-and-pepper hair didn't move, despite the breeze in the air. He lowered his glasses down his distinguished nose and the sky blue eyes that Dash had inherited glimmered back.

"This is a Sunday roast, Dash, of course we do." His dad's British accent always added a layer of dry humor to each sentence. "You can help by getting me another drink."

Dash's mouth opened, as if to say something, but nothing came out. After all, his family didn't know he was sober. Thankfully, the doorbell rang, echoing through the house like choir bells, and his mom moved to go answer. But Dash held a hand up, he'd go. He needed to avoid the bar, and here was his excuse.

When Dash got to the door, though, his older brother was already inside.

"Let myself in." Reece waved a key, then put it back into his wallet.

Dash, meanwhile, had never been given a key to his parents' house. Not that he'd asked for one either. But he wasn't surprised that Reece just magically had it, par for the course. Reece smiled, and his perfectly symmetrical face was made even more so. His brother was born to be a movie star—a tall blond, with a cleft chin, rich brown eyes, thick brows, and tanned skin. He was chiseled and handsome, like their dad, but as confident and charming as their mom. Reece had that very specific movie-star quality that meant a kind of golden light surrounded him, almost otherworldly.

Dash knew he wasn't too terrible to look at himself, but his features were more indie movie, as his agent had told him early on in his career. The scar in his eyebrow, his mother's dark under-eye circles, and the shorter build had made him a perfect quirky lead rather than an action star.

"Wasn't sure you'd make it." Dash's hands found their way into the pockets of his jeans to keep from fidgeting. He couldn't help but be on edge around Reece, even though he wanted nothing more than to just be brothers. "Thought you might be busy with movie prep."

They both walked down the marble floor and toward the living room. "Well, I am *technically* working, since I want to convince you to join the cast of my movie."

Dash stopped walking. Reece had teed up the conversation perfectly for Dash to tell him the truth—he wouldn't be returning to acting—but the words felt lodged in his throat.

"We'll give you an outrageous salary and cut any requirements to do press, which I know you hate." Reece searched Dash's eyes, then puffed out his chest. "It would be fun to work together again after all these years. And for my directing debut, it would mean a lot to have you there with me."

Dash didn't want to disappoint his brother. The fact that he was directing his first film was a *major* accomplishment. But he wasn't about to risk his sobriety.

"I'm not interested in any roles right now," Dash eventually said. His fingers danced with nerves in his pockets.

"No, no. We're not doing the *it's not you, it's me* breakup line." Reece's eyes crinkled as he gave him a thoughtful look. "What am I missing here?"

Dash wiped a hand down his face. "Nothing. I'm just taking a break."

"Okay," Reece finally said. He placed a big, warm hand on Dash's shoulder and squeezed before he dropped it completely and walked off.

Dash had turned down the role. He knew he wouldn't regret saying no. So why was there a needling apprehension that warned him to stay alert?

Their regular Sunday-night dinner was set outside, under the pergola covered in creeping bougainvillea vines. The sun was still bright, though beginning to dip lower in the sky, and the air had cooled ever so slightly. His mother sat at one end of the table, his father at the other, with Poppy and Dash seated across from Reece.

Platters of roast chicken, peas and carrots, Yorkshire pudding, and grilled potato wedges lined the center of the table. And, because Dash was always attuned to what people were drinking, he'd noted that Poppy, Reece, and their dad had Pimms cups, and their mom had a white wine. Dash had slipped away to make his own mocktail—club soda with bitters—which looked like scotch and soda. He wanted the ease of blending in, so as not to be the focus.

"Have you all RSVP'd to the premiere?" Reece asked as he sawed into a piece of chicken.

Their mother, Kitty, pointedly looked at Poppy then Dash.

"My assistant handles the invites and my calendar." Poppy spooned a substantial amount of peas onto her plate. Running a spa kept her busy. "But don't worry, I'll be there."

"It really says something that I'm the only one at this table who answers their own emails." Dash sipped from his cup.

"Yeah, it says that you're unemployed." Poppy playfully jabbed at his shoulder with her fork, but really, it was stronger than strictly necessary.

"How is the speech coming, Dash?" His mom sipped from her glass of white wine. "You're apparently not great at answering your own emails, since you won't respond to my assistant."

William put his elbows on the table and leaned forward. "Kitty, can't the lad have his meal first?"

"I don't think Mom knows how to exist without business, Dad," Dash said with a joking smile. His dad looked to him and smiled back. Dash was happy for his dad, genuinely, as he knew how much awards and recognition meant to him, so he lied. "The speech is coming along."

"Your father got a letter from the royal family to congratulate him already." His mom took another sip from her drink. She was, after all, heavily invested in their father's success—not just because he was her husband but because she was his agent, which was how they'd first met all those years ago. "And the prince is still single…" His mom winked at Poppy.

Poppy stopped chewing the bite of food in her mouth and rolled her eyes. "Mom, don't wink at me like you and I are on the same page here. We went to boarding school together, and he never said a single word to me. Not one. Why would he be interested now?"

"Well, you grew out of the head gear and imaginary friends, for starters." Their mom raised her glass of wine. Reece choked on a laugh.

"If he can't love me at my worst, he doesn't deserve me at my best." Poppy raised her glass back in mock salute.

"Dad, wouldn't it be better if Ang Lee presented you with the award? Or Phoebe Waller-Bridge? Someone you've worked with and can speak to your career more." Dash knew this line of questions would lead nowhere, but he had to try.

"Dash, this isn't just about your father." His mother's fingers drummed along the side of the table. "This will remind people that you're a Montrose. The business is in your blood, and as soon as they remember that, you'll be getting scripts thrown at you."

His mother rarely stopped talking about deals she was working on for their dad, or a role she'd heard about for Reece, or how Dash could pivot into a rom-com leading man if only he'd network more. He'd just hoped that in squashing the deal with Reece, he'd be safe for the rest of the night.

But Dash felt Reece staring at him, and he glanced back. Before he could stop his brother, the words were coming out as fast as a mudslide.

"Don't worry, Mom, I offered Dash a role in my next film." Reece sat back in his chair.

"You did? Well, that's great." His mother beamed, and Dash felt his cheeks burn.

"But he turned it down," Reece said. When Dash looked at him, he cocked his head. There was that competitive side Dash had feared would come out in saying no to the role. Still, he couldn't believe what an ass his brother could be.

Dash glanced at his dad, who looked back with concern. His father had always been unreadable. Dash had never really known where they stood or what William's opinions truly were. Kitty seemed to be the voice of their father, in certain respects, and Dash assumed that what she said was what his dad felt, too.

But he supposed he deserved some of the flaming-hot spotlight being pointed at him. He had turned down a job offer on his brother's directorial debut, after all.

"You're turning down the role?" his mom asked coolly.

"Mom, if he wanted to act, he'd go act." Poppy folded the napkin in her lap. "It's not like you don't pressure him every single Sunday to read a new script you've got. Can't you see that Dash is trying to find himself?"

"Well," Dash started to say, then stopped. He wasn't trying to *find himself*, really. He was trying to keep from falling off the edge of a very dangerous cliff. Less than half of alcoholics in recovery stayed sober, and Dash planned to be one of them. But he was grateful that Poppy had at least *tried* to come to his defense, even if she hadn't been completely accurate in her assessment.

"William..." His mom's voice pleaded, but his father just kept looking back at him, the concern still there. Or was it judgment?

"Kitty, if he turned it down, I'm sure there's a good reason," his dad finally said.

His mom sat back in her chair. It was moments like these, where her gaze turned hawkish and her angular frame became domineering, that he understood why she'd been one of the top agents in Hollywood for nearly three decades and, at one New Year's Eve party, sent Julia Roberts home in tears.

"Okay, then, what's the reason?" she asked.

Dash knew he should say something. Now was the perfect opportunity to bring up his sobriety. He could easily tell them the truth and get the whole awful secret out there. But he kept quiet.

"You have plenty of time to write that speech for your father's award, is what you're saying?" she finally asked. "Dash, I'd like to see a draft by the end of the month."

Dash stiffened at the demand. The thing about writing a speech for his dad was...what would he say? His father's career had soared while Dash was growing up. He'd almost never seen him, save for holidays. It was only now, as his father's career had slowed, that they all sat down for a weekly meal. And even with those few hours, it's not like he and his dad were close or had heart-to-hearts. His father was of a generation of men who didn't share their feelings. And because he'd never been able to open up to his children, he was more of an uncle, or an acquaintance, than someone they knew.

His sister gave his hand a little squeeze under the table, and he squeezed back. The only sound Dash heard was the scrape of his father's knife against the dinner plate. Dash hesitated in responding but eventually said, "Okay."

He just hoped that Sophie was the talented writer he needed to pull the whole charade off.

The next day, he texted Sophie to meet him, and she'd agreed. If he was going to have a speech ready for his mom in a few weeks, they needed to start working on it together as soon as possible.

It was early morning—well, ten was early for Dash—and he inspected the avocado tree while he waited. The tree was completely bare, thanks to the squirrel who terrorized his garden.

The squeak of her front door opening interrupted his thoughts, and Dash turned to see Sophie come out in a visible sports bra and spandex dress which clung to her body as she walked across the lawn. He shouldn't stare—he really shouldn't—but how was he supposed to ignore her generous thighs or the ample cleavage that wasn't covered by the dress? She moved like a cat, each leg slinking in front of the other as she walked.

He tried to remember that this was *Sophie*, Poppy's best friend and a person who, just a few days ago, had barfed all over him. But even knowing those things didn't stop him from taking a step toward her. And was it possible he could see the thick out-line of her lashes, even from so far away? Damn.

She gave him a wave. "Am I interrupting?"

"Not really. Just seeing how my avocados are doing." *And trying very hard not to stare at you.*

"Richard loves those."

Dash eyed her. "Who?"

"Our squirrel."

"*Our* squirrel? Do you mean the terror who eats all of my fruit?"

"Richard is, like, the size of your foot. Get a grip, Dash."

The back of Dash's neck turned hot, and he rubbed a palm across it. "Are you telling me you not only named the squirrel, but you chose Richard as its name?"

"My mom used to love watching Richard Gere movies, and they both have kind eyes." She nudged a fallen avocado leaf with her sandal.

"We'll I'm going to call him Dick for short, because he ab-solutely is one." Dash crossed his arms, hoping the little dig got under her skin a bit.

Sophie's mouth dropped open in shock, and he was pleased by her reaction. "Dash Montrose, you will do no such thing!"

"You clearly don't know me all that well, Soph." He liked the feel of her shortened name in his mouth, like they'd known each other long enough for him to use it. "I'm not afraid to call squirrels out for the dicks they are."

She let out a laugh but rolled her eyes. Maybe she was liking their unexpected exchange just as much as he was.

"Getting some yoga in?" Of course he'd watched her video from the day before and knew how the meeting with her yogi ex had gone, but he didn't want her to know that.

"I used to do yoga a lot and haven't done it in a while. I'm just trying to remember if I *actually* liked it or just did it because my ex did." A slight breeze lifted the hem of her dress just enough for Dash to see a further smattering of charming little freckles. "They say you can't change without making changes, right?"

So she'd read his comment on TikTok, and it had meant something to her. That was…interesting. "They do say that." Dash kept a knowing smirk from crossing his lips. "My mom wants a draft of the speech in, like, two weeks. Do you think that's doable?" He could bring their conversation back to business, and that way he wouldn't think about tracing lines across her shoulders with his teeth.

Sophie gnawed on her lip. "I can make that work. I just kind of need to go back to Ojai this weekend to see another one of my exes. But I can outline the speech on the bus ride up, if that's okay?"

Sophie didn't have a car, one of the appeals of having her as a tenant, seeing as he only had space for his in their driveway. But Dash *did* have a car, and there was an incredible crafting community in the downtown Ojai area he'd really like to visit. He could imagine making a video there would be a nice change on the channel and a value incentive to his followers. Not that Sophie would need to know that, but he could drive her there, go to the shops while she made her connection, and then drive them home.

"Would you prefer a ride? We could talk about my dad and the speech on the way? I need to take my girl for a drive anyway." He realized how that might sound and pointed to his car. "My car, I mean."

"It's kinda far." She crossed her arms and studied him. He worked hard to keep his gaze above her neck.

"Hour and a half, tops." Dash didn't know why he was pushing this so much. He hated asking for her help, and really, he could call her and have this conversation on her bus ride to Ojai. But something about being near her made him want more time.

He was just lonely. After all, even Chris had called him out for being antisocial. So maybe Sophie scratched some deep itch he had to be around another person or something. He wasn't totally sure, but he kept going. "If you want to work on this with me, we have to do it quickly. A drive is the perfect way for me to tell you about my dad, and then you can help translate that onto the page."

He waited for her to respond, knowing that there was a strong possibility she wouldn't want to be trapped in a car with him. But he hoped she would agree to this, and the fact that he was hopeful about something was…new.

"Okay." A smile crossed her lips. "Let's do it."

7

SOPHIE

When Sophie stepped out of her house it was just after ten, but the sun was already blasting down warm and bright rays. She had to hold a hand above her eyes to see Dash by his car.

And, well, a few things came to mind as she gazed at him.

First, there was something quite surreal about the fact that she was taking a day trip with Dash—someone who, only a week ago, she'd spoken all of a dozen words to. Second, that she definitely did not want to spill her matcha tea on those cream seats. She took a massive gulp, then another, and finished the drink off. And third, Dash was attractive. Especially as he leaned back against the car in his dark blue button-down shirt with the sleeves rolled up just enough to reveal glimpses of the tattoos that wrapped around his forearms. There was a workman's jacket slung over his shoulder and he wore faded jeans and aviator sunglasses that made him look like a classic Hollywood movie star.

And maybe it was okay to objectively know that he was sexy, right? He was, after all, an actor, or had been, or whatever, and it was his actual job to look good. So what if Sophie happened to notice his confident stance as he leaned back against the car? Or the way his Adam's apple bobbed as he swallowed? Or how he lowered his sunglasses and smiled a genuine, warm look, just for her?

All those things would've been okay, she thought, except that the smile he'd given her had, in turn, caused a swarm of nerves to erupt. Yes, a swirling, unexpected, jittery sensation in her stomach that was either butterflies or a result of chugging her matcha within the span of a minute.

Either way, neither of those options were great. Butterflies were reserved for people she had crushes on, not a person named Dash who was her best friend's brother and had enlisted her to do a job. Though, if she was being honest, she'd worn a dress that cinched at the waist specifically because she knew it made her ass look amazing. And hadn't she known she'd done that *for* Dash?

"You have a lot of stuff," Dash noted.

She frowned. Did she? Yes, she'd brought a bag for snacks, a purse with her phone (plus credit cards, gloss, sunscreen, and toner), and a backpack with her laptop, notebook, pens, and planner—but those were just the essentials.

"Well, I had to bring snacks." She unzipped the snack bag and opened it wide for Dash to see.

He peered in and pulled one from the top. "Air-dried pineapple?"

"So good," she said. Just the thought of those crispy little wedges made her lips twitch. She wiped at the corner of her mouth, searching for any rogue drool.

He pulled out another option. "Cauliflower cheddar puffs?" He took off his sunglasses completely. "Sophie, did Poppy do this to you? Her gluten-free, sometimes-raw ways have robbed you of all your taste buds."

She jutted out her hip and placed a defiant fist on it. "Why, what would you rather have?"

"Snacks—proper, made-of-chemicals, probably-will-take-years-off-your-life snacks." He leaned into his car, popped open the glove box, and pulled out a bag of sour gummy worms. He ripped the plastic open and deftly popped one in his mouth. He moaned as he chewed.

Then, as if remembering she was there, he broke the lustful, sugar-induced moment and held the bag out to her.

"I'm not really a sour person," she said. Though, she had to admit it was kind of cute to see him so excited about neon-colored candy.

"Suit yourself." He grabbed a handful of gummies and popped two into his mouth.

Feeling the need to prove how great her own snacks were, she tore open a bag of dried chickpeas and ate a handful. Then she tucked the snack, her purse, and backpack on the floor where her feet would be. She sat in the passenger seat and buckled herself in. He slid the sunglasses back onto his face as he walked around to the driver's-side door. Dash started the engine, and it purred through her entire body. He adjusted his grip on the steering wheel, and she watched his bicep flex underneath his shirt. Not that she was staring or anything.

They pulled out of the driveway. The caffeine from the matcha was starting to kick in and caused her leg to bounce in the seat as she asked, "Can you tell me about your dad? I know what Poppy's idea of him is, but what comes to mind when you think of him?"

Dash's hand moved on the steering wheel, rubbing the leather against his palm. "I'm not really used to talking about him." There was an edge to his voice she couldn't quite place.

She'd need Dash to feel comfortable if she was going to help him with the speech, so she offered, "I'm not used to talking about my dad either. He wasn't in the picture. All I know is he moved to Florida when I was a baby and apparently started a new life and family there. The only time I ever heard from him was when Nina got on a cooking show and he magically popped up, suddenly wanting to be in our lives. But neither of us were interested in getting to know him, especially considering the timing."

Then she stopped talking and waited to see if Dash would respond. Or, if she'd once again just been word-vomiting, as she often did. But then, to her delight, he spoke.

"To be honest, my dad wasn't really around either." He glanced at her out of the corner of his eye. She'd heard as much from Poppy. "He's kind of this larger-than-life person because, in a lot of ways, he feels more like a movie star than my dad. I've seen him talk more on-screen than to me directly."

She wanted to reach over and grab his hand, but she didn't. Sophie worked hard to keep her face neutral. She didn't want to make Dash feel bad, and she didn't judge him. She took in a deep breath and leaned back against the comfort of the chair. "I know it's not the same thing, but I was raised by a single mom. She worked nonstop to make sure we had everything we needed. My sister was really the one who raised me. And I adored my mom—we spent a lot more time together once Nina could help her financially—but I do understand what it's like to miss your parent. Especially now that mine's gone."

Sophie's mom had passed away almost a decade ago, and while she'd grieved, she would never really recover from losing her.

"I'm sorry about your mom," he said. And to her surprise, he reached over and squeezed her hand.

"Thank you" was all she could think to say. Her hand practically burned from the spot where he'd touched her.

"The thing about my dad is," he said, "I didn't know him. So I didn't know what I was missing, really."

A little corner of her heart broke off for Dash. Because she hadn't known her dad at all either, but Sophie had had her mom. And as much as her mom had worked, she'd still tucked them in every night. She read them books, and when Sophie was old enough, they read romance novels together. And Sundays were their family time. She'd never been in Dash's shoes, but when she looked over, he didn't seem fazed.

"What was your relationship with your mom like?" he asked.

"My mom was the absolute biggest cheerleader I've ever had, and the first person who told me I could be a writer." Sophie softly smiled, the way she always did when she thought of her mom. "She encouraged us to do what we loved, which is why not being able to write is kind of killing me."

Dash let her words sit before he added more. "Don't get me wrong, I had a really charmed childhood—going to sets, awards shows, meeting every celebrity you can think of. My life wasn't bad," he said. "But it's hard for me to talk about my dad because he just...wasn't there for *me*."

"As you know, I'm an award-winning speechwriter." She smirked, and he gave her an amused look back. "We'll figure this out." Her hand landed on the armrest, almost touching him, and then she pulled it back.

"So long as you can find a way to make something out of nothing." He readjusted the sunglasses on his face, and his strong jaw flexed.

She really hoped, for Dash's sake, that she could. She wanted nothing more than to deliver a speech that would impress not only his whole family but also him. When she looked out her window, she no longer saw the endless stretch of buildings that signaled Los Angeles. They were on the highway, with cars zipping past, but there were also endless stretches of green and billboards for upcoming fast-food stops. She took out her phone and pulled up the list of questions she'd made for Dash. "Okay, is there something your dad has always dreamed of doing but hasn't done yet?"

"Can I plead the Fifth?" Dash asked. "I absolutely don't know the answer to that question."

"Okay, no worries. I've got more!" Sophie scrolled down her phone. "What does your dad value most in a friendship?"

"Well, my dad's only real friend is my mom, and she's..." He drifted off and didn't seem like he intended to finish the thought.

"Okay, well, it's cute that your parents are best friends." Sophie shifted slightly in her seat, batted her curtain bangs away from her eyes, then asked, "Okay, third time's the charm, I hope. I just want to know one thing you genuinely like about your dad."

He sighed so deeply she couldn't tell if it was him or the engine rumbling through her seat.

"Dash, as you know, I'm a great writer, but I do need *something*. Even if you just make it up!"

"Okay, my dad is terrified of sharks," he finally said. "Like, deeply, horrifyingly scared of them. But on his first *Mission Forever* film, there's a scene where he jumps out of a helicopter and into the ocean. He had to land in the water, then climb onto this boat, and he was so terrified but wanted to do his own stunts for his first starring action role, so he just did it. He decided he wasn't going to be afraid of sharks that day. So he took a shot of whiskey, dove into the ocean, and pretended like they were in a water tank and not on the open sea. I kind of loved how badly he wanted to be an action star, that even his deepest fear couldn't keep him from making it happen."

"I love sharks," Sophie said, straightening. "Did you know they don't have bones?"

He squinted at her. "Just so I'm clear, you love tractors and sharks."

"You say that like they aren't all related."

"Sharks and tractors are related?"

"They're both wildly misunderstood, Dash." She made sure to sound deathly serious.

Her phone pinged with a new text, and when she glanced at the screen, she saw a new message from Ned.

Ned: See you soon.

She swallowed down the ball of dread that had gathered in her throat and tried to focus on the road ahead of them. She'd been enjoying the car ride with Dash and had almost entirely forgotten that she'd soon be face-to-face with her high-school boyfriend. She didn't want to have an uncomfortable conversation with Ned, but it was shaping up to be something she couldn't avoid.

8

DASH

When Sophie came back from the gas-station bathroom and buckled herself in, Dash held out his hand and said, "Gummy me."

"Excuse me," she shot back. "Please, don't be vulgar. I am a *lady*, sir."

"You're right." He put his hand on the steering wheel, shifted slightly in the seat, then reextended his hand. "Gummy me, *please*."

"That's more like it." She placed a handful of sour gummy worms in his palm, the edges of her nails just skimming him, and he popped the candy into his mouth.

"You have to try one," he said through a mouthful. "Just one, otherwise it's not a proper road trip."

She glared at him but, to his amusement, she reached her hand into the bag and pulled one out. "Is this what you want?" She shook the gummy worm at him, a disgusted look on her face. "You want to watch me eat this sugary little worm?"

"I absolutely do." He popped another one into his mouth and

smiled. She tilted her head back and dangled the worm above her lips before dropping it into her mouth.

"Are you happy now?" She chewed and her face contorted as she tasted the sour and sweet of it.

"Are *you* happy now?" he said back.

She continued to chew. "These are good, actually."

"Told ya." He raised his eyebrows as he maneuvered the car back onto the highway. They were getting closer to Ojai, but he wondered if there was some way he could convince her to just hang out with him. He didn't want her to miss an opportunity for growth and more content, exactly, but he liked being next to her. He hadn't talked to someone else for this long a stretch of time since...he couldn't remember. And he'd told her about his dad, which he never brought up with people.

"How do you think your experiment is going?" Dash asked.

"I have four thousand followers, which isn't nothing," she said. "I just don't feel closer to finding an answer for my book. I mean, seeing my first ex was fine, I guess? I'm just not used to analyzing my behavior that way, and I'm not totally sure I'm doing it right."

"Do you think this ex we're driving to see might help?" He snuck a glance at her, which he realized he'd been doing a lot of while they were driving. She was easy to look at.

"He was the first person I ever dated." She brushed the sugar off her fingertips. "But I think his memory of our relationship is a little different from mine. I don't want to think about it too much. I might end up psyching myself out."

Dash nodded. He could change the subject. "What's the best date you've ever been on?" Why the hell was he asking this ridiculous question? "Just because, ya know, you're revisiting all of these exes."

Great save, Dash, that doesn't make you sound weirder. He read-justed himself in the seat and let out a heavy sigh. He was not used to small talk.

"Oh, hmm." Sophie tapped her index finger against her chin. "Well, Ned grew up on a ranch and was into horseback riding. He took me riding one time and it started to rain, but we ended up having fun."

The image of Sophie in the rain and on a horse was doing something very specific to Dash, and he reached a hand down to release some of the pressure against his jeans.

"Oh, but Jewel always brought me to interesting places, like, they loved rock climbing, so they taught me how to climb on a weekend trip to Yosemite." Sophie cocked her head as she thought a bit more. "Hmm...but Carla knows a lot about astronomy and took me stargazing at the planetarium once, which was also super sweet."

"Which ex is Carla?" Dash hadn't heard that name before.

Sophie shook her head, then studied her hands as she answered. "She was my longest relationship. We dated for close to a year. If there's anyone who I could see a second chance with, it's her."

He frowned. Something about that made his throat go completely dry. Was he actually jealous? No, he couldn't be jealous of the fact that Sophie had dated someone and might want to date them again. Still, he was suddenly choked up. He reached for the bottle of water in the cup holder, undid the cap, and took a sip. "I'm hearing a lot about what all of your exes like, but what about what you like?"

Sophie blinked, then sat back in her seat. "How do you mean?"

"Like, if I were to take you on a date, where would you want to go? How would you want to spend the day?" He was phrasing this in a very weird way, because apparently, he wasn't capable of a normal conversation when he was with Sophie. He should just let her do the talking from now on.

Sophie stared at him, then shrugged. "Well, I mean, obviously I love books. It would be cool to do, like, a literary tour of LA. Maybe hopping around to different places? Like Joan Didion's house in Hollywood. And Nora Ephron used to love eating at Langer's Deli downtown. And then getting to visit all my favorite bookstores—Book Soup, The Last Bookstore, Chevalier's, and ending at The Ripped Bodice, which is my actual happy place. That would be a perfect day."

She gazed off somewhere in front of them with the hint of a smile that caused the apples of her cheeks to pop. He imagined what it would feel like to make her happy like that, like she had nothing in the world to ever worry about.

"It's cool that books are your life. Not everyone finds their thing that way." Dash certainly hadn't.

"Do you want to be acting more?" she asked.

No, he absolutely did not. Just the thought of having to read a script made his shirt collar way too tight. "No, I'm done with acting."

"Oh." Sophie sounded genuinely surprised.

And then he realized he'd told her something he hadn't yet told the rest of his family. He seemed to have a problem when it came to Sophie, in that all his closely kept secrets were spilling out. First the mention of his TikTok account, and now his plan to leave acting permanently. Only Chris, and now Sophie, knew the truth—which was probably not the smartest decision, given that Sophie might tell his sister.

"Please don't tell Poppy that, though. I don't want her to worry." He glanced at her, and she gave him a concerned look. "My parents want me to be acting, but I never liked being in the spotlight. It was their dream, not mine."

"Are you really *done* with acting?"

Dash sighed. The problem with sharing this decision was that it was complicated. He wasn't just quitting acting because he was bored. He'd decided to leave the industry to save his life. "I'm done," he simply said.

She fiddled with the silver pinkie ring on her hand. "I've

seen all your movies. They were kind of what got me through high school, if I'm being honest."

That wasn't the first time he'd heard a similar sentiment. He'd come of age on-screen, and a lot of his fans had grown up along with him.

When he glanced at her, she blushed and quickly looked away. The color in her cheeks only highlighted the freckles that dotted them. He wanted to rub his thumb across her skin and feel the flame of her there, but he stopped himself.

"You created these incredible characters. And if I was having a bad day, I knew I could turn on a movie and escape with you for a bit. I felt like I knew you, in a way. That probably sounds weird." She laughed, then searched his eyes for a reaction.

The truth was, she didn't sound weird to him at all. If he didn't know any better, it sounded like she might've had a crush on him when she was growing up. Why was that making him feel self-conscious and proud at the same time?

"Only a little weird," he finally said. Dash's mouth quirked up, and he fought to suppress it.

"What do you want to do, if you're not acting?"

He cracked his neck. He always felt like a loser when faced with this question. But this was Sophie, and for whatever reason, he trusted her not to judge him. "That's the zillion-dollar question. My parents projected onto me what my life would be, so now I'm having to sort out who I am without their input. It's harder than I thought. It probably sounds ridiculous to say. I'm thirty-six and should know what I'm doing, but I'm still figuring things out."

"So am I." Sophie smiled, and Dash was surprised by how grateful he was to see a kind of warm, understanding look cross her face. "It's sometimes like everyone already got their membership to the Adulting Club, except me. I don't know what I'm doing either. Don't feel bad about it."

And, for the first time since deciding he was done with acting, he really *didn't* feel all that bad about it.

"What would you do, if you weren't writing?" He shifted in the seat and pointed the air vent toward his face. His whole body had warmed from accidentally telling Sophie about his career change. He wasn't used to opening up, and it made him sweat, literally.

"That's just it," Sophie said. "Writing is the only thing I truly want to do. It's this big, wild dream my mom always wanted me to achieve. And getting a book published made me so happy because I knew she'd be deeply proud. Just knowing people read something I wrote lit this fire inside me. And I don't know that there's anything else in the world that would make me feel as fulfilled as writing does."

"Then, that's what you have to keep doing," he said. "Don't ever give up."

Sophie was so quiet that all he heard was the whoosh of the wind around the car as they continued to drive. When he turned, she watched him, her expression appreciative. But he'd never done well with other people's emotions, so he avoided her gaze and refocused on the road.

Only he couldn't ignore how hard his heart raced as they flew down the highway together.

When they pulled off at the Ojai exit, Sophie looked out the window, and he saw what she saw—grand mountains set against a blue sky dotted with comically puffy white clouds. The place was idyllic and quaint. The air was warm, but also crisp with the smell of lavender coming from the slight breeze, and it made him relax instantly.

"I'm getting small-town vibes." Dash spotted a billboard for the upcoming town parade and strawberry festival. "Is the town mayor a golden retriever?"

She laughed so loudly that it hummed in his ears and made him smile. *He'd* made her laugh.

"You're thinking of Idyllwild, and they really do have a dog as the town mayor. But it's still small here. You really couldn't get away with much." She instructed him to turn down a side street and smiled at something ahead of them. When he followed her gaze, he saw a vine-covered structure with a placard out front that read Bart's Books.

"There she is," Sophie said. "My mom and I used to come to this bookstore once a month and buy dollar romance novels. She always dreamed that I'd have a book in here someday."

Dash pulled up to the curb and killed the engine. "It must be cool to go into a bookstore and know that you're on the same level as all of these other amazing authors."

"I don't know if I'd say I'm on the *same* level." She straightened her shoulders. "Sometimes walking into a bookstore makes me feel like an impostor—like I snuck on the ride without having to pay first. Maybe I shouldn't be in any bookstores."

"I read *Whisked Away*, you know." He turned to her. Why hadn't he told her this before? Well, he didn't want to seem like he'd been spying on her, he supposed, or reveal that he most definitely had to take a shower after reading her particularly steamy sixty-nine scene.

"You did?" Her mouth hung open.

"Yeah, I had to see who I was renting to." He took off his sunglasses. Sophie looked almost touched by the fact that he'd read her book when, really, reading her words had been nothing but pure joy. "I loved how you described the LA food scene. And the proposal at the end was really sweet."

"Thanks, Dash." A rosy flush rushed up her neck as she twisted the pinkie ring again.

Maybe he didn't need to keep pumping her up, but making her smile was exhilarating, and he wanted more of that, so he added, "You're a great writer, Soph. I'm glad you're fighting for your dreams. Not everyone does."

She held his gaze, and he felt trapped by the rich hazel of her eyes. He really had to stop noticing how they changed color depending on what they were focused on and how gold they appeared when she looked at him: that wasn't going to do him any favors. He didn't so much as blink as he stared back, certain that time had slowed. It was then that he realized he really, really liked her. If this were one of his movies, the music would swell, he'd lean across the armrest, gently weave his fingers through her hair, grasp the back of her neck and move toward her lips—

Her phone pinged with a new text, which made her look away and sever their connection.

Dash blinked rapidly and shook his head. He'd had a full-on fantasy sequence going on, and if he didn't keep his feelings in check, he'd do something neither of them could take back.

"I should go," Sophie said, pocketing the phone. "I'll text when we're done?" She searched his eyes for confirmation.

He didn't want her to leave, though. He wanted her to get back in the car so they could keep talking about nothing and everything. And, if he was being honest, he didn't like the idea of her meeting up with some ex she could still have feelings for. So when she got out he said, "Soph?"

She turned back. "Yeah?"

There was that little canine tooth, cresting the corner of her lip and teasing him. Was it possible to find a tooth attractive? Yes, apparently, it was. He so badly wanted to pull her back in, but she wasn't his, not even close. So he cleared his throat and simply said, "Good luck."

She paused, as if waiting for more. And maybe he should've told her that something felt like it was shifting between them. He no longer saw her as just his sister's friend, and he wanted to figure that out with her. But after a beat of silence, she just turned and headed toward the bookshop. He should've driven off immediately, but he found the thought of leaving her almost impossible.

SOPHIE'S TIKTOK
Ex number two
Name: High-School Sweetheart
Occupation: Sommelier
Length of relationship: Eight months
Reason for breakup:
Disagreement over who Buffy should've ended up
with—I was Team Spike and he was Team Angel
Weeks until book two is due: 5

"Crushes are bizarre, aren't they?" Sophie stood outside the entrance to Bart's Books, in front of a simple wooden door with a carved sign hanging from the top, flanked by ivy vines on both sides and an overhang draped in thick green flowering strands. "In high school there were people I liked and pined after for years. Years! I would just stare at the backs of their heads, write their names in little hearts, and try to partner with them on school projects, and this was totally acceptable. But as an adult? I don't think staring would be as welcomed." She blinked a lot, then added, "Even if it would be fun."

Sophie cleared her throat. "Anyway, High-School Sweetheart was my first real relationship, but we were more like friends who watched *Buffy* and went to school dances together. Leave me any thoughts you have in the Comments."

Sophie's smile faded as she turned to look toward the store.

COMMENTS:

@lalalifebookclub Team Spuffy over here too. I think it was his hair. Or cheekbones?

@hadeelthereader Spike is the only hot vampire ever. Fight me on that.

@1995forever I once had a crush on a cartoon ghost. His name was Casper. I still have a crush on him, actually.

    @nostalgiahour Can I keep you?

      @1995forever Why did I almost faint at those words?

        @nostalgiahour idk, but you're kinda cute

          @1995forever oh…you too.

            @nostalgiahour oh… 😃

@tokcrafty2me I'm Team Sophie

9

SOPHIE

Sophie walked through the entrance to Bart's Books and leaned against a wall for support. She'd filmed her TikTok video as quickly as she could—not as fast as she'd run from Dash's car, but in a rush, nonetheless. Because after the way he'd looked at her with those aviators halfway down his nose, his full lips quirked up in a smirk, and the hint of tattoos poking out from under the rolled-up sleeves of his button-down...

Holy tingling lady bits, Sophie had found him attractive before, but now she *might* have a crush on Dash Montrose, her landlord and best friend's brother. No, she...she definitely had a crush on him. Physically, emotionally—she was all in.

A hot summer breeze kicked up the smell of old books. She inhaled sharply, closed her eyes, took in another deep breath, and let the overhead sun warm her face. *This* place had always been so magical—an outdoor bookshop with endless rows of red-painted shelves. Sophie followed the vines that wrapped around the courtyard from one shelf to the next, wandering over to a section with softcovers in pastels.

Which is when she stopped in her tracks. There, standing

next to a shelf and holding a copy of *Whisked Away*, was Ned. He noticed her and a steely expression crossed his face. Well, she'd been nervous to see him before, and now those nerves were absolutely confirmed. Ned hated her or something. He placed the book back on the shelf, rocked on his heels, and gestured toward an empty patio table. "Shall we?"

Sophie supposed they would, even though confrontation was something she actively avoided. Now that she was here, and just a few feet from Ned, there was no getting around talking to him.

They sat in the courtyard and the hard metal of the chair pressed into her back. Ned rested his chin on his fist. To Sophie, he still looked like the guy she'd dated in high school—skin tanned from working outside, leather bracelet, thick black hair, and high cheekbones—but he'd added a beard and a collared shirt.

"How are Isabella and April?" Sophie figured she might as well keep trying to dodge why they were really meeting, and Ned's sweet moms were almost a bigger draw than Ned was, back in those days.

He took in a sharp breath and brushed a yellow flower petal from the table. "They keep talking about retiring and selling the ranch, but I'm not sure they ever will."

"Will you tell them I said hi?" She could almost picture their kitchen table, where she'd sat for a meal so many times.

"Sure." They locked eyes, but then Ned looked off as his thumbs twiddled on top of the table. She waited to see if he would talk first. Like, apologize for saying something untrue, for example.

But after several long and silent moments passed, Sophie sensed that Ned wasn't going to bring up his comment—*Weird, since you told me you loved me*—so she decided to just put it out there. "Okay, so obviously, I saw your message."

"Obviously." He steepled his fingers and waited for her to continue.

"Right." She fought off the urge to sigh. He'd always been a bit dramatic, and here he was stirring the pot again. "And, you know, I was a little shocked to see you say that because it never happened."

"Yes, it did." He quickly replied.

"Okay, when did I tell you that?" She started to feel like she was back in their high-school cafeteria, and they'd played a game of gossip telephone but he'd gotten the password wrong.

"Right before you broke up with me."

She shook her head. She did *not* remember ever telling Ned that she loved him. "But when did I tell you the words *I love you*? Because that one definitely didn't happen."

Ned crossed his arms and leaned back into the chair. "I didn't want to do this, but I have receipts. My moms kept my room intact, and the Valentine's card you gave me was still in my desk drawer when I went to look for it." Ned stood up and pulled a card out of his back pocket. He handed her the slip of pink construction paper with a red cutout heart, two googly eyes, and a mouth with fangs. A vampire Valentine, of course. When she opened the card, there was a message in her handwriting that read *Happy V-Day! Lurve ya, Homeskillet!*

This was definitely a *Buffy*-inspired card from her to Ned. And while the words were absolutely ridiculous, she couldn't ignore the message. Why hadn't she remembered this card at all until now? Seeing the card did jog some kind of vague memory of making it, and she let out a sigh as she held the evidence in her hands that she *had* told Ned she loved him—well, *lurved* him.

"Look, it's not a big deal." Ned took off his baseball cap and swiped a hand through his hair before tugging it back on. "But I saw your video, and I was just like, wow, look at Sophie conveniently forgetting things, as usual."

There was a joking edge to his voice, but what was Ned going on about now? "I do not forget things. What are you talking about?"

"You forgot that card." He nodded to the card in her hand and, well, touché. "And you also forgot to return my calls after you dumped me. I know I never told you I loved you back, but that was no reason to be rude." Ned's shoulders slumped, like he was reliving the memory all over again.

Sophie was about to respond but paused, because maybe there was a grain of truth to what Ned was saying. Yes, she'd broken up with him and used *Buffy* as an excuse. But maybe part of her had also ended their relationship *because* he'd rejected her... She hadn't considered that before.

"I'm sorry if I was rude." She shrugged, at a bit of a loss as to how to make things right. "But writing *lurve ya, homeskillet* in a card is not *exactly* the same thing as telling someone you love them."

"I guess we can agree to disagree." Ned briefly looked beyond her, like he was remembering something, then his attention came back to Sophie. "But you broke my fragile high-school heart and then avoided me like the plague. You hurt my feelings."

She opened her mouth to protest, but weirdly saw pain still lingering at the edges of Ned's expression. Their adolescent relationship had felt more like a friendship to her than anything truly romantic, but maybe Ned had felt differently, which wasn't something she'd considered. "I'm so sorry," she eventually said. "I didn't know that."

"Look. I've moved on. I'm happily married." He held up his left hand and revealed a shiny gold band. "I just wish you hadn't avoided talking to me back then. I thought we were friends."

"We were friends," she said.

"It didn't really feel that way when you just kept ignoring me." And there it was: Sophie had absolutely hurt Ned's feelings. Their breakup had been so long ago, the thought he might still hold a grudge hadn't even occurred to her.

"Do you want to talk about it?" she offered. Out of all the things Sophie had expected coming into this meeting with Ned, her being the villain wasn't one of them.

"You don't have to therapize me, or whatever they do out in Los Angeles," he joked.

"I don't therapize, I only accessorize." Sophie held up her red laptop bag, which *did* match her red dress.

This made Ned laugh, which she was grateful to see. She'd forgotten what an incredibly wide and mischievous smile he had.

"I need to ask you a question." Sophie leaned across the table. She wanted to steer them back to the experiment.

But then Ned's phone began to loudly ring. "One sec." He took the phone out from his pocket. "It's my wife. She's picking me up after this."

Ned pushed himself up from the table and walked away as he answered. Sophie exhaled, a bit relieved that he was gone, even if only for a minute. She knew these meetings with her exes would be emotionally draining, but she hadn't realized just how much unfinished business she might have to wade through. And she and Ned definitely had some.

Sophie grabbed her phone to distract her, and when she glanced at the screen, there was a text from Dash.

Dash: Car won't start...

Well, that was a plot twist she hadn't seen coming.

10

DASH

Dash stood under the awning of an olive-oil store called You're Oil I Need, where he'd bought a lemon-infused blend that was supposed to do wonders for the skin.

He had not anticipated that his happy place would be downtown Ojai, but he'd also nearly bought one of every candle at the Candle with Care store next door. Retail therapy was working wonders for his mood and making the tiny trunk of his sports car rather crowded.

Which was why he'd decided it was time to collect Sophie before he ran out of room for her, too. The day was turning out to be...*fun*. A word he hadn't really used or thought of in some time, but he was enjoying himself.

Only, when he went to start the car...the engine did not turn over. No matter how many attempts he made.

After texting Sophie the bad news, he'd googled auto-body shops that worked on classic cars, but there didn't seem to be any nearby. He stared at his phone, unsure of the next best move. A TikTok notification popped up, and he clicked into the new message.

@craftycindy bad news: it's so hot here that I have to do
my next video in a bikini

Dash couldn't help but lick his lips. Cindy was cute, no
doubt about it, and she was definitely flirting with him. Since
he couldn't keep flirting with Sophie, he might as well funnel
his feelings into someone else.

@tokcrafty2me if you're trying to make knitting go viral,
you might have found the answer

@craftycindy ☺

@craftycindy what are you doing at this very moment?
Should we FaceTime? I'll give you a bikini preview…

A loud horn beeped as a pickup truck pulled up next to his
car. Then Sophie opened the passenger door and hopped out,
which was made stranger when a random guy and a very pregnant woman got out of the driver's side.

Dash raised an eyebrow at them. Without having to ask the
obvious, Sophie went ahead and made the introduction. "Dash,
this is Ned, and this is Brittany, Ned's wife."

Ned tugged the brim of his baseball cap as a greeting.

"Sophie said you're having car trouble?" Brittany wore a fitted violet maternity dress and her straight, fiery red hair fluttered behind her in the wind. She was impossible to miss. "My
dad is a mechanic, and I know just about everything when it
comes to an engine. Could you pop the hood?"

Dash would happily oblige because, truly, he had no idea
what to do in a situation like this beyond calling a tow company. He may have taken great care of his car and massaged oil
across her paint to maintain the shine, but a mechanic he was

not. He popped the hood, and Brittany got to work inspecting the engine while Ned dutifully stood next to her.

Dash stepped back and onto the sidewalk to give them space, but also to stand next to Sophie. The easy smile she gave was almost as warm as being next to a kiln.

"How did it go?" He took the opportunity to be nosy. He was, admittedly, a little relieved that Ned was married, but he'd keep that thought to himself.

She tucked a loose strand of hair into her bun as she answered. "Uh, yeah, kind of a disaster. Ned and I got in a fight. Or a disagreement? It was hard to tell. And I didn't get to really dig into our problems or ask my questions." Sophie shook her head and let out an exhausted breath. "This just feels like a total bust."

"I don't know, the car ride was fun." The words slipped out of Dash, and his chest tightened at the realization that he'd just revealed the secret truth that he'd enjoyed spending time with her. Sophie watched him with the same level of interest as a kitten who'd just discovered a laser pen, but Brittany interrupted.

"What we have here is a cracked hose." She pointed into the engine. Dash broke his gaze on Sophie, then stepped off the curb and toward the car. He looked down to where she pointed, where a hose was visibly disconnected. "You're going to need a new cooling hose before you can take her on the road again. Don't worry, I know a guy who can fix this."

"How long does that take?"

"If they have the part, probably just two hours." Brittany squinted against the bright sun shining down on them, then closed the hood.

"My brother has a tractor and a chain," Ned offered. "He can tow you to the shop."

Dash felt inclined to say, "Don't bring up tractors in front of Sophie. She has a Pavlovian response."

Sophie's elbowed him. "Please don't mention my kinks in front of company."

This was a private joke between them. He couldn't remember the last time he'd met a new person and grown close enough to have one of those. Which must be why a little shot of adrenaline ran through him and caused his fingers to dance in his pockets.

Brittany ignored them, or didn't care, as she continued to talk. "By the time we get the car to a shop, they inspect it, and give you a price, it's going to be five, and they'll tell you to come back tomorrow."

Dash grimaced and ran a hand through his hair. This was not ideal. He'd planned for a day trip and didn't know what this was turning into, exactly. "So, what, we'll need to stay here?"

"I'm so sorry, Dash." Sophie's hand felt cool on his bicep, and he involuntarily flexed against her grip. Her eyes flitted from his arm to his lips before she dropped her hand and blinked rapidly. "You brought your car all the way out here. I feel awful."

"I should've taken her in for a tune-up before the trip." He shrugged, mainly because there wasn't much else to do.

"What should we do, if they can't fix it today?" Sophie asked Dash. "There are a lot of nearby hotels."

He was about to respond, but Brittany did that for him.

"It's the Ojai music festival this weekend." Brittany fanned her face with her hand. "All of the hotels are booked solid. We have a guesthouse—it's small, but all set up. My mom is going to stay with us for the first few months after the baby comes."

"I can't ask you to let us stay at your place," Sophie protested.

"I know we got off on the wrong foot today, but we were friends once. It's really not a bother for you to stay the night." Ned rubbed Brittany's back as he spoke.

"Dash?" Sophie angled herself away from them and spoke softly enough so only he would hear. "I don't love this any more than you do, but I don't know that we have another choice."

Dash did not really want to stay at this random couple's home, even though Brittany had done him a massive favor by inspecting his car. He just didn't know her or Ned.

"It's not a problem," Dash said. "I can call hotels near Ojai and we can Lyft there."

"You don't want to say no to a pregnant woman, especially a hormonal one." Brittany slung an arm around Ned's waist. "You're staying with us."

Sophie shot him a look, and he tried to read her expression. Something about the way her eyes slightly widened told him resistance was futile.

"Okay, we'll be happy to stay, then," Dash finally said.

The promised tractor came twenty minutes later, and despite them being on the main street with all of the local shops, no one seemed fazed in the slightest to see an enormous piece of farming equipment rumbling toward them.

Except for Sophie, whose smile stretched across her face as she bounced on the balls of her feet. "That's a John Deere 7R 350," Sophie whispered, as if the tractor might hear. "Won Tractor of the Year last year."

"How do you know that?" he said, laughing.

"I'd been toying with writing a book about a tractor-riding shero." Sophie crossed her arms and nodded to the tractor. "Research was needed."

"Admit it." Dash leaned in so close that his lips brushed her ear as he said, "You have a subscription to *Tractor Weekly*."

She flushed and fought back a smile, and he lowered his sunglasses down the brim of his nose for added effect. She turned back to the tractor, then said, "It's a monthly magazine, for the record."

He suppressed a too-big grin.

Brittany and Ned's house was set in the mountains, surrounded by farms with acres of land, blooming citrus trees, and fences made from massive, fallen rocks. She parked the truck in front of a garden path that led to the house, and just behind was an endless sea of vineyards with emerald leaves and deep brown twisted trunks.

When Dash stepped out, the air was warm from the late-afternoon sun, but not hot. His phone vibrated with a new message.

@craftycindy Don't leave me hanging

He quickly typed back, Rain check, then pocketed his phone.

Brittany led them toward a small cottage just off to the left. But when she opened the door, Dash realized, maybe at the same time as Sophie, that this was a studio with one bed.

"Is there another room?" he asked, but the only additional doors he saw led to a bathroom and another into a closet.

"Another room?" Brittany asked. "Aren't you two together?"

"No," they both answered at the same time. Dash looked at Sophie and she looked back, her face paler than usual. Now that he had a real crush on Sophie, the idea of being in a bed with her was...well, a bit daunting.

"Oh." Brittany glanced between them with a frown. "Well, we don't really have any other space. Our main house is just our room and the baby room."

"Right." Dash took in a deep and resigned breath, then looked to Sophie.

"Only one bed," she said, each word sounding like its own sentence. "Well, isn't that something."

The sunflower-yellow burst around her irises seemed to flare gold back at him, and he cocked his head, wondering what the hell she was thinking at that exact moment.

11

SOPHIE

One bed. They only had *one bed* that they would have to *share*?!
This was absolutely impossible. Sophie never believed the *only
one bed* trope could happen in real life—it was a fantasy, a series
of ridiculous events that would lead the main characters to share
a bed, forcing them together even if they didn't want to be.

And this was also the exact moment she'd figured out she
had a real crush on Dash? If things were happening for a reason, then she could not imagine what lesson the universe was
attempting to teach her.

Do not covet thy best friend's brother.

Remember to only find people attractive who are available.

You shall not have sex with Dash.

The real problem was that those damn butterflies immediately responded as soon as they'd heard she'd be sleeping next
to Dash, fluttering up like loose pages in the breeze. Because
if she was in a bed with him, she might get close enough to
study the tattoos that wrapped around his arms and dipped underneath his boxers...

Sophie pinched her shoulder blades together, trying to be

present, but when she looked up, Dash's eyes were glued to hers, and a little shiver passed through her from all his undivided attention.

"There are towels, spare toothbrushes, shampoo, and soap in the bathroom, too, if you want to freshen up." Brittany walked toward the bathroom and flipped the light on inside. "I'm going to see if Ned and I have some spare clothes you can wear for the night."

Sophie nodded as Brittany left the bungalow. And then they were alone, with nothing but silence as they both seemed to avoid moving altogether. She looked over at Dash, but he watched the door. He sucked in his bottom lip as his brows knit together, and she realized this might just be a little too much for him.

"Is this okay?" Sophie took a step forward but stopped herself. The space was cozy and intimate, and they were already practically on top of each other. Well, now she had *that* image in her head to navigate. "We don't have to stay here. I'm sure we could get a ride to a hotel outside of Ojai."

"Yeah, I..." But Dash stopped himself, then looked at her. "Sophie, I don't know if you've noticed, but I don't really get out much."

And she laughed, because him making a joke about the situation felt better than him running as fast as possible.

"I guess I'm a little on edge from all of the surprises." He wiped a hand over his face.

He did *look* exhausted. They'd spent most of the day traveling, and she knew how much Dash loved his car and was probably worried about it the way one might fret over a sick child.

"What if I let you chill in the room alone for a while?" Sophie was an introvert with extroverted tendencies. She needed to recharge her batteries after spending too much time with other people, too. She understood where Dash was coming from. He could take the room, and she could go for a walk.

"I'm not overwhelmed by you," he clarified. And something about the way his gaze lingered on her, as if to reassure her, made her breath catch.

I'm not overwhelmed by you, the words repeated in her head. His tone had been firm, like he needed her to understand his intentions. But what were those, exactly?

"Okay." She licked her lips and tried to shake the confusion from her thoughts. "Want to catch the Pink Moment?"

His gaze searched the space, as if looking for her reference. "The Pink Moment?"

Sophie and Dash made their way across the yard and toward the edge of the property line, where a field of gnarled grapevines sat in the shadow of the looming mountains. The sun was just beginning to set, casting the rocky mountainsides in a shade of dusty pink. The light warmed every inch around them, and Sophie's mouth opened as she took the view in. She hadn't seen an Ojai sunset—the Pink Moment—in years, and she turned to tell Dash as much, but he was already looking at her. He quickly blinked and turned back before she could say anything. She lingered on him for a few moments—at the dimple in his chin and the small, perfectly round mole centered on his cheekbone. She studied the semivisible tattoo on his left bicep—a longhorn skull with the horns pointed forward—but forced herself to look away and back to the setting sun.

Even though she was focused on the mountains, she was close enough to smell the overwhelming wet-earth scent of Dash. And as he took a deep breath in, then out, she noticed the rhythm of his breaths. What would it be like to be wrapped up in his arms, pressed against that chest and feel the rise and fall of him as they breathed together?

"There it goes," Dash said.

Sophie followed his gaze to the mountains where the sun had finally dipped behind the rocky crest and the sky was being swallowed by charcoal light.

"Hey." Ned's voice cut through the air. Sophie turned as he approached with a bottle of wine and two glasses. "Sorry I came in hot at the bookstore."

Brittany emerged from their house with another wineglass and called out to them, "I told Ned that bringing your old Valentine was weird. Who does that? Petty people, that's who."

"She did tell me that." Ned rolled his eyes, then handed Sophie a glass and extended one to Dash.

"I'm good." Dash shook his head no.

"You sure?" Ned tilted the bottle. "I'm a sommelier, and this is a special bottle. It's twenty years old and aged beautifully."

"Even I'm going to have a little sip." Brittany's head tilted slightly.

"I'm good, thanks," Dash said coolly. Sophie couldn't help but notice how his entire body had gone rigid, so different from when they watched the sunset.

Ned poured wine into Sophie's glass, then his own. They sipped and looked out toward the mountains. Eventually, Ned said, "So you're a writer, too?"

"No, I wouldn't say that." Dash's hands went into his pockets. He rocked back on his heels. "I used to be an actor, but now… I don't have a steady job yet. I do a lot of gardening and some crafting."

Sophie almost choked on her wine. He was a crafter? News to her. He hadn't so much as mentioned that he… What did crafters do? Macramé?

"What do you make?" Ned asked.

"Mostly ceramics, but sometimes I work with candles, soaps, and body wash."

"You do?" Sophie's voice sounded way too surprised but, well, she was surprised. The guy lived next door to her, and they'd spent more than an hour alone in the car together, but he'd never brought up anything about ceramics. "You never told me that."

Dash looked at her, amused. "That's because I can't get a word in, most of the time."

Ned snickered loudly.

"Sophie, I think I know why you and Ned didn't work out—you both talk too damn much." Brittany looked directly at Dash. "I can't get him to shut up half the time, *and* he talks in his sleep. I never have peace."

"Wait until the baby arrives," Ned said. "You'll think of this time as peaceful then."

"We did four rounds of IVF to get this girl." Brittany rubbed her bump. "When she's here, she can scream as loud as she likes."

"Congrats." Sophie waved a hand at Brittany's belly and then gave her a warm smile. "My sister, Nina, froze her eggs this year. She said the whole process was hard, but obviously worth it in the end."

"Definitely." Brittany nodded.

Ned and Brittany shared a look, and Dash leaned over to Sophie.

"Do you talk in your sleep?" His breath smelled sweet, like honey.

She didn't think so, as no one she'd dated had ever mentioned it, but she said, "You'll have to tell me if I do after tonight." Their eyes met, and she nearly laughed at how forward she'd sounded. She'd *really* need to watch her words if they were going to share that bed.

"You look a little familiar, Dash. Did you act in anything I'd know?" Brittany asked.

Dash shook his head, as if dismissing the idea. "Mostly indie movies."

"Well, everyone's seen *Holiday Bound*." Sophie elbowed him but found he didn't playfully elbow her back.

"You were in that?" Ned asked.

"Yeah." Dash scratched at the back of his head. "I played the little brother."

"The little brother..." Brittany's eyes darted around the lawn, as if searching for him. "The one who brings ice cream to bed and comes downstairs covered in chocolate?"

Dash seemed to fight back a smile. Sophie was relieved that he was warming up, especially since they had a whole night ahead of them.

"Oh, wait." Brittany's eyes narrowed. "Wasn't the little brother the *real* brother of Reece Montrose?"

Dash paused before answering. "I am, yeah." He looked down at his feet, and Sophie realized, too late, that maybe she shouldn't have mentioned the movie at all. Maybe he was embarrassed by all the attention, or something?

"That is wild." Brittany's hands came up to her mouth. "We're with Hollywood royalty."

Sophie tried to shoot Dash what she hoped was an apologetic look, and he pursed his lips back, seeming to accept.

Ned lifted the wine bottle and peered at it. "You sure you don't want some?"

Dash didn't immediately respond, but his focus was on the glass.

"You know, I'm actually not feeling well." Dash sent a hand through his hair. "I'm going to lie down."

He looked to Sophie briefly, and she sensed he wanted to say something, but he didn't. Instead, he turned to walk off toward the cottage.

"Dash?" Sophie called after him. She didn't know why, but the look he'd given suggested that there was more going on. Maybe he really *was* just not feeling well, but she needed to see for herself. "Let me just make sure he's okay." Sophie handed Ned her glass and hurried after Dash.

The sun had completely set, and the trail back to the bungalow was lit by overhead strings of twinkle lights. The ground was uneven beneath her feet, but she took care not to deviate from the pavers lining the path.

"Dash?" she called out to him again, but he didn't so much as turn to acknowledge her.

12

DASH

He'd heard Sophie call out his name. Of course he had. At this point, anytime she spoke, he paid attention. Still, he hadn't stopped. What he needed was to get back to their room, close the door, and wait there until morning came. Then they could head home and pretend he hadn't just fled a group conversation as if being chased by hornets.

He wasn't going to drink. He wouldn't break eighteen months of sobriety just because he was a little stressed at the idea of having to share a bed with Sophie or because someone happened to bring up his family. He wouldn't.

Still, he needed to put distance between himself and the bottle. He didn't want any unnecessary temptations. When he got to the room, though, Sophie had caught up and closed the door behind her. She wasn't tall, but her curves took up space. Not that he should be sneaking glances at the top of her dress, where her cleavage was pushed up and toward him…

"Hey." Her hands easily rested on her hips. "You okay?"

"Fine, just needed to get out of there." Not exactly a lie, but also not the whole truth.

"Can I ask you something?" Her eyes were heavy with concern, and he couldn't help but notice the faint lines at the edges. He nodded yes, and she continued, "You seemed upset out there—not like yourself. What was going on?"

He waited for another lie to come, but instead the truth tumbled out. "I don't drink." He said the words to a corner of the room but eventually returned his focus to her. And to his relief, her eyes were clear and gentle, not even a flicker of judgment there.

"Do you mean, like, ever?"

In that moment, he knew that if he told her the truth, he would be safe. He could trust her. He took a breath in, then out, and finally said, "I've been sober for eighteen months."

The words hung in the air: humid and sticky and making Dash limp from the embarrassment of having to reveal them.

But Sophie did not seem fazed as she calmly sat on the edge of the bed. She eventually asked, "Does Poppy know?"

"No one in my family knows. Just Chris, who's my best friend, and now you."

"Oh." Her brows furrowed.

He sat on the bed just next to her. "I'd appreciate it if you didn't say anything to them, if that's okay. My family is important to me, but I can't trust them with this."

"Of course," she quickly answered. "I won't."

At Sophie's words, an unexpected shiver ran through Dash, like releasing this weight had also taken away some of its power. Chris had told him that when he was ready to open up to the people in his life—mainly, his family—he'd feel relief, along with dread and apprehension, of course. But he didn't feel dread, not as he looked at Sophie and her eyes softened.

"That must be really hard," Sophie continued. "To have this big thing that they don't know about."

"Sometimes." *All the time.*

"Thank you for telling me."

Why had he told her? He hadn't told anyone new in so long, but he'd confessed to Sophie. And something about her knowing this truth made his whole body tingle with lightness. Like a door had just opened and the shimmering sun was finally washing over him. Sophie was his sun.

She gave him a warm smile and squeezed his open palm. If this was how Sophie reacted, maybe his family wouldn't be so bad.

"I've tried really hard to not be in situations where I might be triggered. I know people will continue to drink around me, but in these early days I'm just trying to stay sober and not get distracted."

And then her expression shifted to something akin to disgust, as she said, "I made you take care of me when I was hungover."

"You didn't make me do anything." His hand found its way to her shoulder, and he squeezed for reassurance.

She looked at his hand, then up at him, and swallowed. "I think it's really cool that you're sober."

Something about her saying that made him roll his eyes grudgingly. She was trying to empathize, which was sweet, but she didn't have to take pity on him.

"No, I'm serious!" She inched closer and put a hand on his knee. "Committing to anything is hard. And you're smart enough to know something had to change. That takes a lot of courage. You're an impressive person, Dash Montrose. You'll just have to accept that fact."

And he stared at her, and she stared back, and they stayed frozen like that for a few beats more. There was no judgment from her about anything he'd said, only a heat he couldn't quite place. Then her eyes danced from his mouth back up his face, and she licked her lips. And he'd never ever in his entire life wanted anything more than to have her. And maybe he was imagining it, but she seemed like she wanted the exact same thing. Without thinking through what he was doing, he reached a hand up and rested it against the back of her head, and no movement he'd ever made had felt this natural. His fingers touched the soft hairs at the nape of her neck and goose bumps erupted across her flesh.

His breath grew shallow as he asked, "Can I kiss you?"

And he knew as soon as the words came out that he couldn't take them back, and kissing Sophie would change everything, but he didn't care. All he wanted was to pull her toward him and see if she tasted the way he imagined: lime and sun and salt.

"Yes, Dash." She said his name, and it was coated with a layer of something thick and sweet, too.

His thumb grazed the side of her cheek as he looked into her eyes to check that she really was okay with this.

She smirked back. "Dash," she breathed out again.

The whisper of his name made him want her even more. Her lips met his, and she tasted like a sip of warm tea that heated his entire body. Her wide bottom lip pressed against his mouth, then her lips parted, and so did his, and their tongues met.

He couldn't keep them this far apart, even though it was only a few inches, really. He reached a hand around her waist and pulled her toward him. And, to his delight, her legs parted and she hoisted up her dress and straddled his lap.

Her hands went to his face, and she trailed her fingertips along the scruff of his jawline. "I didn't expect this."

And he hadn't either. He had fantasized about her, of course. After all, the mere thought of her sizzling gaze made him hard. But he hadn't expected anything to happen between them, especially because he wasn't sure when he'd feel comfortable enough to be with someone while trying to stay sober.

He knew, logically, that he would eventually date. But asking someone to handle all the complications that came from dating a newly sober person was intimidating. And, frankly, he didn't want to have to explain his sobriety repeatedly while trying to date. But Sophie wasn't someone he'd planned to connect with at all. She'd just happened to need him, and he'd helped, and now he needed her.

"Should we talk about this? Or about how you're feeling? I'm okay, but if you want to stop—"

He pressed his lips to hers because he was done talking. He knew why Sophie wanted to talk things through—she had a hard time *not* talking—but for now, all he wanted was to keep kissing her. He overthought almost everything in his life these days: second-guessed interactions with people, worried about what his family might think, or what to do with the rest of his life. But he knew with crystal certainty that he wanted to kiss Sophie, and as her fingers dug into his arms, he knew that she wanted to kiss him, too.

His hands wove through her hair and pulled out the bun she'd so carefully crafted on top of her head. He let her hair fall around them and that citrus scent of hers enveloped them both.

Later he would figure out what they were to each other. But right now, all he wanted was her—and that was better than any high he'd ever felt.

He could keep kissing her for the rest of the night, but he pulled back. His thumb grazed her cheekbone, and she searched his eyes.

"What's wrong?" she asked. Her grip on his shoulder tightened.

"Absolutely nothing." Except for the fact that he hadn't expected a make-out session, and he wasn't ready for anything more than that either. Even if his body pleaded otherwise. "It's just been kind of a crazy day."

Sophie hesitated but eventually nodded. They untangled themselves, and he stood from the bed. "I'll get us water." He didn't look back at her as he walked toward the bathroom. He knew he should feel ashamed for what they'd done. If Poppy found out, she'd be so hurt. But the feel of Sophie against him hadn't felt wrong at all. It felt like he was waking up to something he hadn't known was missing, and that realization scared him more than anything. Because he hadn't needed or wanted anything in so long, but he wanted more of Sophie.

13

SOPHIE

Sophie could not sleep. Obviously she couldn't just drift off, because not only was Dash gently snoring next to her but whenever she closed her eyes the only thing she saw was him.

Dash weaving his fingers through her hair.

Dash's charmed expression as she straddled his lap.

Dash cutting their make-out session short with the weird excuse of needing water.

Gah. She shouldn't obsess over what was going through Dash's head, but overthinking was also something she did extremely well.

And it wasn't just Dash who was playing on a loop. Whenever she took a mental break from them, her mind wandered to her unfinished conversation with Ned. Maybe it was the lack of sleep, but a little worm of dread had wriggled into her thoughts. Was she the bad person in their relationship? Had she completely ruined their friendship all those years ago?

As soon as soft morning light trickled in through the curtains, Sophie quietly grabbed her laptop bag and let herself out of the guesthouse. If she was going to have insomnia, she might as well try to get some writing done. The air was still cool as the sun began to crest the mountains, and despite the lack of sleep Sophie felt wired. There was a long, wooden table in the shared courtyard, and she sat down at it.

She opened the draft of *The Love Drought* that was just waiting for her final scenes to be written. She had twenty thousand words to go, and then she'd be done. Her meteorologist and storm-chaser leads had experienced their all-is-lost moment, and now she just needed to bring them back together so they could find their happily-ever-after. Typing those words out should've felt like seeing the finish line after running the bulk of a marathon—the end in sight. But as Sophie stared at the last page she'd written, a kind of numbness overtook her. Nothing about her characters or their relationship in this book felt natural or earned, just forced. And she found that while her fingers were poised over the keyboard, ready to put the words to paper, she couldn't just fake their love story.

"Hey." Ned's voice was soft. She turned to see him coming out of his house with two mugs of coffee. "Thought you could use a little fuel."

He handed her a mug, and she was grateful for the coffee and the excuse to not stare at her current work in progress. Her palms warmed as she sipped. "Thank you."

"Was everything okay with Dash?" He straddled the bench next to her.

"Yeah, just wasn't feeling well." She'd never been great at lying and took another sip to hide her expression.

"Sorry to hear that." Ned glanced at the rising sun.

"I wanted to apologize." Sophie put her coffee down on the table and closed her laptop. "You were right. It was mean of me to just cut you off in high school. Subconsciously, I think I wanted to be loved so badly, and I was trying to force that on us. When you didn't reciprocate my feelings, I just bailed. I'm so sorry."

Sophie briefly rubbed a spot on Ned's knee to try to reassure him that she was being sincere. He scratched at his hair before responding.

"You know, you were always writing. And all your stories had these overly romantic, optimistic versions of relationships, even back then." Ned gave her a faint smile. "Sometimes with us, you would slip into this idealized version of me, too. Kind of projecting who you wanted me to be instead of seeing who I was."

Sophie found herself leaning forward to listen to him, because he was making a point she hadn't yet considered. Sure, Sophie lived inside the stories she created while she was writing them, but did she really create alternate realities in her real life, too?

"Do you think that's why we never fell in love? I wasn't seeing who you really were?"

"I just think you have crazy-high standards." He shrugged. "But I do wish we'd stayed friends. Neither of us had many back then."

Well, that was true. They'd both been loners. And when she lost Ned, she had lost someone to talk to.

"If there's ever anything I can do to make it up to you, just tell me."

Ned hesitated before responding but eventually looked up and gave her a curious look. "I'm sure I'll think of something."

Sophie wanted to make sure they left on good terms, so she added, "Everything obviously worked out for the best. You have Brittany and a baby girl on the way."

"And you have Dash." He motioned toward the guesthouse, and Sophie glanced over. She wondered what Dash was doing at that moment. Was he awake? Actively avoiding her by hiding behind the curtains?

Sophie hesitated before eventually saying, "Right." She didn't move to correct Ned, even though she should. Maybe it was the fantasy part of her brain, but she wanted to live in the illusion that Dash was hers, and she was his, for a little longer.

The illusion was shattered almost instantly when Dash emerged from the guesthouse an hour later. He had the same scowl on his face Sophie had seen so many times before, and while she wasn't shocked to see him looking a little rough around the edges, it was still a stark contrast from the Dash she'd known hours earlier.

"The repair shop called." He held his phone up for evidence. "She's ready."

The drive home was quiet. Sophie usually filled the silence, but instead chose to stare straight ahead. It was a good thing she was strapped into her seat, because if there was any more tension in the car she might spring through the window from it.

Sophie would honestly love to go back to the effortless chatter they'd had the day before, but now she wasn't sure how to act around Dash. Where were they supposed to go from there? And based on Dash's still-present scowl, it was entirely possible that he regretted their night together. She couldn't wrap her head around what he was getting from their situation anyway. She'd puked on him, talked his ear off about tractors, and indirectly been the cause of him being stranded with a broken-down car. She understood her attraction to Dash—he was basically the real-life version of the brooding men she saw illustrated on romance covers—but had he only made out with her because he was feeling vulnerable?

She had no idea. But her phone pinged and snapped her out of the staring contest she was having with the road. She blinked and snuck a look at Dash, who watched her out of the corner of his eye. Was he just counting down the minutes until they got home so he could pretend this whole thing never happened? She pulled the phone from her dress pocket and had a new notification in her group chat.

Nina: How was the trip?

Sophie typed, I'm only just heading back now, actually...

Poppy: Don't tell me my brother left you. I will kill him.

Sophie wanted a sinkhole to appear in the floor of the car and swallow her up. Poppy was her best friend. Dash was her best friend's brother. Sophie was...a monster. A terrible friend. What had she been thinking by straddling Dash's lap? Best friends shouldn't ride their best friend's brother's dicks...right?

Her stomach churned at the thought of Poppy discovering the truth. Their friendship wouldn't survive the fact that Sophie had been so selfish and betrayed her. As those thoughts swirled through her, Sophie blurted out, "We can't tell your sister."

Dash did not immediately agree, the way she'd assumed he would. Instead, he kept his eyes on the road—either being a great driver or finding an easy excuse to avoid her—and simply said, "Okay."

"Okay? Just, *okay*? If she finds out, I'm pretty sure she'll kill me. Maybe both of us?" Sophie's shoulders went up to her ears at the thought. "You've seen how she gets when she's mad. One time, at the spa, someone on staff accidentally ate her vegan queso, and Poppy had to lock herself in the meditation room because she didn't want to shout while there were clients in the middle of sessions."

She was talking very quickly, but it was all true. Poppy was not a forgiving person. She held grudges. And she and Dash could never, *ever* tell Poppy about the night they'd had.

"There's nothing to tell, really. We just kissed." He shrugged, but Sophie frowned. Sure, she supposed they had *just kissed*, but...hadn't it been more?

"Did you get the answers you needed from Ned?" Dash continued.

Sophie blinked at the mention of her ex's name. Had she gotten the answers she needed? "Well, he told me my standards are too high. I don't know, maybe he's right. I guess I can be—"

Dash cut her off by loudly blowing air through his lips. "Men tell women they have high standards when they can't meet them. Your standards are exactly as they should be. He's just not good enough for you."

Sophie's cheeks burned hot, but she wasn't sure if it was because what he'd said sounded like a compliment or that he'd defended her. Dash being on her side made her straighten in her seat, like he was physically lifting her up. Which was when she knew she needed to ask the question she didn't actually want an answer to. "So what should we do about what happened last night?"

Dash's grip tightened on the steering wheel, then he looked at her, and time slowed as his gaze met hers. She'd seen this heartfelt expression from him before in one of his movies. Was he putting on a show for her now, or was he being genuine? She couldn't exactly tell.

"I like you, Soph," he said.

"I like you, too." She smiled as she said the words back. Maybe their kissing *had* been more. Sure, Ned had accused her of living a fantasy life, but this was starting to feel like a fantasy coming true. Except as the words came out, she instantly wanted to kick herself: Dash's face shifted into something unreadable. This was the moment she'd feared was coming—the rejection—still, she somehow wasn't prepared.

He licked his lips before continuing. "I'm just not in a place where I can get serious with anyone right now."

"Right." Her index finger absentmindedly tapped at her pacemaker. "Why—why is that?"

She knew the *why*, though. It was the same reason all of her relationships ended: there was something deeply wrong and flawed about Sophie.

"I've only been in recovery for eighteen months." His voice had lost all the softness it once held, and instead he sounded almost mechanical and completely unlike the man she'd grown to know. "Technically, it's okay if I date after twelve months. But I don't feel ready to do that yet. All of my energy has to be focused on staying sober."

"No, I—I get that." She tucked a piece of hair behind her ear and looked down at her feet. Part of her *knew* they couldn't exist outside of that room in Ojai, but hearing it still hurt.

"I'm sorry, Soph." His hand gently fell to her knee, and his warm palm easily rested against her cool, freckled skin. "I know you're looking to fall in love, and I won't get in the way of that."

Right. The whole point of meeting up with her exes was so that she could eventually fall in love and get back to writing the books she and her mom had always dreamed of. Her career and future were on the line. So what if kissing Dash had felt like the only right move she'd made in months? Her night with him was a distraction, if anything. And she needed to cut him loose before she lost sight of her end goals: finding a way back to writing.

Still, she needed some clarification. "So, what are we, then? I know last night wasn't serious or anything…" She lied, because while last night had just been kissing, the whole thing had felt special, somehow. She'd sensed that he didn't let just anyone behind the high walls he'd built, but she'd made her way to him. He didn't seem like a casual-fling kind of person but, apparently, he didn't do serious either. So what the hell had their night been?

"We're…friends." He looked to her, as if for reassurance. "And I hope we can stay friends."

Sophie nodded back, even though she did not kiss her other friends or grab their asses while she ground against them. The part of her that had opened itself to Dash started to close again.

A kind of resignation filled her throat instead of the frantic butterflies she'd had hours earlier.

"I just can't risk—" he shook his head "—I can't risk relapsing."

"No, I don't want that either," she said emphatically. Suddenly, she felt more than a little selfish for wanting anything from him. She didn't know much about sobriety—she made a mental note to do research—but she didn't want to be the reason he couldn't stay sober. And she didn't want to lose him as a friend either. She liked being around Dash. And she wouldn't hold it against him that he couldn't date her.

But then, what was she going to do about that part of her that still wanted to grab his ass?

She shook that thought off. "We can just pretend last night didn't happen."

He began to slowly nod. "Okay."

"Okay," she quickly repeated. Though, part of her still clung to the small hope that a plot twist would pop up and Dash would tell her he'd just been kidding and they should absolutely continue to pursue this. But he didn't say anything further.

As the car sped down the highway, she was numb from Dash's words and the rumbling engine gently lulling her. For some reason, her conversation with Ned began to replay in her mind. *You would slip into this idealized version of me.* Had she just completely done the same thing with Dash? She'd fantasized so much about what they could be that now, when faced with the stark truth, she couldn't accept it.

Her phone began to ring loudly. And when she looked down, Nina's name was on the screen. She was close to shaking from her conversation with Dash, so she took in a deep breath before answering. "Hey, Nina, sorry I didn't respond to the group chat. I'm fine. We're heading back from Ojai now."

"Yeah, okay, whatever." Her sister's voice was dismissive, which was…strange.

"What's wrong?" Sophie asked.

"Did you tell Ned that I froze my eggs and am having IVF?" Nina said. "*Celeb Weekly* just posted an exclusive scoop about it, and he's their source."

"I... What?" Sophie sat forward, but the seat belt stopped her with a forceful tug. She remembered the conversation with Ned and Brittany from the night before, after she'd had a glass of wine. She'd told them about Nina's experience, which wasn't hers to tell, but she'd felt safe sharing it with them. Had he really betrayed her trust? Sophie had told Ned that if she could ever do anything to make it up to him, she would, and he'd said he'd think of something. Was this the something?

"You know how much bullshit I have to deal with around this." Nina's exhausted voice came through. "Now every question I'm going to be asked is if I'm pregnant. How could you do this?"

Sophie screamed inside. She wanted to turn the car around and go scream for real at Ned. Her hand gripped the armrest and her voice was shaky as she replied, "Nina, I'm so sorry."

Then the line went dead.

14

DASH

"Do you want to talk about it?" Dash pulled his car into the driveway. He'd heard enough of her call to get the context: Ned had sold a story about her sister to a tabloid. "I can't tell you how many times someone I thought I was close to sold a story about me to the press."

This was true. He'd been betrayed by close friends, exes, and plenty of people he'd only interacted with briefly, including a Lyft driver who'd told a reporter that Dash "stole all of his free ginger chews." Which was absolutely correct, but Dash had missed lunch and needed a snack was all.

"Ned won't answer his phone." Sophie opened the car door, got out, and slammed it shut. "Sorry, didn't mean to slam that. I know he was mad about how I ended things in high school, but he grew up with me and Nina. I can't believe he'd do something like this."

"Money changes people." Dash got out of the car and stood with his hands at his hips. He wasn't happy either. He'd been through the same emotions before when a story leaked about him, but it was another thing entirely to watch someone else experience that level of betrayal.

"My sister is everything to me. She's the only family I have." Sophie's voice started to choke up. She slid her phone back into her dress pocket and rested her palms on the frame of the car door. "She's been through so much already, and she doesn't deserve this. What if she never talks to me again?" She wiped a tear away from the corner of her eye.

Dash wasn't sure he knew how to comfort her. His family wasn't exactly cookie-cutter, and he wouldn't say any of them—except maybe Poppy—were his everything. He also didn't know Nina well enough to reassure her that she would talk to Sophie again. But as Sophie choked back tears, Dash found that he could no longer just stand and watch. So he moved around the car and wrapped her in a hug. She let her head fall against his shoulder, and they fit as closely as if their bodies were the nesting pottery bowls he sometimes made. He closed his eyes, and his hand brushed a strand of hair behind her ear as they stood together.

There was nothing to say in a situation like this. The damage was done. But with a sickening new realization, it dawned on him that if he hadn't encouraged Sophie to try this TikTok thing in the first place, maybe she wouldn't even be in this mess. She definitely wouldn't have gone out of her way to see Ned. Perhaps Dash had made her life a bit worse by being in it.

"I never should've told you to lean in to TikTok. The internet is truly a trash heap." He pulled away from her. "If you don't want to work on the speech anymore, I would totally understand." He *did* understand, but for some reason his grip on her shoulders tightened.

"Do you *not* want me to work on it?" She dabbed a tear away from her cheek.

"No, no, I'm—" His words evaporated like water on the burning concrete driveway. He didn't love Los Angeles in the summer. It was too hot and too dry, and now he was starting to sweat around his hairline. He wiped his forehead with the back of his hand as he tried again. "I want you to work on it. I just also want to make sure you're okay, especially after..."

"You mean because we made out?" A little spark of playfulness flickered across her face, and while he was relieved, he also wondered if she was intentionally poking at him.

"Because of that, yes." He rubbed at the longhorn tattoo on his bicep—a piece he'd gotten inked after leaving rehab—the forward-facing horns represented looking to the future, which is how he wanted the rest of his life to be.

The present, though, was Sophie, and a warm breeze brushed through her hair, whipping long tendrils along the side of her face. She was gorgeous: her cheeks had a flush, her breasts swelled as she breathed in and out, and those eyes—her absolutely dazzling almond eyes surrounded by thick lashes that focused solely on him. He was lucky she even bothered to look his way.

"You are a really great kisser, so I will miss that." She chuckled, but he almost heard a sadness there. "But we're okay, Dash. I totally understand. I mean, I don't *totally understand* where you're coming from, but I would do the same thing if I were in your situation. We're okay."

Sophie smirked, and Dash spotted her canine tooth—the one that had nibbled his neck the night before. And while he knew he needed to move forward and away from Sophie, there was an undeniable sense of loss that had settled in his throat.

He'd kissed so many women throughout his life—on set and off—forgetting her should've been easy. But Sophie said he was a *great kisser*—no, a *really great kisser.* And why did the thought of never getting to brush his lips against hers again hurt so damn much?

A light breeze swept across the lawn, and the ends of her dress swayed to reveal a hint of her thighs and the freckles that trailed up her legs. What would it be like to just slide his hands from her heels, up her calves, then just up, up, up...

"Dash?" Sophie's voice cut through his thoughts. He swallowed his desire and looked up, only to realize she'd been watching him, too.

The problem was that absolutely ridiculous red floral minidress she'd worn for their road trip. Ridiculous because it was short enough to highlight her curvy legs, and the sweetheart neckline was doing an excellent job of emphasizing her breasts. He could almost see the faint buds through the fabric...

"I'll come over when the speech is done, and we can run through it, okay?" She clearly wanted to leave, and he was the one who had a problem now.

He had no one to blame but himself, seeing as how he'd firmly planted the *just friends* stake in the ground. So he nodded a reply. But as she turned to walk up the steps to her place, he found he couldn't keep his mouth shut. The truth bubbled out of him like lava: hot, thick, and unstoppable.

"I don't know that I can be friends with you," he called out to her.

She turned back and her mouth hung open, maybe in surprise. "What?"

Exactly. What was he thinking? Well, he wasn't thinking was the problem. He was just letting his feelings do the talking, which he never normally did but he found he couldn't stop them from gushing out now that he'd opened the hose. "I don't know how this is going to work. I mean, *look* at you."

She looked down at her dress, then back up at him. "I looked," she said. "What are you saying here, Dash?"

Ugh, and the way she said his damn name, like the mention of him tasted sweet on her tongue. Why had he thought, even for a minute, that he'd be able to turn off his attraction and just go on like nothing had happened between them?

He couldn't. Maybe he'd been single and sexless for too long, or he wanted more of the adrenaline he'd felt from kissing her, but he couldn't just be around her and not touch her.

"How can we be friends when I know what you taste like?" He was more than a little amazed by his own bluntness, but her mouth was sweet citrus, and he wanted a little bit of that for himself.

She swallowed, tucked a loose strand of hair behind her ear, then looked up at him. A kind of steady flame had settled in her eyes, so when she spoke, heat came out with her words. "You don't know what I taste like. Not really."

His eyes instinctively darted down her ridiculously short dress. No, he didn't know what she tasted like *everywhere*, but his dick really wanted him to find out.

"You're right, maybe we can't be friends. But maybe we can be friends who..." She licked her lips as her gaze traveled up his body, lingered slightly at his chest, then eventually met his eyes.

His breath caught. He wanted nothing more than to get on his knees, pull down her panties, and explore her with his tongue, but he couldn't let himself get close to her that way... not unless *she* wanted him.

"We're both adults and clearly attracted to each other." She smoothed her hands down her dress. "We can just get this out of our systems so it's not a big thing. We don't need a full-blown relationship. No one has to know about it. No commitments, just sex."

Dash's jaw had maybe completely unhinged itself and he must've stared at her with a dumbfounded expression, because she started talking again.

"Or I've just totally humiliated myself, and I'll ask you to forget the conversation entirely. I'll walk back to my place, and we can return to not talking to each other." She ran a hand through her hair, which was in a messy bun, and her fingers got caught at the hair tie and then she had to awkwardly extract them. She let out an exasperated sigh.

He couldn't help but laugh. Did she seriously think he didn't want the exact same thing?

"Dash, it's not funny!" Her fingers furiously tried to fix her hair as she spoke.

"Do you actually think that I could even—for a second—not want to touch you?" He took a step toward her. Her head shot up, and she eyed him.

Part of him knew he *should* go home and leave her alone, but he couldn't just forget her. Sophie had been the first person he'd felt genuinely attracted to since getting sober. She'd gotten him out of his routine and given him space to see what life could be like if he let other people in, and he had those pesky feelings for her.

Maybe they could stay friends, with the bonus of sex. If he cut Sophie off now, he wasn't sure how he'd react, but if he kept her in his orbit, he could continue to let whatever this was run its course safely.

So when he moved to her and took her face in his hands, he asked hopefully, "Are you sure about this?"

She nodded, and he brought her mouth to his. There was nothing soft about his approach this time—no more tentative kisses to gauge how eager she was. He knew she wanted this just as much as he did. And he needed more of her. She wrapped her arms around his neck to pull them closer, and a little moan escaped her lips as the needy centers of them met.

His mouth traveled across her chin and to her neck, where he lightly traced his tongue down the length of her collarbone and in between her cleavage. He traced a finger across the scar on her chest before lightly kissing the spot. "Will you tell me about this someday?"

"Yes, but right now I just need you to take my clothes off," she breathed out.

Then he pulled at the sleeves of her dress, and she helped

him maneuver her arms out of it, letting the fabric fall and rest at her waist.

"You wore this just to mess with me, didn't you?" he asked as he trailed his fingertips lightly across her shoulder.

She shivered under his touch as she said, "Yes, yes, I absolutely did."

"You'll pay for that."

"Prove it," she said.

And so he would. He pulled at the fabric of her lace bra, took her breast in his hand, and gently licked the nub of her nipple. Then he tugged, and she let out a small, "Oh, God," as he sucked her into his mouth.

"You taste so good." She was soft but perky for him, and his fingers claimed her flesh greedily. She grabbed a fistful of his hair as he brought the bud to his mouth again.

He glanced around the property, which was surrounded by hedges. His space was private, even though they were in the middle of the city. Plus, he didn't see the point of going inside, not when the sun had turned her skin golden and warm.

He carefully knelt in the grass in front of her, pushed her dress up, and saw the most absurd pair of panties he'd ever laid eyes on.

"Little pink hearts?" He looked up, and she grinned wickedly back.

"Look closer. They have smiley faces, too." Her hand found his hair, and she pulled at the ends.

He hooked his thumbs under the top edge of those panties and pulled them off slowly.

She stepped out of the panties and lifted the hem of her dress for him. She knew what she was doing just as much as he did, and that made him even hotter for her.

"I'm going to make you feel so good." His fingertips trailed down her thighs, past her knees, then back up again. He looked up, his head between her legs, and her eyes smoldered back.

She opened her mouth, then closed it.

"What?" He wanted to dive right in, so to speak, but not if she was having second thoughts. "Should I stop?"

"Not to be dramatic, but if you don't keep going I might actually need a new pacemaker." She tapped the scar on her chest.

"So this is a life-and-death situation, then?" He was still on his knees, but he was getting the impression he wouldn't have to beg.

"Please, Dash," she said. "Please."

15

SOPHIE

"Oh!" Sophie exclaimed as she steadied herself by fisting a hand through Dash's hair.

Much like everything that morning, she truly couldn't have predicted standing in her yard, topless, and being eaten out by Dash. It was a little hard to plan for these things!

"Tell me how to make you come," he said.

She looked down at the beautiful curve of his distinguished nose, the dimple on his chin, and his strong arms holding her in place. Then she licked her lips and wondered if asking for her absolute favorite thing would be too much of a reach, considering he was already doing a great job on his own.

"Can I ride your face?" she asked, then scrunched up her nose. She'd never been so forward with what she wanted during sex. She wasn't self-conscious, exactly, but she'd always worried about offending her partner by voicing the need for something different. She'd had plenty of great sex, but she'd usually let her partner explore her without interruption. This time, though, she wanted to tell Dash exactly what would make her come because she needed him to do that.

His eyes glazed over, and he cracked a naughty half smile. He lay down in the grass, his lips still wet from her, and she fell to her knees next to him, then hitched a leg over his head until she was on top of him. His mouth found her slit quickly, and he began to lightly trace her nub with his tongue. The combination of his light tongue flicks and the slightly cool breeze sent tingles through her.

If she'd known that outdoor sex would be this hot and fun, she would've tried it before. Or put it into one of her books. Maybe she should if she ever was able to write again… He plunged his tongue into her, making her thoughts stop entirely. She moaned loudly as he asked, "What will the neighbors think?"

Which…why was that making her want to come even more? Did she want to be caught? No, she would be absolutely mortified if someone walked in on them or peered over the tall fence, but that idea of being caught was undeniably doing something to her. She moved her hips a few inches up, then back, allowing him to lick the length of her.

Then she rested a hand on the grass behind her. His free hand caught her wrist and held her there as she continued to ride his face.

"You're so wet," he said in between licks.

Sophie realized, as she pinched her own nipples, that she had almost no inhibitions with Dash. She didn't feel self-conscious about the way her body looked, how she tasted, or the little sounds she made. She was just in the moment and loving every bit of what he was doing.

When she reached one hand toward his belt and trailed her fingers over his bulge, he murmured "Fuck" underneath her.

As soon as he made her come, she planned to return the favor. And she was getting close. Her legs tensed, and she let her head fall back as she continued to glide her hips up and down. The sun warmed her cheeks, and she closed her eyes against the bright heat.

She groaned as she leaned back farther and his tongue dove into her while his middle finger traced circles over her clit. She bucked her hips back and forth while he continued to eat her out and tease her bud. The tension was building too fast and too quickly.

"I'm almost there." She sat forward because she wanted to watch Dash as she came. His eyes closed as she wove her hands through his hair.

"Come for me," he said. And those words, laced with the rich command in his voice and watching him from above, sent her over the edge.

"I'm going..." she breathed out. Her eyes closed, then opened, as little embers of pure bliss rocked through her.

Her breath came out in ragged gulps. She was never at a loss for words the way she was then—just wanting to stay on top of him until all the pleasure drained from her.

"That was so hot," he said eventually.

She looked down, and the hem of her dress was around Dash's chin. She reached behind her again and found the firmness of him. But when the tips of her fingers began to slip underneath the waistband of his pants, his hand stopped her.

"I haven't been with someone in a very long time." His eyes locked onto hers, and she swallowed. "When I do have sex again, it's going to be exactly how I want it."

"Oh." She broke their eye contact. He did *not* want to have sex with her in the middle of their yard, which was fine, she supposed. But she was still topless, and her panties had landed on the branch of a rose bush.

So she pulled her bra straps and dress sleeves back up, then walked toward Dash's garden and gingerly plucked her panties free—a few petals falling loose as she did.

A frantic series of chitters made her glance up, and she saw Richard in a branch of the avocado tree. His hands clung tightly to the branch as he screamed at her.

"That damn squirrel takes all my fruit and then has the audacity to watch us?" Dash pushed himself up to sitting, then winced as he readjusted to being on both legs. "Get lost, Dick!"

The squirrel seemed to listen and quickly maneuvered from the tree onto the fence and took off at a sprint.

"He didn't mean that, Richard!" she called out after the squirrel. Though, she was still in a bit of a daze as she eyed Dash's shirt, which was drenched in what was probably his sweat and hers. It clung to his torso, and she blinked hard at the sight of his muscled chest.

"So, um..." Well, she didn't exactly know what to say. It was probably close to noon, judging by the sun, and she'd just let Dash give her the strongest orgasm of her life. But they weren't going to date. They'd had a little fling. And she was still his tenant slash speechwriter, but she very much wouldn't mind riding his face again...

"I can see your wheels turning." Dash swiped a hand through the hair she'd tugged moments earlier. "Was that okay?"

"Oh, yeah." She kind of choked out a laugh, still in disbelief that any of it had happened in the first place. "But are you okay? I mean, I know you're worried about staying sober and—"

He cut her words off with a wave of his hand. "Nothing about what we did felt wrong. Trust me, I will tell you if it starts to be too much."

She tried to focus on putting her underwear back on because, really, being the only half-naked person in their yard felt unbalanced. But his words were doing quick rotations through her head: *If it starts to be too much*, as in...maybe there would be another time, or this wasn't the end for them?

"Are *you* okay?" he asked.

"Oh, uh, yeah." She shimmied her panties on. "That was really unexpected."

"I know." His hands fidgeted at his sides. "I just...couldn't imagine not touching you."

And then she blinked more, because something had clearly opened in Dash and he was being the kind of honest and vulnerable person she wrote about in her books. Which *so* wasn't who Dash was. He was funny, but openness was not his usual mode.

She didn't know what to do with this version of him—the one who complimented her and couldn't keep his hands to himself. Especially because he'd made it clear that they wouldn't date, and she'd said she was okay just banging the feelings out.

But Sophie had never done casual before. She dated people, then slept with them, in that order. If this was a normal relationship, she'd probably go have a cuddle or a meal with her person. But people who were just having sex probably didn't engage in those things.

She decided to act like she knew what she was doing, though, because the last thing she wanted was for Dash to think she couldn't handle their arrangement. She needed more of him, and if faking like she was okay would get her that, then she was about to win an Oscar for Best Sex Buddy.

"I should go. I have to feed Rain Boots—my fish—and uh, organize my books, and finish this speech for your dad." She grabbed her phone, which she'd dropped in the grass.

"You could stay." Dash was doing the thing where he shifted from one foot to the other, and she wasn't totally sure if that meant he was anxious, or mad, or just nothing at all. But she figured he'd need space just as much as she did to figure out what had happened.

"No, no, no, no, no." Her voice had become loud, too loud, really. She cleared her throat, then gave him her best *I'm cool with this* smile back. "Okay, well, thank you for the...thing. It was very nice." She shook her messy bun, knowing she was not doing particularly well at stringing words together. "I'll text you when I have a draft of the speech ready."

"Sounds good." His jaw tightened, and she nodded, trying to convey the air of business as usual.

Then she turned and told herself that all she needed to do was reach the front door. As soon as she did that, she could go inside, lock herself in, and scream, or whatever she needed to work through the last few hours.

As she walked, her phone pinged. She swallowed down the apprehension that it might be Nina texting to inform her they were no longer sisters. But when she checked the screen there was a text from Carla.

Free Wednesday? I can have my schedule cleared.

Sophie's jaw clenched. She *was* free that night, but how could she see Carla after the weekend she'd spent with Dash? Then again, Dash was meant to be a casual thing. He explicitly told her that he couldn't be in a real relationship. And wasn't finding love the whole point of everything she was doing right now? She couldn't just ignore the fact that all Dash was available for was a friendship with the occasional hookup. She couldn't prioritize him over Carla, who might want to give their relationship another chance.

Sophie took out her keys and unlocked her door, not bothering to see if Dash was still there. She couldn't look at him while holding her phone with a text from Carla without her brain overheating. She closed the door behind her and leaned against it.

If she started something back up with Carla, then she couldn't see Dash, physically at least. There had to be rules if she were going to juggle two people at once...right?

Absolutely ☺

Sophie typed back to Carla. When she hit Send, there was a knot in the pit of her stomach. She should be happy that there was a potential second chance on the horizon, but she couldn't stop herself from glancing out her window toward Dash's place.

TEXT CHAIN BETWEEN SOPHIE AND NINA

Nina: Hey, could you call me back?

Sophie: I'm so sorry, Nina. It all just slipped out.

Nina: We need to actually talk about this. No text apologies.

Nina: Hello?

Nina: How am I the one begging you to talk to me?

TEXT CHAIN BETWEEN SOPHIE AND POPPY

Poppy: I saw the article about your sister...you okay?

Sophie: Nina's going to kill me. I feel like I can't talk to her right now. She's too pissed off.

Poppy: She just needs time. Your sister loves you.

Sophie: I know. I'm going to give her a minute to cool off.

Poppy: Is your writing thing fixed yet?

Sophie: Oh, you mean my failing career? No, I still have writer's block 👇

Poppy: I keep telling you to sage the house...

Poppy: whispers :::sage the block away:::

Sophie: Are the sage growers paying you for this product placement?

Poppy: it's called being a visionary, look it up

SOPHIE'S TIKTOK
High-School Sweetheart Recap
Weeks until book is due: 4 (and a few days)

"You might notice that I'm wearing a face mask." Sophie pointed to the green mask covering her entire face. She wore a blush-pink robe and tightened the wrap around her waist. "I'm needing a bit of self-care today, because after the last few days, I feel like I'm about to truly explode."

"My ex-boyfriend from high school, as it turns out, is an actual piece of trash and sold something I told him in confidence to the tabloids. So now my sister—" Sophie stopped herself. "No, I'm not going to talk about her any more than I already have. But let's just say, my life is a mess. Messier than usual.

"And to top it all off, I'm starting to realize that I might have some real issues. Like, fear of rejection and low self-esteem... It's just a lot. Like, I have all of this data coming in from meeting up with my exes, and now I have to actually figure out what it all means. But I'm afraid that what it means is that I probably need a lot of expensive therapy, with money I don't have."

Sophie sat on the lip of her tub and sighed. She tapped a finger against her now-dry mask and continued, "So, anyways, yeah. I'm just taking this afternoon to decompress and try to mask-away all the pain because I'll be meeting up with my next ex soon. Drop some self-care tips in the comments."

COMMENTS

@bookishatwell I read friends-to-lovers for self-care. Out loud. To my cat. Don't judge me.

@bookrecsbymel Have you ever sniffed a book for self-care? Because that shit WORKS.

@tokcrafty2me be kind to yourself, change is hard

16

DASH

Dash had made the clay too wet, again. It slipped through his fingers and slumped in a heap on the wheel, exhausted from being overworked. His phone was propped against the opposite wall to capture a time-lapse video for a TikTok post—all standard routine when he had a crafting day. But he wasn't focused on any of those things, really.

He hadn't had a good night's sleep since his weekend away with Sophie, and his brain was short-circuiting from the two cups of coffee with extra sugar he'd had to compensate.

He had to be borderline delirious. How else to explain that Sophie's perverse little canine tooth kept flashing through his thoughts? Or how the peach-colored freckles that dotted her shoulders seemed like they'd make an interesting pattern for his mug? And then there was the way she'd said his name— *Dash*—all breathy. Why could he still hear her saying it, even now? He hadn't seen her in a few days, but she was haunting his thoughts.

He was clearly on edge from the change in his routine and the new surge of feelings, or something. And now he was attempting to craft those feelings away. Even though he certainly didn't need another coffee mug—he had a gorgeous set he'd made earlier that year—he'd taken out the clay and added water, because that's what had come to him.

But before he could plan out the next step, his phone pinged. He stopped the video recording and saw a message.

@craftycindy getting your hands dirty?

Normally Dash would respond back with something flirty or quippy. But now, seeing her name didn't feel right. The idea of engaging with her on any kind of flirtatious level made him uneasy. He wasn't dating Sophie—he knew that—but even flirting with someone else didn't sit well.

@tokcrafty2me making a new mug set, actually ☺

He kept the text simple, factual, no hidden innuendos. Before he could go back to filming, another message came through.

@craftycindy when are you going to show me your mug, tho?

Dash cracked his neck, a little annoyed that she was trying to coax more out of him. She had occasionally suggested Dash show his face, but he never had. He knew what she looked like from her videos, so it seemed a little unfair in some respects, but remaining anonymous was important to him.

@craftycindy I won't reveal your identity, Batman.

She wasn't going to let this go. And maybe it was wrong, but Dash thought there might be a way to shut the whole flirtatious thing down quickly, so he replied.

@tokcrafty2me lol, my girlfriend is the only one who sees my mug

@craftycindy Girlfriend? Since when?

@tokcrafty2me It's pretty new

@craftycindy Does she know about the drinking, Dash?

He nearly dropped the phone. What had she just said? Dash reread the message, certain that the lack of sleep was causing him to stress-hallucinate. But no, she had said his name. How did she know who he was? Had he accidentally revealed his first name somehow? His heart raced as he tried to determine how to respond, or if he should respond.

@tokcrafty2me Dash? You have me confused with someone else.

@craftycindy We're meant to be together, Dash Montrose. Will she love you like I can?

Dash swallowed down a lump of pure terror. He was no stranger to stalkers. His family had dealt with their fair share throughout the years—one had even broken into their house looking for his dad when Dash was a kid. If this woman somehow knew his full name, did she also know where he lived?

Calling the cops absolutely crossed his mind. But then he'd have to reveal his TikTok account to them and turn over the messages where he confessed to being an alcoholic, and he wasn't convinced they'd keep any of those facts a secret. He'd been in Hollywood long enough to know that everyone could be bought, for a price.

So instead, he took off his apron, grabbed his keys, wallet, and phone, and made for the door. He couldn't be alone in his house, not while knowing that Cindy had figured out who he was. He needed to talk, but there was really only one person for that.

"Hey, buddy, you know I don't like to do this, but I'm going to have to cut you off."

Chris's hand clapped on Dash's back. When Dash glanced up, he was met with furrowed brows and plenty of concern, which made him clutch the plastic bag closer to his chest.

"I haven't even gone to the chocolate section yet." They were in Gimme Some Sugar, a beautifully curated candy store in West Hollywood that had just opened next to Lisa Vanderpump's bar, Sur. Which also meant that, even though it was the middle of the day, they could hear (and feel) the blast of frenetic pop music from the iconic bar next door. Dash was surprised that he didn't have a headache from the bright fluorescent glow of the overhead lights, but maybe the black-and-white candy-striped overhang, or the metallic bins that lined the shop like sugary presents, had all conspired to keep his brain focused on the promise of candy.

"Your bag is completely full." Chris bounced slightly to rock Luna in the carrier. "And I don't think Luna is going to sleep through another nineties pop anthem. They're too catchy."

"I told you I have a stalker, right? I need to stress eat. You and Luna can wait outside." Dash wasn't exactly desperate to stay in the store, but he needed to be out of his house and away from reality for a little while.

"No, my friend, this is my intervention. I'm cutting you off." Chris gave a hand signal for Dash to stand up and, reluctantly, he did. Dash paid for his candy, and they walked out.

The busy West Hollywood sidewalk was wide and cluttered with restaurants and shops. Dash popped a gummy crocodile in his mouth and chewed, the instant hit of sugar giving him a rush of dopamine. Out of the corner of his eye, he saw two guys walk out of a MedMen dispensary. One of them gestured toward Dash and whispered something to the other. Great, he'd been spotted. Dash angled the baseball cap lower on his head to cover his eyes as they walked.

"Do you want to talk about how you're kind of going from zero to sixty?" Chris kept a protective hand on the baby carrier as they walked.

Dash swallowed his candy. He'd told Chris about Sophie, their time in Ojai, and his front yard... And then he'd told Chris about how his online friend had turned into a very real stalker. He'd gone from someone with absolutely nothing happening in his life, to a lot of somethings happening. He didn't want to delve into those again, though, so he tried to deflect.

"What does everyone have against sugar? It's delicious." Dash popped another crocodile in his mouth to emphasize his point. The candy was already sticky from the heat outside, and he licked his fingers.

"You know I'm not talking about the candy." Chris stopped under the shade of a blooming jacaranda tree that had littered the sidewalk with wilted purple petals. "You originally wanted to get a new tattoo, which we're not doing. You and I both know that you need to take change slowly. You're not erratic, but this new thing with Sophie has thrown you off. And you need to focus on making sure you're safe from this person who has somehow figured out who you are."

He *had* wanted to get a new tattoo of a pixie tangerine, like one of the ones above Sophie's fireplace. He liked how bright they were, and they reminded him of their Ojai trip.

Dash felt deflated, like all of the steam he'd built up had just been released from his body. Yes, Chris was right: he was kind of flailing. And he didn't really know what to do about Cindy, the stalker crafter. But he couldn't delete TikTok, because it was his only way of contacting her, and he didn't want her to potentially retaliate. He'd just have to take his situation one day at a time.

Eventually he said, "You're right. I'll stop seeing Sophie and fix this other problem, too."

"You're allowed to date, Dash."

"But not her." Dash could not start something—well, more than he already had—with Poppy's best friend. Not only because he'd be messing up his sister's friendship but because he respected Sophie too much to drag her into his bullshit.

"Why not?" Chris's tone had gone from friendly to accusatory. Luna fussed against him, so they started to walk down the street toward Dash's place. "If you're going to tell me again that it's complicated, then I don't want to hear it."

Dash licked his lips as he thought on how exactly to answer this. He didn't want to tell Chris that he was afraid he couldn't give Sophie everything she deserved—a loving marriage—because Chris had managed to have exactly that. But Chris never really appreciated that they were very different people, and Dash would always be a disappointment. "Because I'm going to fuck it up, the way I always do."

Chris clicked his tongue at Dash. "You're being way too hard on yourself."

They reached Dash's gate and stood outside. Dash sucked in his bottom lip and leaned against the metal door. "I'm not." Dash knew his strengths, and being reliable wasn't one of them.

"What about when you came over the other week to help me and Mira? You're amazing with Luna. You make shit better— that's what you do." Chris's hands were on his hips, and he gave Dash a look so stern that he could almost see what kind of a dad Chris would be in Luna's teenage years.

"I also make everything worse. I've ruined my parents' precious Hollywood dynasty."

"Two things." Chris held up a finger. "One, your sister isn't an actress, so if you ruined the dynasty, so did she. And two, your parents don't know how hard you've worked to get to where you are now because you haven't told them your story. And you know that your story is powerful. Once you share it, you're going to change lives for the better."

"If I did tell them, they'd just know me as the jobless alcoholic versus merely the jobless son they already have." Dash shoved another gummy into his mouth and focused on angrily chewing.

But Chris crossed his arms and leveled Dash with a glare. "You need a meeting."

Dash swallowed a lump in his throat and looked off. Why had he called Chris? Of course he'd suggest a meeting. But this wasn't about drinking at all. Dash was fine and in control. He didn't need a roomful of strangers to help him out of this situation. He wanted to end the line of thought immediately. "I'm fine."

"You're not, and if you don't go to one, then I'll bring you to one. In fact, let's just go right now." Chris was stubborn, always. So stubborn that he'd already started to walk down the street in the direction of the meeting place.

"Fine, I'll go." Dash held up his hands, as if in surrender, but he was not going to a meeting. "Just not today. I have to figure out the TikTok thing."

Chris turned back and released a frustrated sigh. "Then, when?"

"Tomorrow. I'll go to one tomorrow." Dash shoved a handful of gummies into his mouth, not caring which ones he was even eating. His brain worked overtime to block out Chris's words, *you need a meeting.* He didn't need anything except to get back in his house and lock the door, the same thing he'd done for all the prior months that had kept him on a straight path.

"I'm going to follow up and make sure you go."

As Chris stared Dash down, the pedestrian gate opened and Sophie came out. She wore one of her signature dresses that fluttered in the breeze and revealed slivers of dewy skin. Her hair was down, and he smelled the tangerine scent of her.

She looked between Dash and Chris, and a surprised smile flashed across her face, but Dash immediately went cold at the thought that she'd potentially heard them. Maybe she'd heard every single word Chris had said and thought that Dash was on the edge of slipping up. She could be totally disgusted by his lack of control over his addiction issues. She was probably thinking of how lucky she was to not actually be in a relationship with him.

"Hey, are you Chris?" Sophie approached him. Chris nodded, though Dash could tell that his friend was still heated from their conversation. "I'm Sophie. I've been hoping we'd meet. Dash has told me so much about you."

And then, because she was Sophie, she went in for a side hug so as not to disturb Luna. Chris looked to Dash as he quickly hugged her back.

"Nice to meet you, Sophie." Then Chris gave him a pointed look. "Dash, we'll talk tomorrow."

They watched as Chris walked toward his car. Sophie nodded as she said, "That's an excellent vanity plate."

Dash looked, too, though he already knew the letters on the plate: *DADG ERS*. "He used to play left field for the Dodgers before Luna was born. His dad jokes came quickly, as you can see."

"The real role he was born to play." Sophie gave a tight smile, then flicked the clear bag of candy at his side with her index finger. "So it was an eventful dude-bro outing, then?"

"Very bro-ish. We watched NASCAR while eating raw steak." Dash raised an eyebrow at her.

She gave him a withering but amused look back. "Dash, please, easy on the dirty talk."

Her playfulness made the conversation with Chris melt away.

His hand instinctively reached for hers. He thought to pull it back, but then her fingertips traced a little line along his thumb.

"Everything okay?" she asked.

"Yeah, I bought about three pounds of candy, which should last me through dinner."

She gave a knowing smile. "That sounds right."

"Where are you headed?" He didn't want to lose the feel of her next to him. "I have some free time now, if you wanted any video help?"

She shook her head. "I'm, uh, meeting up with Carla."

His breath caught, then he cleared his throat. "Oh, okay, cool." Her grip on his hand loosened, and his hand flexed at the lack of her palm against his.

Sophie was meeting up with her exes. Why should this one be any different? His hands turned clammy, and he rubbed them against his jeans.

Maybe it wasn't a date? Maybe she was just looking for more closure? Though, Sophie had told him that Carla had been the one ex she'd seen a future and potential second chance with. He couldn't stand in the way of her finding happiness, even if it was without him.

Still, there was a burning acidity in his throat that had started to bubble up. He couldn't ignore the fact that he had feelings for Sophie—he absolutely did. But he had no right to act on those, or to lead her on, when the only thing he was looking for was to stay out of trouble. Sophie was complicated: she was his tenant, and Poppy would kill them both, like Sophie said.

He would focus on the future, not on what had happened between them. And besides, if he ever got in another relationship again, he'd need simple, straightforward, and drama-free— the exact opposite of what being with Sophie would entail.

"Okay, well…" Sophie blinked rapidly, but he couldn't help but feel like there was sadness in her eyes.

She gave a little wave goodbye, and he mumbled a quick response before she turned and walked down the street toward her potential second chance.

Good. She should walk away from him. Without trying, maybe he'd given her the out she needed to save herself from getting hurt. And he should be happy that she didn't want any part of him, but his jaw still clenched as he watched her vanish.

17

SOPHIE

Sophie wanted to turn around and talk to Dash, because she'd absolutely heard Chris mention that he needed a meeting and she was concerned. But their conversation had been private, and she had no business intervening. Plus, she was sure Dash *would* go to a meeting—he'd told his best friend he would, after all.

She rolled her shoulders as she attempted to stop thinking about the way Dash's firm grip on her palm had held her steady. But the fluttery, warm sensation Sophie had grown used to feeling whenever Dash's name popped into her head returned. She felt enveloped by it, the way she did whenever she reached a particularly emotional scene while reading a book. She could easily be swept away by the idea of him and what they could be—living in the fantasy world she often did. But she knew the truth was they would never move beyond the friends-with-benefits fun they had.

Sophie needed to turn over a new page and focus on Carla. If there was any chance of tonight going well, then she couldn't think about Dash. So she might as well commit with a video.

SOPHIE'S TIKTOK
Ex number three
Name: Doc
Occupation: Cardiologist
Length of relationship: Eleven and a half months
Reason for breakup: My issues
Weeks until book is due: 4 (and one day)

Sophie continued to walk down the street as she spoke to her phone. "I have a date tonight with my third ex, who we will call Doc. I had a long relationship with Doc, and she was the only person who has ever told me they loved me. But for some reason, I couldn't say those words back. Well, not *for some reason*. I kind of know the reason, which is that I never felt good enough for Doc."

Sophie stumbled as she hip-checked a sign, clutched her chest, and looked back to where she'd tripped. The sign was for valet bike-parking. "Okay, did you see that? Only in LA will you see a sign for someone to valet your bicycle..." Sophie shook off her annoyance and continued to walk.

"Anyway, I'm trying to piece together everything I've learned so far, and I'm starting to wonder if in my relationships and life I just kind of lose myself. Like, do I even need to be meeting up with these exes, or should I just be putting in more work and digging deep to find the answers? Because so far, my first ex shut me down and told me to just look ahead. Ex number two totally effed me over. And the ex I'm seeing tonight... well, who knows.

"So how do I fix this? How do I bring more of myself to the table in my next relationship?" Sophie's head tilted back as she said, "Basically, anytime I think about my situation, just one song comes to mind. DJ, play 'I Knew You Were Trouble' by Taylor Swift for the people at home."

Sophie stopped filming, added in the Taylor Swift anthem, and posted her video. She started to walk again and was determined *not* to think about Dash. But she instinctively glanced at her screen to see if he'd texted. He hadn't. She inhaled sharply and prepared to put the phone away and bury down her disappointment, but then she saw a new notification of a comment on her video that made her smile.

@tokcrafty2me you are perfect.

Sophie arrived early to dinner—twenty minutes early, to be exact. Tardiness was a pet peeve of Carla's, so Sophie power-walked the mile to Santa Monica Boulevard and the sushi restaurant where they were meeting.

In doing so, though, she'd rubbed her toes raw against the new slip-on sandals she wore—closed-toe, heavy, and not at all appropriate for Los Angeles in the summer (but they looked too cute not to wear). So she limped on the sidewalk in front of the restaurant and watched as a rather angry man shouted into his phone and pointed to an illegally parked Ferrari in the process of being towed.

The air was warm, despite the setting sun, and a thin line of sweat dappled her hairline. Sophie touched a finger to remove it. She wouldn't be the first one at the table, but she also wouldn't be late. Her options were hiding between two enormous and overloaded dumpsters in the alley behind the restaurant or... Yup, she was in too much pain to go any farther, so that was her option and the one she took.

She scanned both sides of the alley to make sure no one was watching, then took her left shoe off and instantly sighed. Her pinkie toe was as round and red as a raspberry, and she rested her bare foot on top of her right. Her head fell back against the building's stucco wall, and she closed her eyes as she wiggled her toes in the hot summer breeze.

Even though Sophie had published a book, worn her very best minidress, and used a flat iron to add waves to her hair, she was still a big wad of nerves. She hadn't seen her ex in two years, and she wasn't feeling confident.

Because Carla wasn't all that easy to impress. She was a cardiologist to the stars, came from money, had traveled the world, and read literature with a capital *L*. She was almost as intimidating as the blank page.

"Sophie?"

She startled and her head pivoted toward Carla's voice. There was her ex, Carla Shah, standing on the sidewalk with her glasses lowered down the bridge of her nose and her mouth open in confusion. Tall and slim, with a wavy chocolate-brown shoulder-length bob, she wore high-waisted silk shorts and a white button-down top. Her lacy black bra was just visible through the shirt, and the subtle sexiness made her even chicer.

Sophie attempted to remove herself from the dumpster situation but stumbled against one of the trash bins. A loose bag fell from the top and cascaded across her head and shoulders in a trash-filled shower.

"What the—" Sophie shouted. Her hands scrambled to brush away the pieces of paper, plastic containers, and old food. Her voice was thick with humiliation as she said, "I think there's wasabi in my eyebrow. This isn't happening, is it?"

"Unfortunately, it is." And then there were Carla's hands, which flew around Sophie's face, clearing off trash and picking a used wet wipe out of her hair. "What were you doing back here?"

"I don't know!" Sophie did know, though, but didn't want to say *Hiding from you.* Once the trash was cleared from her body, including a packet of soy sauce she'd had to pluck from her cleavage, she moved away from the dumpsters and attempted to salvage the situation.

"Could we just pretend this never happened and start with me saying that I really love the new haircut?" Sophie asked.

And, to Sophie's relief, Carla let out a generous chuckle, then closed the gap between them and pulled her in for a hug before she could even respond. The vanilla bourbon of her perfume surrounded Sophie as she hugged her back. Being wrapped in Carla's arms felt familiar and safe, just as she'd remembered.

And as Carla guided them both into the restaurant, a firm hand on Sophie's lower back, for a moment it felt like no time had passed. But then, she remembered Dash's hand on her back as he...

"You okay?" Carla asked.

"Yup." Sophie willed the memory from her thoughts and forced a smile. "More than okay."

The restaurant was all low lighting meant to imitate the soft glow of candles, and chill hip-hop music played in the background. At the table next to them, two women posed for a selfie together while a waiter entered their order into an iPad.

Carla sat and crossed one long leg over the other, her skin gleaming as if buttered. Sophie could remember the feel of being caught up in those legs, but she dismissed the thought quickly.

"This place is secretly owned by Leo DiCaprio and impossible to get reservations for," Carla said in a low tone. "But his cousin is a client." She shrugged, like it was no big deal that she'd called in a favor to Leonardo DiCaprio's cousin for their date.

Sophie leaned across the table, aware of how it would emphasize her cleavage, and said, "Since you were nice enough to get us in, then I'm going to be nice and let you order for us."

Carla had always loved ordering for them—she was a self-proclaimed foodie. She licked her lips, then said, "You won't regret this."

"Unless you order too much food." Sophie raised a brow,

and a grin crossed Carla's lips. On their first date ever, when Sophie was trying to impress her, she'd eaten all the sushi that Carla had ordered—too much—and proceeded to feel nauseous immediately after.

"You just have to remember to share what I order," Carla said.

"Sharing is wildly overrated."

Sophie was surprised that the conversation was easier than expected. Part of her had anticipated that this dinner would mostly be hashing things out, something they'd never had the chance to do, but maybe they could just move past their old issues and start fresh.

Carla reached across the table and tucked a loose strand of hair behind Sophie's ear. The graze of those fingertips shot a little shiver down her, and Carla let her hand linger as she studied Sophie's face.

"That wasn't another soy sauce packet, right?" Sophie joked.

"No, it's just really good to see you," Carla said.

"I've missed you." Sophie flinched, as she hadn't meant to say that out loud—it was a thought she'd have about once a month, then bury. Carla had been the one person she'd never gotten over. A relationship that stuck in her mind and when she got lonely, or tangled up with a vibrator, she often pictured Carla there with her. Though lately, when she thought about touching herself, it wasn't Carla's face that came to mind...

Carla's eyes flitted over Sophie's breasts, then back to her mouth, and she licked her lips. "We have a lot to catch up on. I was surprised to see you telling the world that love wasn't real."

"Oh, that?" Sophie fake laughed, then shriveled as she remembered that Carla had seen *the video*. "Just trying to spread the good word."

"So you still haven't fallen in love, huh?" Carla asked.

"I haven't. I think you know I haven't." Sophie wondered if she should say the thought that had come to mind. But before she could stop herself, the words tumbled out. "I could have, though, with you."

Carla studied her. "I didn't get that sense when we were together."

Sophie had absolutely nothing to lose, so she pressed on, "You never even told me why you broke up with me."

Carla smoothed the fabric of her shorts across her thighs. "Sophie, do you remember the first time I told you I loved you?"

"Yes." She did. Of course she did. They'd been lying in bed with their bodies tangled up in the sheets and each other and been just drifting off. And Carla had reached over, pushed hair behind Sophie's ear, then whispered, *I love you*. And Sophie knew she should say it back. They'd been dating for six months. That's what you did when someone loved you. But the truth was, she hadn't loved Carla back. Or maybe she had. She wasn't sure what her feelings were, but she couldn't say the words. So instead, she'd kissed Carla long, and hard, and then made love to her. The only way she could express what she'd felt.

And the next morning, over tea and croissants, Carla told her she didn't need to hear it back until Sophie was ready. But then a month passed, and another, and eventually Carla ended their relationship.

"You were so closed-off with your feelings. But I thought that if I gave you a little push, you might fall with me." Carla's gaze flicked over Sophie's face.

"I'm sorry." She instinctively reached a hand toward Carla, then stopped herself. "I wanted to get there, but I needed more time."

"I don't really know what to say to that." Carla rested her hands on the arms of her chair. When they'd dated, Sophie knew every single expression Carla made, and what each one meant. But now, Sophie couldn't read her at all. "We dated for close to a year, and if you don't know whether you love someone after a year, then there's probably a bigger issue. I don't want to be mean about that, but it's true."

"There is an issue, you're right," Sophie admitted. "That's what I'm trying to work on now, and I'm aware that it's completely a me thing. I'm just hoping that you might be willing to give me a chance—"

The sharp ring of a cell phone interrupted them. Carla hesitated, then frowned and pulled her cell out. "Shit, I have to take this. Work." She caught Sophie's eye with an apologetic look, then stood and walked out.

Sophie exhaled sharply and sat back in her seat. She didn't know why she felt exhausted, exactly. If anything, she should be energized about being in the same room as Carla. But the way that Carla used to make her giddy didn't seem to be kicking in. Maybe she'd been so worked up and stressed about what *could* happen leading up to their date that her body was just starting to catch up?

Sophie checked her phone and saw a new message from Nina. She sucked her lip in. It's not that she was avoiding her sister, exactly, but she knew that Nina was still (rightfully) pissed off, so she thought it best to give her some space.

You are coming to see me on set tomorrow. No excuses.

Well, now she had no other choice. Even though she'd hoped Nina might take time to cool off, she suspected her sister was still very much in the land of being mad. She gave the text a thumbs-up, put the phone in her pocket, and went back to waiting.

The waiter dropped off a bowl of edamame, and Sophie nibbled at one. As she looked up, Carla walked toward her.

"I've been trying to take more time off and set work boundaries," Carla said as she sat back down. "But I have a few patients who've decided boundaries don't exist for them. Apparently, I need to make a house call tonight."

Carla's shoulders pinched up around her ears in a shrug, and she grabbed a piece of edamame. "Do you mind if we take dinner to go? I'm so sorry, Sophie."

"It's okay." Sophie waved away Carla's apology and smiled back to reassure her. Sophie had, after all, been one of Carla's patients once upon a time, which is how they'd initially met (though, Sophie got a new doctor as soon as she realized there was more to explore with Carla). So she understood that when there was a medical issue, people needed her.

"I'll drive you home." Carla signaled a waiter to bring their check.

"You don't have to do that. I can call for a ride."

"No, no, I insist. I'd like more time with you." Carla's hand reached across the table, and her fingers threaded through Sophie's. Sophie waited for butterflies to swarm, but none came. So she swallowed down something that was either edamame or apprehension as she held hands with her ex and wondered why things felt so very different between them.

Which is how Sophie ended up in a Tesla with a to-go box of sushi on her lap. When they pulled up in front of Sophie's place, Carla parked the car.

"I'm sorry we had to cut the night short." Carla's hand reached again for Sophie's, and she willingly gave it.

She should've been thrilled that Carla wanted to spend more time with her, so why wasn't she?

"Maybe we can see each other again, like, for a date?" Sophie cautiously asked. She knew that something didn't feel exactly right about being with Carla in that moment, but they also hadn't seen each other in a very long time, and maybe they just needed to warm up again. She wasn't going to throw away the opportunity to find love because it didn't feel as exciting as when Dash held her hand.

"I'd like that." Carla gave a generous grin, and Sophie softly smiled back.

Good—they'd have another date, and another chance to try this out. If Sophie really wanted to fix her writer's block, falling for Carla might be the only real way to do that.

"You're really hard to say goodbye to," Carla told her. Then she leaned across the car's console, brought her fingers to Sophie's chin, tilted her head up and…kissed her. One tentative, soft kiss. And Sophie returned the kiss, just as tentatively.

She wanted to feel the spark of absolute electricity she'd had with Carla when they were together, but as she kissed her back, and harder this time, she didn't feel the same jolt. She reached a hand behind Carla's neck and pulled her close, willing the chemistry between them to show up.

But then Carla pulled away as she said, "Guess you missed me, huh?"

"Of course," Sophie said. And she *had* missed Carla, so why wasn't her body reacting the way her mind had? She forced a warm smile.

"See you soon?" Carla asked.

Sophie nodded, then she opened the car door and stepped out. The night air had turned everything cool, and she shivered as she watched Carla drive off.

When she got into her house, she had no intention of going to bed. She felt wired as several thoughts crossed her mind.

That was a lackluster kiss.

Dash's lips taste like honey.

Nina might murder me.

What she suddenly wanted to do more than anything else was write—a feeling she'd had for months but hadn't been able to act upon. Only now, there were words swirling around her and the only way to silence them was to put them onto the page.

She sat at her work desk and cracked open her laptop. An

open document was already waiting, and without overthinking what she was going to type, she started to write.

Hello, my name is Dash Montrose, and I am absolutely thrilled to be standing on Hollywood Boulevard in the summer heat and wearing a three-piece suit...

18

DASH

When the car came, it was ninety degrees out, but Dash was still in a suit because it was something his mother had insisted on. A driver opened the back door and, as he stepped in, he heard his brother before he saw him.

"Which outlets will be there?" Reece gazed out the window.

"All of them." His publicist, Justine, didn't look up from her phone.

Dash raised his eyebrows as he sat next to Reece, and Reece nodded back. Dash's phone pinged.

Luna and I are going to a meeting later. Free to join?

He ignored the text from Chris and quickly pocketed the phone. He should be at a meeting instead of going to a premiere—he knew that—but he wanted to be there to support his brother, and his mom had insisted he go.

"Who will I be talking to?" Reece pressed.

"All of them," Justine said again.

"Are you actually listening to my questions, Justine, or just

saying *all of them* for everything because you think I'm annoying?" Reece had a smile on his face that suggested he knew
what was coming and was excited for it.

"It's called multitasking, Reece. Some of us don't always
need to hear the sound of our own voice."

Dash let out a chuckle at his brother's expense, and Reece
frowned back.

"I deserved the spanking, but I didn't know it would sting
that much," Reece said to Dash. Then he turned to his publicist. "Justine, I'm obsessed with you. You know that, right?"

"I do." She finally looked up, almost annoyed. "Now, have
some water. We'll be there in ten."

Reece had always been one to follow orders, so he took a
bottle of water from his side and cracked open the lid. "But
you'd tell me if I were being difficult, right? Like, is the fact
that you have to remind me to drink water really annoying?"

"We've had this conversation before." Justine finally put her
phone down, folded her hands in her lap, and looked at him.
"What's annoying is you asking me every five minutes if you're
being annoying."

"Don't ever leave me," Reece said.

"Keep paying me, and I'll stick around." She grabbed her
phone again and began to type.

"Isn't she great?" Reece asked Dash, loud enough so Justine
could hear, but she explicitly chose to ignore him.

"Thanks for the ride." Dash changed the subject and ran his
hands across the leather seat.

"The studio pays for these. Why not add an extra stop?"
Reece eyed Dash's suit. "The bow tie is a bold move."

"Mom had it sent over, because apparently I'm still not old
enough to dress myself."

"I don't dress myself either, but Mom isn't my stylist." Reece
tugged at the ends of his jacket and grinned. He was classically
handsome in a black suit with a button-down shirt and pocket

square. He might as well have *Hollywood Leading Man* stitched across the collar. "I'm glad you're here for the premiere. It really means a lot."

"Happy to," Dash said.

"And I'm sorry I put you on the spot the other night at family dinner." Reece's jaw clenched, like he was anticipating blowback. But Dash had never been confrontational with his older brother, even if he *did* deserve it.

"Don't worry about it," Dash said quickly.

Reece gave a genuinely appreciative look. "And besides, I need as many people as possible to tell me how good I look. Right, Justine?"

"Compliments cost extra."

"Fine." Reece took his phone out and began to type. When a new alert sounded on Justine's phone, she looked up.

"You look very handsome, Reece. And you, too, Dash."

"Hey, I only sent you the Venmo to compliment *me*," Reece said.

"I know, but I complimented Dash for free because he *does* look handsome."

Dash stifled a laugh, but Reece didn't look at all amused. "That one hurt, Justine," Reece said.

"For what it's worth, I think you look fantastic," Dash offered. "Don't tell, but this look is better than Dad's 1985 Oscar acceptance speech."

Reece brought a hand to his lips in surprise. "I'd never tell him that, not unless I wanted to lose my life."

The car stopped in front of a long red carpet where white pops of light flashed as cameras began to point and click. Dash sucked in a deep breath.

Justine stopped texting long enough to catch Dash's eye. "Dash, go first. One of our PAs will escort you to the photo op."

Dash rolled his shoulders back. He wasn't surprised to be

the opener for his brother, that's what he always was—the appetizer before the main course. He just wasn't looking forward to getting out of the car and seeing looks of disappointment as the media circus realized he wasn't Reece.

Reece's square jaw tightened as he glanced at Dash. "I'll see you in there?"

Dash cracked a smile. "You were born for this. And, if you weren't, then Mom would've sent you back. Just remember that whenever you feel like a fraud tonight."

Reece clapped him on the shoulder. "See? This is why I gave you the ride, and not Poppy."

Poppy would never do a red-carpet line and was likely entering through a secret back entrance, but Dash kept those thoughts to himself.

The driver came around and opened the car door, and a blinding number of flashing cameras forced Dash to look at the ground as he stepped out. He locked his mouth into a tight smile, the way his media training had taught him—stay brooding, stay mysterious, and play the role.

The PA waved him over toward the line for photos. There was an energy to a red carpet that was hard to deny—a kind of anticipatory buzz.

Dash turned at the sound of loud applause and knew before he saw that Reece had finally stepped out of the car. A slice of tension lifted at the reminder that Dash was not the focus tonight, his brother was. And, more likely than not, his presence here would just be a blip and potentially forgotten. It would be a welcome change when, in a few more years' time, people stopped asking for his photo at all, but for now, as he queued up to walk the red carpet, he was still *someone*.

Dash stood with the PA at his side but wished that Sophie could be there with him. His fingers tapped at his thighs, and he longed for her hand to take his and still the nerves in his chest. She'd know what to say to calm him down, the same way she'd known what to say in writing his dad's speech. In reading through her pages, she'd managed to capture Dash's dry humor and made him feel seen in an entirely unexpected way. Spending time with her was easy, unlike all the dating he'd done when he was wasted. Not that he and Sophie were dating, exactly.

But Dash had never dated sober. In fact, dating and drinking used to go hand in hand—he couldn't go out without having something to take the edge off. But when he was with Sophie, he didn't feel the need to drink or try to be someone he wasn't. She accepted him for who he was. He should've been thrilled to finally find a person he could open up to, but he also couldn't be responsible for someone else's happiness, not when he was still trying to find his own.

He didn't like wanting to be around her—something about the way his brain latched on to her reminded him of how he felt when he drank. What if Sophie became his substitute addiction, and then they didn't work out? How would his brain and body react if she took herself away from him?

Just in time to rip him from his thoughts of Sophie, the PA shouted into his ear, "You're next!"

And then he was on the red carpet, standing in front of a wall-length step-and-repeat poster covered in the title of Reece's movie, *Final Judgment Day*. Dash walked onto the carpet and angled his body slightly, the way his former publicists had taught him, to show off his good side—the one without the scar in his eyebrow.

"Over here, Dash!"

He turned to each voice that shouted his name and cracked a soft, barely perceptible smile that would photograph well and enhance his cheekbones. He hated that he knew so much about his angles but couldn't remember what he'd had for breakfast.

"Dash, where have you been?"

"What's next for you?"

"Is it true you're going to be in your brother's new film?"

"Dash, can you confirm that you were recently seeking treatment for drug abuse?"

Dash's heart stopped, and so did his breathing, or at least it felt like that. Except for his mind, which whirred frantically at the words he swore he just heard. *Drug abuse. Seeking treatment. What the actual fuck?*

His mouth opened, but he forced it closed and swallowed down a panicky lump in his throat. What would his mom do in that moment? She wouldn't react. She'd almost not hear the question and just continue to pose. But he was having a hard time *not* reacting. He was starting to shake—a little vibration— and he shoved his hands firmly into his pockets as he walked off the carpet and toward the hallway that led to the theater.

Dash's vision blurred as he picked up the pace and nearly sprinted toward the signs for the bathrooms. The smell of buttery popcorn nauseated him. He passed other people in suits and gowns along the way, knocking shoulders and muttering apologies. He just needed to be completely alone. So when he went into the single-stall bathroom, he locked it behind him and leaned against the door.

He took in deep, panicked gulps of air. He couldn't calm his breathing, and there was a ringing in his ears. He wasn't sure if he could even make sense of his own thoughts over the deafening sound.

How had a reporter found out about his stint in rehab? Who had told them? There were strict NDAs the staff at the facility had signed to make sure no one ever found out he'd been there. AA was anonymous, and while he supposed someone in the group could've leaked his secret, what awful person would do something like that?

He hadn't told anyone, other than Chris and...*fuck*. His goddamn TikTok stalker knew he was in recovery.

He pulled out his phone, opened the TikTok app, and went to his messages.

@craftycindy Don't ignore me.

@craftycindy what did I do wrong?? You trusted me, what changed?

@craftycindy is it your "girlfriend"?

@craftycindy I can find her too, you know

@tokcrafty2me Leave me alone or I will call the cops

He bit the bottom of his lip so hard he tasted blood. That had been his last message to her. A threat to call the cops—which he had no intention of really doing. Had that pushed her to tell the press his secret? What else did they know?

Then there was a knock. And two more. And finally, his mom's terse voice through the door. "Dash, open up."

He swallowed back another new lump in his throat, unlocked the door, and let her in.

She swiftly shut and locked the door behind her. She towered over him in stilettos, and he avoided her gaze.

"You ran." Her tone was measured and matter-of-fact. "When that reporter asked you about abusing drugs, you practically ran off the red carpet."

He didn't answer. Kitty always knew every single thing that went on with her children, but he couldn't bring himself to say the words out loud. He'd wanted to tell his mother about being sober, but on his own terms and his own time, when he was ready. And in that moment, standing in a blue suit with the bow tie she'd picked for him, and sweat pooling under his arms in the fluorescent bathroom lighting, he didn't feel ready to talk about his addiction issues.

"I see." Kitty's hand went to her temple, and she lightly

touched a spot there. Then she shook her shoulders out and put a hand on Dash's arm. "Are you okay?"

He looked up, surprised to hear concern in her voice. "I'm not, no."

He hadn't expected to tell her the truth, but when his mom knew something, she was like a human lie detector, and there was no sense in hiding from her in that moment.

She exhaled sharply, then wrapped him in a hug. He let her, and as she held him there, his body began to shake, but this time he was fighting against tears that he couldn't hold back. And he cried into the shoulder of her dress for what felt like several minutes.

"Your dress." He pulled away from her and there was a large wet stain across her shoulder.

"There are jackets for this exact kind of thing." She stroked a hand through his hair. "Dash, look at me."

And he looked, because when it came to his mother, he tended to do whatever she told him.

"I love you very much." Her eyes held his there, and for a moment, he wondered if this would be the Hallmark moment that some people in AA experienced when they spoke their truth.

This, however, was Kitty Montrose, and she didn't do sappy. "There's no nice way to say this, so I'm just going to have to say it. This night is not about you, Dash."

The words slammed into him, like an accusation that he'd somehow tried to take away attention from his brother. He hadn't even wanted to come. He'd been asked to attend, and now his mom was suggesting he'd intentionally tried to make this about him?

"I know that," he quickly fired back.

"Tonight is about Reece. This may be one of the biggest moments of his career—the start of an action franchise, just as your father had—and we can't have it overshadowed by what's going on with you."

His jaw set tight. He wanted to leave. He wanted to be home and away from the chaos his family always managed to bring with them.

"I'll go," he said. He moved to brush past her, but she stopped him with a firm hand on his shoulder.

"You're going to come out of this bathroom, and when you do, a PA will lead you out a back door where there will be a car waiting. The car will take you home, and I will tell your brother that you weren't feeling well. Then you and I will talk on Friday. I will handle this."

He didn't know what to say. She'd planned the whole thing before even coming into the bathroom, already certain that Dash couldn't continue to be there. Already knowing or thinking that he would cause a scene and ruin the whole night for their family, tarnish the golden reputation she'd built for them.

Dash was the problem. He was the person always threatening to ruin something, and he didn't belong anywhere near them.

All he could do was give her a single nod in return. She squeezed his shoulder, though any warmth was gone as he unlocked the door and pushed it open.

The PA was waiting for him, just as his mom had promised. And his dad also stood there, in a gray fitted suit, but his normally bright eyes were dull and creased with concern. Dash glanced at him briefly, then looked away, not wanting to see any more judgment than he'd already received from his mother. He pursed his lips and followed the PA toward a door down the hall.

"Son." He turned at his dad's voice.

Dash opened his mouth, but before he could answer, his mom called out, "William."

They both turned. She met them, grabbed William's arm, and whispered into his ear. His dad hesitated as he looked to

Kitty, then Dash. Eventually he grabbed Dash to bring him in for a hug.

Dash had not been hugged by his dad since...well, he couldn't remember when. And he stood frozen to the spot as he let his dad embrace him. "Your mother means well, even though it doesn't feel that way all the time. I hope you know that. She assured me we'll fight this." Then his dad pulled back but said into his ear, "Be strong."

Yes, *Be strong, Dash*. Words he'd heard so many times when he didn't want to be on set, or auditioning for a role, or at some event he'd been asked to attend. Dash shoved down whatever hesitations he had, turned away from his parents, and walked toward the open door that would take him home.

19

SOPHIE

Sophie should've gone home. But she'd already waited two hours, so what was one more?

She sat on a bench as the summer heat burned the concrete and sent warmth up through the soles of her sandals. Even the shade from the overhead palms that lined the sidewalk didn't provide any kind of relief. She was outside Formosa Cafe, a historic landmark that was a restaurant and bar. The interior was all wood paneling, terrazzo floors, and red booths that gave off a classic Hollywood vibe, which was fitting, since stars like James Dean and Ava Gardner used to drink there. Sophie had also drunk at the bar before, and she could use one of their green tea martinis to cool down.

But today the spot served as a shooting space for her sister's show, *Second Chance Kitchen*. Enormous production trucks lined Santa Monica Boulevard, the backs of them open and carrying electrical equipment. There was also a wardrobe truck filled with outfit options for Nina, and a hair-and-makeup trailer for the cast.

And while Sophie wasn't sure where her sister was, she planned to wait so they could finally talk out the mess she'd made.

"Can I help you with something?" a cheery voice asked.

Sophie eyed the guy in his early twenties, who was short with the most gorgeous dark curls she'd ever seen. He held a latte with her sister's name written on the side in one hand, and a clipboard in the other. She guessed he was part of the crew.

"I'm Sophie Lyon," she replied. "Nina's sister?" She said the last part as a question because, really, would Nina still be calling her a sister at this point or something less nice? Like, Most Likely to Spill Your Secrets after a Glass of Wine, for example.

"Oh, shit!" He covered his mouth with a hand. "I'm sorry, I just recognized you."

Sophie couldn't help but brighten. She was rarely—well, it'd only happened once—recognized out in the wild for her book. "You read *Whisked Away*?"

"Is that a TikTok thing? I love that you're meeting up with your exes. So brave. If I had to see my ex, I'd need a few beta blockers to get through it."

His words sank in, and Sophie realized he had *not* recognized her for being an author but for being a person on TikTok. Which was...not the best feeling, considering she was trying to save her writing career, not become an influencer. "Brave, yes," she mumbled.

"Sorry to fangirl." He scanned the clipboard at his side. "Does Nina know you're coming?"

"She does, Tyler." Sophie had clocked his name tag and hoped that by being nice he might take pity and bring her inside to the air-conditioning. "I've been waiting for her, actually."

"We're running a bit behind schedule today, so I'm not sure when she'll get a break." Tyler clutched the clipboard to his chest.

"You know I don't take breaks."

Sophie and Tyler turned at Nina's voice.

Her sister walked toward them as a ray of sunshine broke through the rows of trailers and hit Nina in just the right way so that the glitter from her eyeshadow nearly blinded Sophie. She wore a plum, long-sleeved jumpsuit that hugged her curves and a pair of kitten heels. And while her makeup was meant to look natural and approachable, her high cheekbones always gave her the look of someone who could destroy your life with a blink.

And Sophie was certain that Nina might very well do that to her. "Damn, Nina," Sophie said. "This outfit makes me want to wear pants, and you know I don't mess with those."

"Tyler, I'll take the latte and meet you on set." Nina kept her eyes on Sophie as she spoke.

When Tyler left, Sophie launched in. "Nina, let me explain—"

"I gave you a chance to explain, but you ignored me. So now it's my turn to talk." Nina sipped from her latte. "I love you more than anything, but whenever things get hard, you bail. You were so terrified of talking to me about what you did that you avoided me. I'm your sister. Do you know how that made me feel?"

Sophie licked her lips, but even her tongue seemed to have shriveled in the heat. As usual, her sister was absolutely right, Sophie had avoided her. Though Sophie hadn't actually meant to, she supposed she *had* hurt Nina.

"It made you feel like shit?" Sophie glumly replied.

"Yes, like shit. So I made you wait because you deserve to have your feet in the fire, too. How does it feel?" Nina crossed her arms and sipped from the latte.

"Hot." Sophie swallowed, though she didn't even have saliva in her mouth at this point. "Like, very hot."

Nina's jaw clenched, then she rolled her eyes and reached into a back pocket where she pulled out a small bottle of water. She tossed the bottle to Sophie, though Sophie completely missed and had to bend over and pick it up off the ground.

After gulping down the water in a few hearty sips, Sophie said, "I'm sorry."

"You better be sorry. You totally blew up my spot."

"I know." Sophie dabbed her fingers at her inner elbow, which was somehow sweating. "I didn't mean to—"

But Nina interrupted her, "Leo and I are pregnant."

Sophie frowned. What was her sister even talking about? "You're…"

"Yeah." Nina cracked a smile. "One of those frozen eggs got put into a surrogate. She's twelve weeks along. We tried a few rounds of IVF, but the toll it takes on you…" Nina's smile faded as she shook her head. "I just couldn't do it anymore."

Sophie was…well, she was flabbergasted, really. Her sister was going to have a baby? Yes, she'd known that Nina had frozen her eggs, and that might mean that she'd eventually use them. But she hadn't known that Nina and Leo had already tried IVF, or even considered a surrogate. How could she not know any of this? "You didn't tell me" was all she could think to say.

"I didn't want you to worry, and as we both know, you can't keep a secret." Nina shrugged as she took another sip of her coffee.

Well, okay, she *had* accidentally revealed Nina's secret, but she'd managed to keep Dash a secret, hadn't she?

She wanted to be happy for her sister. She *should* be hugging her and telling her how excited she was to be an aunt. But she was hurt. Nina keeping a massive secret like this made her feel like her sister didn't trust her. "I really am sorry."

"I know you are. And I'm sorry that I didn't tell you sooner." Nina's expression softened slightly. "You're going to be an amazing auntie to this girl. And I expect you to be there for me, for her, for us. So no more ghosting. Okay?"

"A girl? You're having a little girl?"

Nina's cheeks flushed with excitement as she nodded. Sophie was happy for her sister, but also, in that moment, she felt infinitesimally small. Nina had an actual career, a loving husband, and a baby on the way. Whereas Sophie's career was about to shrivel up and die, her longest relationship was with her pet goldfish, and she was currently obsessed with a man who had made it abundantly clear that they'd never amount to anything.

"So can we move on from this?" Nina asked. "We've cleared the air. Now you know everything. No more secrets?"

Sophie nodded, though she was going to keep Dash a secret, because she didn't know what they were to each other, and hadn't she disappointed her sister enough for one day?

On the walk home, she needed to talk to someone about her *No Good, Very Bad Day*. And really, she did miss her best friend. She wasn't going to tell Poppy about Dash, but maybe it was still okay to reach out and just vent.

Sophie: I'm having a bad day ☹

Poppy: Can you meditate?

Sophie: Not immediately, no

Poppy: 10 self-affirmations out loud. Studies show it makes everything better

Poppy: like, in general, I'm summarizing

Poppy: also, Botox boosts your mood so lmk if you want to come in for a treatment ☺

Sophie: lol

Sophie: Thank you, as always

Poppy: ♥

Even if Sophie *had* wanted Botox, she couldn't afford it. But mantras were free, and she'd picked up enough from being best friends with Poppy to know that affirmations helped her, on occasion. So what was the harm in reciting a few on the way home?

20

DASH

Do not text her. Do not look toward her window. Don't even think *about her.*

Dash told himself these things, but the truth was that the only reason he'd come outside was in the hopes that Sophie might wander out, too. His red-carpet fiasco had left him with the kind of stomach-churning dread that made him want to throw things. Which was likely why he was craving a dose of Sophie's sunshine and optimism.

As he stood with a shovel in his hand and upended dirt for a new antisquirrel fence he planned to install, even he had to admit that it was kind of a nice day. Sure, the heat was unrelenting, but he was shaded by the branches of the fat avocado tree. The sky was the kind of blue you couldn't quite capture with a paint color, and he heard birds singing like he was in some Disney movie.

He licked his lips and stood up as beads of sweat cascaded down his back. He was about to go in for a break when he heard the pedestrian gate open and then her voice.

"I am worthy of love," Sophie said to herself.

He watched as she closed the gate behind her.

"I am strong, emotionally and physically." She walked toward her place. "I can write another book, damn it."

Dash hadn't realized that he'd been inching closer to the sound of her voice, like a homing device, when what he needed was to give her space. But as he turned to head back to his place, he stumbled over the shovel. He cursed as his shoe met the metal. When he looked up with a wince, she noticed him.

He'd expected her to smile or even laugh at his clumsiness—one of her normal lighthearted reactions—but she barely raised a hand to wave. As he eyed her, he couldn't help notice her deflated hair, the unmistakable red burn across her shoulders, and the way her feet dragged like bricks as she walked. If he didn't know any better, he'd guess she was out of sorts.

"Hey." Her eyes went owlish. "You heard me doing my mantras, didn't you?"

"I did." He picked up the shovel and threw it, rolling his eyes in the process. "Hard time writing?"

"It's just one of many problems. It doesn't make any sense. I wrote your dad's speech and thought that was this big breakthrough where I'd be able to get back to my book." She had written that speech and shared it with Dash, and he'd already sent it to his mom without making any changes. "The book is due in less than a month, and it's like my brain is an ice cube that refuses to melt. Even though the rest of me clearly has." She lifted the side of her dress and, as if for emphasis, the dress fell limply at her side.

"Do you need some aloe for your shoulders?" His hand reached up, as if to try to soothe them, but he forced the hand back.

"I deserve the burn." Sophie gently rubbed her own shoulder. "I went to see my sister this morning. She was really mad about the whole Ned thing."

"That wasn't your fault, Soph. I mean, I know you told him

about Nina, but that's because you expected him to be a decent human being." His hands were on his hips now in the Angry Dad pose, but he couldn't help feeling a little on edge—he didn't like anyone making Sophie feel bad.

Her lips twitched, as if wanting to say more. It was unusual for her to hold back, so he pressed. "What happened?"

"We were talking, and it became clear that she's been keeping things from me. Like, big life things. And I was just kind of hurt about that, ya know?" She wiped the back of her hand across her forehead. "I thought we were close. She's my only family, and it's weird to think she doesn't trust me."

"I don't know your sister well, but from my experience, families aren't perfect. They're really complicated and messy." He stuck his hands in his pockets, thinking of his own dysfunctional family. "I'm sure you both are close, but that doesn't mean she won't fuck up and accidentally break your heart. The relationship you have with Nina is like anything else, and you have to expect there will occasionally be bumps."

"Yeah, I guess you're right." She attempted a smile, but what came out was more of a grimace.

Disheartened Sophie was new, and he wouldn't have minded if it wasn't so obvious that she was miserable. His first instinct was to help because he sensed that she needed some. And when it came to Sophie, he inexplicably wanted to make her happy.

"Okay, I've got an idea. Let's get your laptop and head out." The suggestion came quickly, but as the words settled he realized that he missed being around her, and he'd just created an excuse to be next to her again.

"And go where?" She let out an exhausted sigh, but her expression turned curious as she twisted a loose piece of hair around her finger and watched him, waiting to hear more.

When they pulled into a parking spot at Glow, Sophie turned to Dash and exhaled sharply. "Not to rain on your spontaneous parade, but you do know we need appointments to be at the spa, right?"

Dash killed the engine and unbuckled his seat belt, then stepped out of the car. Despite her protests, Sophie slung on her backpack and stepped out, too.

"You forget that I'm the owner's brother, and you're the owner's best friend." He had some newfound confidence as he came around to her side of the car to meet her. "They'll make something work."

"We'll see about that, Montrose." She hadn't called him by his last name before. And, as it turned out, he liked the sound of that just as much as when she said his first name.

They walked toward the spa entrance, so little space between them that they knocked shoulders, but he didn't move to correct it and neither did she. He enjoyed the way they touched and tore apart, like magnets seeking each other.

"Maybe a new environment will help your brain melt, or whatever it is you need to write." He shrugged, but she watched him with interest. "And worst-case scenario, you spend a day at a spa. Not too terrible."

"Admit it, you just brought me here because you wanted the free macaroons." Her hand reached for the door handle.

"Well, they are really yummy."

"They're my sister's." She pulled the front door open, and they both walked through it.

Sophie looked proud of that statement, and he was glad she'd turned some kind of corner and could smile about Nina.

Admittedly, Poppy wasn't as pleased to see them as Dash had anticipated. She came into the waiting area carrying a green juice with her assistant in tow and reminded Dash that he couldn't just show up to her place of work and make demands. But, in the end, they paid for day passes, handed over their cells—per the no-phone rule—and had been given lockers with robes and slippers, along with unlimited use of the spa facilities.

When Dash stepped out of the men's locker area and into the coed relaxation room, his eyes adjusted to the low lighting. Salt lamps lined a path on the floor that led to white sofas and chaise lounge chairs, and the scent of mint and eucalyptus permeated the air. The place wasn't empty, but most everyone was covered in a blanket with an eye mask. No one so much as stirred as he padded to an empty chaise and sat down.

A man in tennis shorts and a Glow T-shirt approached. "Can I offer you our hibiscus and yuzu tonic?" He extended a shot glass filled with a fizzy pink liquid.

"I'll take one," Sophie said.

Dash looked up to see Sophie in the same plush robe with silk tie that he'd been given. She grabbed a shot glass off the tray and took the lounge chair next to Dash's. She sipped and licked her lips as she settled in. "Oh, you'll like this, Dash." She grabbed a shot glass for him. "It's a little sweet."

"And antiaging," the man said.

Dash frowned. Was that antiaging comment directed at him? He took the shot glass, the first time he'd held one since getting sober. But he knew this wasn't the same, even though his body reacted to the feel and look of the glass in a knowing and longing kind of way that irked him.

"I'll take this over the Botox." Sophie drank down the rest of hers.

Dash wasn't looking forward to drinking an antiaging potion but pinched his nose and swallowed his in one gulp. He braced for the impact of something decidedly too healthy but, to his surprise, it *did* taste sweet.

"Are you shocked that you didn't immediately turn into a carrot stick?" she whispered.

"It could still happen." He kept his voice low, too.

She smirked.

"You brought your laptop?" He readjusted the soft collar of the robe. Maybe he needed one of these for himself.

Sophie picked a bag up from the floor, put it on her lap, and gave it a firm pat. "What did you bring?"

He pulled a book from the pocket of his robe.

"You brought a romance novel?" Sophie eyed him with a confused expression.

"When you were packing up your laptop, I saw it on your bookshelf and liked the cover. So I'm borrowing it, I guess." He shrugged.

Sophie shook her head and leaned back in the chair. "Well, get ready to bawl your eyes out. Abby Jimenez can really write a tearjerker."

"What?" He leaned forward, and she pivoted toward him. The side of her robe fell open slightly, revealing a long stretch of her leg. He shook his head and refocused. "Isn't this a romance?"

"Yeah." She opened her laptop. "And sometimes there's crying in romance."

Dash wasn't a big crier. "Well, I'm not afraid of a few tears."

"Bawling. Your. Eyes. Out. I guarantee it." They held each other there for a moment before he decided to break the tension.

"Get to work, already," he said as he cracked the book open.

Out of the corner of his eye, though, he caught her watching him. Eventually, she settled back in the chair, and her hands hovered over the keyboard. He waited for the telltale tap of fingers against keys but heard none.

"I'll just try a quick sauna visit. BRB." She placed the laptop next to her on the chair and pushed herself up, and he watched her hurry toward the locker area. Once she was gone, he settled back and exhaled. He wanted nothing more than to be able to flip a switch and help her find that passion for writing again, but she was the one who had to commit words to paper. All he could do was be there to support her until she did.

Ten, maybe fifteen minutes passed. When she came back,

he was deep into the second chapter of the book but looked up to ask, "Better?"

She nodded, then sat on the lounge chair and placed the laptop on her knees. Her fingers drummed along the top of the keyboard, as if imitating the act of writing without actually doing it.

"What if you tried writing about a spa?" Dash softly asked. When he took acting classes, a lot of them were method, and he'd had to work with what was immediately in front of him. Maybe if Sophie treated her writing the same way, it could help unlock something. "You're here, sitting in one. Don't they say to write what you know?"

"I'm supposed to fix the book I already wrote," she said.

"You can always go back to that book. Just do what feels easiest now and return to the hard stuff when you're ready." Dash had approached recovery in a similar way. Some things had felt easier to him, like developing a routine, while others he'd shoved into the corner for a later date, like telling his family the truth.

She eyed him but eventually gave a shrug. This time, when he returned to the book in his hands, he heard the light tap of fingertips meeting keys. It was a sound he had anticipated would bring him pleasure, but when an unmistakable flood of warmth filled his chest, even he was surprised by how soothing her triumph was to him.

And over the next few hours, he became acutely aware of every sound Sophie made: when she went quiet thinking through a line or an idea, when she got up to take a steam room or sauna break, and when her head fell back and onto the lounge chair in frustration.

As she slowed her typing and began to nibble the tip of her index finger, he decided to make himself useful. He stood up, and made his way to the snack bar. In typical Poppy fashion, none of the snacks were his version of a good time. But still, he knew they were things Sophie would love. He grabbed a hot-pink plate and used a pair of tongs to pile on dried apricots, date bites, and something called a detox bar. As he turned around, he came face-to-face with Poppy, who cocked her head in an inquisitive way.

"You never come here, even when I offer to give you free services." She crossed her arms. "Speaking of, do you want to try some filler for those under-eye circles?"

She playfully poked at his cheek, and he swatted her away. "You're right, it's so weird that I never come here when it's always such a nice experience." He glanced over to where Sophie sat. She'd stopped typing altogether, and he wanted to bring her the plate of snacks as writing fuel.

Poppy glanced to where Sophie was. "So, you and Sophie are friends now?"

He frowned. Maybe they were friends. He'd said they'd be friends. And now they were hanging out. Of course, he had also nearly come in his pants as she rode his face the other day, but...that wasn't something Poppy needed to know about. "Yeah, I guess we are."

"And she's writing again, huh?"

"She is." Why did he feel personal pride about that? He wasn't the one writing, she was. Still, just by being next to her he felt like he'd been part of her process in some way.

"Good job. Maybe you aren't totally worthless."

"Let's not get ahead of ourselves."

"You should come here again. I like seeing your face." Poppy gave him a pat on the shoulder.

And Dash liked being there, too. He realized that he and his family rarely came to Poppy's spa, even though it was wildly successful. His parents always prioritized the Hollywood industry above all else, including their daughter's self-made business. Dash was going to make a point of trying to visit and support his sister more often.

"I will," he quickly said.

Poppy smiled at him. "Take care of her. She's in a vulner-able place," his sister said before heading back through the Employees Only door.

Dash swallowed down a little lump of apprehension as he looked back to Sophie. He wanted more than anything to be the person who could take care of Sophie. But how could someone as flawed as he was be trusted with someone as important as her?

21

SOPHIE

Sophie had turned a corner. She'd glanced down the road of the blank page, started typing, and turned right onto a street filled with words. Two thousand of them, to be exact. Sure, she'd started a totally new project instead of focusing on the one she was under contract for, but she'd filled up pages—plural. She felt so exhilarated by the feel of the keys under her fingers that she hardly noticed when Dash set a snack dish down on the side table next to her.

But, of course, she *did* notice because there was Dash's earthy scent.

"Thanks." She grabbed a dried apricot from the plate and met his gaze.

"How's the new project?" He sat back into the lounge chair; swaddled in the robe, with his legs crossed at the ankles, and a book in his hands, Dash looked positively cozy. Adorable. Sophie had to stop herself from shutting her laptop and climbing into his lap for a cuddle.

"Probably garbage." She chewed the piece of fruit. "All of my first drafts are. But it feels good to see words on a page again."

She gave him a pure and genuinely pleased smile because that's exactly what she was.

"It's nice to see you excited like this." His eyes danced across her face, and she felt herself flush.

She looked down at her screen and the battery power was now in the red. Which was probably for the best anyway. Her hands were starting to cramp from trying to remember how to work, and she wasn't sure she could take the heat of Dash's gaze on her for much longer.

The man was like a damn human sauna. She'd need a bucket of ice water to stop thinking about how underneath that robe he was only wearing a pair of boxers...

"I didn't bring my charger," she quickly said. Sophie closed the laptop and ran her hands over the top of it. She had written. She was still a writer. There was hope.

"Should we head out?" Dash had already swung his legs around and stood.

Sophie sat up and tucked her laptop under her arm. She was ready to leave, but Dash stopped her. "Don't forget to take your organic gluten-free collagen bar for the road."

He tried to hide his cocky smile, but she clocked it as she snatched the bar off the plate and shoved it into the pocket of her robe. As she stood, they were eye-level, and she tried not to think of pulling his robe off with her teeth.

Not an easy thing to *not* think about, really.

As they left the spa, the summer swelter had cooled and the sun set behind them, turning the sky to the color of orange clay.

"You have no idea how amazing it feels to have written pages after going so long without having produced anything." Sophie buckled herself in beside him, and he revved the engine as they backed out of the parking lot. "I have to thank you for getting me out of my own way. I wouldn't have written anything today if you hadn't helped. You're a good man, Dash Montrose."

Dash, who was maybe not that great with compliments, deflected. "What did you write about?"

"I did what you suggested and started something new. I'm still stuck on my book, but I started a few pages from the point of view of a spa owner. I think she'll fall in love with one of the employees. Maybe it could be my book three." She playfully raised her brows.

Wind whipped softly through the open windows of the car and blew Dash's hair over the top of his sunglasses. Her gaze lingered on him for a moment too long, and when he looked over she had to quickly turn away, hoping he hadn't noticed.

"If you're writing about a spa, is there a happy-ending massage scene in there somewhere?" Dash sounded cheeky, but Sophie also sensed some heat behind his words. Or was she still so worked up from seeing him in a robe that she was adding that heat in?

"Only if I want to have a lot of fun while I'm writing, yeah." She chuckled back.

Then they both went quiet. So quiet that all she could hear was the road. But there was unspoken tension between them, something almost chemical.

And that chemical attraction could no longer be ignored. "I guess I might need to do some research," she finally said. She placed her hand on his knee, and as he looked over, his eyes burned back at her.

Sophie had just said that, hadn't she? She'd implied that she could practice a happy-ending massage on someone…and that someone could be Dash.

Maybe she'd turned feral at the sight of him reading a romance novel, or that yuzu tonic had more than just vitamins in it. Either way, she'd developed a borderline-unhealthy curiosity about the noises he'd make and the pleasure that would flash through him as he came.

The problem was she had no idea if her feelings were one-sided. But he'd floated the idea of them being friends with benefits, so she wanted to redeem some of those VIP Member perks.

As her hand rested on his knee, she waited for a sign, any sign, that he might be interested in more. Like, say, him acknowledging that her hand was there. But instead, he pulled into the driveway, parked the car, and killed the engine. Which likely meant that all signs pointed to a big unfortunate *no*.

He gently lifted her hand away from his knee, and her stomach sank at the realization that she was being rejected by him. Again. Would she ever learn? Was this another part of her deep issues with intimacy?

Eventually he said, "I haven't done this in a long time."

She wanted to tread lightly, as she was (sadly) unable to read his mind. "By *this* do you mean…?"

He sighed. "I haven't *been* with someone in a long time."

Her brows furrowed, because he hadn't told her no, exactly, and his words seemed to imply that he would be open to *her* being the next *someone*.

"I see. Well." Sophie took off her sunglasses and her eyelashes fluttered as she chose her words carefully. "The thing about a sensual massage is that all you have to do is lie there, so the stakes are low for you."

His eyebrows rose, and she laughed.

"We don't have to do anything you're not comfortable with. And you'd be helping me, too. Book research, and all." She held up her backpack and patted the laptop inside, as if for evidence.

Dash took his sunglasses off and folded them in his lap before he looked back up. "Well, I'd hate to hinder any progress you're making on what is sure to be a very juicy new novel."

The flutters she'd become so used to when she was around

him returned in full force. He watched her through hooded steely-blue eyes, and she froze at the intensity of his stare.

Eventually he broke the silence. "My place or yours?"

"What a line," she replied with a laugh.

He laughed, too. "I told you it's been a long time."

She looked toward her door. "I don't know that I'm ready to introduce you to my son, Rain Boots, yet. Let's do yours."

Dash gave her an amused look, and she felt a kind of cautious hope that made her nervous. Because she knew she couldn't expect more than what Dash was able to give, but she would take what he had for now.

When they got to Dash's house, he quickly led Sophie to his room, and she was surprised by how much…stuff was there. Dash's neatly made bed was against a wall accented with a muted brown, yellow, and red patterned wallpaper—which re- minded her of an early film he'd made with Wes Anderson— and on the opposite side was a long dresser, topped with dozens of ceramic dishes and vases. Above those were framed movie posters of Dash's films, and on the floor were piles of DVD screeners. Even the ceiling had something going on—gorgeous dark-wood exposed beams in neat rows.

She picked up a ceramic tray from the dresser and turned it over in her hand. "This is cute. Where'd you get it?"

"I made it," he said.

She blinked at him, still holding the tray. Then she brought it closer and examined every side. "I know you said you crafted, but these are… I mean, you could sell these, like, in stores." She carefully placed the tray back on the table. "Poppy could even sell these at the spa—you'd both make a fortune."

"I couldn't ask her to do that." He placed his palm against the wall, and Sophie's eyes followed the line of his arm.

She didn't know how to do this with him—how to be in a room and not be next to him. The oval window was open, and a warm breeze came through that made the place smell like fir and wet earth. She moved toward him as she said, "You wouldn't have to ask her. If she knew you were this talented, she'd beg to sell them."

When she stood a few inches from him, he ran a hand up her arm and a trail of goose bumps erupted at his touch. He eyed them, then her. "We don't have to do anything. I just want you to know that."

"I know we don't have to." Sophie stepped toward him, so they were eye to eye. If she'd learned something from the past two weeks it was that she'd spent most of her relationships trying to be what the other person wanted. But she was done hiding who she was. Sophie wouldn't try to be perfect for Dash. She was going to speak her mind, because she knew Dash could handle it. "All I want is to get you naked, lie you down on that bed, and trace the lines of your tattoos with body oil." She licked her lips at the thought of it, then said, "Does that sound good?"

A flush crossed Dash's cheeks, and she was so surprised to see him caught off guard that she let out a chuckle.

"Whatever you want," he eventually replied.

They weren't one and done, and maybe they didn't need a label. Their whole *thing* could just be to go with the flow and have fun. In fact, because they were friends with no added relationship pressures, she started to think she was more comfortable around Dash than she'd ever been with anyone else.

Dash took a step back to peel his shirt off and over his head. Sophie exhaled sharply as she eyed his beautifully inked torso, with lines that dipped into the top of his pants. He was a work of art.

"Usually, I leave the room while my clients undress, but I'll stay, just in case you need assistance." She had never been much into role play, but something about being in the room with Dash—an actor—made her feel like she could try.

And her words *did* seem to do the trick, as his mouth quirked up and he tugged at his belt buckle. "Might need a professional's hand here."

She stepped close and slowly released the belt from the buckle, then pulled it out and away from him. She tossed the belt over her shoulder and watched as Dash unbuttoned his jeans and took the zipper down. As he pushed his pants off, his boxers came, too, and she saw the hard length of him.

Sophie had seen a few dicks in her time, but this was…a cock. Hard and thick, and bouncing from the attention. She brought a hand to her lips to cover her gasp of delight.

"Show-off," she said.

"Once a performer, always a performer." He made a cutesy shrug.

She removed her hand from her mouth and finally locked eyes with him. They both shared an easy smile. Dash's chest rose and fell as he stared back. She sensed they were both ready, so she cleared her throat.

"Lie down, please." She gestured toward the bed.

He turned to do just that, and her eyes went wide at the sight of his bare ass; two firm and round apples perfectly placed on top of his legs. Sweet sassy-assy, what was she supposed to do, ignore the ripe fruit? If she was Eve, she'd be making pies already.

Dash lay across the bed, and Sophie stood at the edge. "Close your eyes and try to relax." And so he did. She took a moment to admire the whole of him—his set and square jaw, firm chest, subtle abs, the coarse hairs under his belly button, the indents at his hip bones, the beautiful tats that swirled across his arms, on his lower stomach and upper thighs. For the time being, he was her someone, and she wasn't going to waste a moment.

She turned to the bedside table, saw the oil he'd bought in Ojai, and grabbed the bottle. She warmed the oil between her hands and brought them to Dash's nose. He took a deep inhale. "That's a lemon oil we like to use here at the spa. It should awaken your senses."

"I definitely feel awake."

She bit her lip at just how awake certain parts of him were. She started by rubbing smooth firm circles across his chest, then worked her way to his nipples, where he peaked under her touch.

Then she slowly slid her slick hands down and stopped at the tattoo below his belly button—the words *You Chose* in a cursive font. She traced each letter with the tip of her finger, and he tensed against her touch.

"You chose?" she asked.

He lifted his head and looked down at himself. "Something I got to remember that I'm in charge of my own destiny. I chose to change, but I can choose to drink again, too. I work every day to make the right choice."

She traced the words once more, which were now infused with new meaning. She dragged her fingers through the coarse hairs just above his hardness, and his body twitched beneath her.

"Firmer," he commanded.

He wanted firm? Oh, she'd show him firm. She reapplied oil and took him at the base and brought her grip all the way up the thick length of him. A moan escaped his lips as she slowly brought her hand down, then back up once more.

He stiffened, and the vein at the underside of him throbbed along her hand. As she slicked down, then back up, she began to pulse with longing, too. What would it be like to have him at her entrance, waiting to plunge in?

"How's the pressure?" she asked.

"Better."

Not satisfied with that answer, she cupped his balls with her free hand and gave them a gentle tug. He hissed.

"Much better."

She smirked.

"Good." She twisted her grip as she reached the top of him and elicited another low moan. She had to know what he tasted like.

So she bent down and put the tip of him into her mouth. He was both salty and sweet, and her mouth tightened as she flicked the sensitive seam of him with her tongue.

"I'm going to..." he started, but then his whole body tensed beneath her. She lifted her mouth and began to pump her hand steadily around him.

"Release that pressure," she encouraged him.

She watched how his whole body twitched from her touch. His eyes opened, and his gaze locked onto her as he began to spasm against her hand. She aimed him to the side of the bed, and he came in hot, quick bursts. His moans were deep and ragged, and his body was still slick with oil and a new sheen of sweat. When his cock finally stopped pulsing against her, she gave him one last longing tug.

Eventually his gaze came back, and she was surprised when he sat up and wrapped a hand behind her neck to draw her in for a kiss. He was so sweet and gentle at her mouth, like an unspoken thank-you. Her hands found the sides of his face, and they continued to kiss, slow and firm.

When he pulled away, something vulnerable was in his expression. "You okay?" he asked.

She couldn't help the smile that broke across her face. Could this man be any sweeter? "More than okay. Are you?"

"Yeah." Then he sucked in his bottom lip as he asked, "Now, what are we going to do about you?"

"Something hot, I hope," she blurted out.

He laughed, then sat up and leaned into his palm, which caused his triceps to pop. "What would make you feel taken care of, Soph?" He ran his knuckles along the side of her arm, and she shivered.

Dash moved to the side of the bed and placed her between

his knees. He pressed her body up against him, and she felt him harden. "This okay?" he asked.

She nodded, then grabbed the hem of her dress and lifted it up and over her head. He let out a heavy exhale as she unhooked her bralette.

He cupped her breast and brought his mouth to her nipple. Her head fell back as she let out a happy sigh. She'd missed that tongue, and his full lips, which sucked her into him. He pulled her body close so she could feel that he was hard again. She moved a knee onto the bed, and he lifted her and placed her on his lap, his hardness meeting her mound. She instinctively ground against him, and he moaned into her breast.

He wrapped an arm around her waist and moved them both onto the bed. Then he lay back into the pillows and brought her down with him, so her breasts hovered perfectly over his waiting lips and her mound met his dick.

He lifted his hips so that his hardness reached her clit, and she throbbed back, wanting more. He was so slick from the massage oil, and she was so wet with anticipation, and as she rocked against him, they moved as smoothly as if he was already inside her.

But the cotton fabric of her panties was still between them, and she needed to feel him gliding up and down her clit, in between her lips, and grazing her wet entrance. She attempted to take them off, but then his hands moved to her waist, and he tried to wrestle the fabric off himself.

He wasn't moving fast enough, though. "Just rip them off," she said forcefully.

Then she heard the tear of fabric as he pulled the panties off and away from her.

"Ah." She breathed out as she easily settled against him. "That's what I want."

She braced her hands against his toned chest and glided her hips up far enough for the tip of him to meet her entrance, then back down so her clit nudged his head. She rode him up and down, stopping her bud at his tip to move in slow circles against him. And she let out little moans as she felt the pressure build.

"I'm close," she said.

She bucked her hips up and rode along the tip of him, then ground in a slow circle, the way she liked. And just as quickly as he'd come for her, she felt the sparkling, hot release of all that pressure as she moaned and twitched. "Oh. Dash." She breathed out, letting her body fall against his as she continued to tremble from the orgasm.

"Sophie, I…" He stopped himself from whatever he wanted to say.

"You can tell me." She sat up and took his hand in hers.

"I know I can, which is maybe the strangest part of all of this. Not because you're strange, or anything. Wow, I'm starting to ramble the way you do."

"Uh, easy on the compliments, Dash. You're going to make me swoon here."

He laughed, but then his expression turned serious. "What I'm trying to say is that it's easy to joke, because then we don't have to think about it. But that was a big deal for me. And I'm just really happy. I like being around you."

His gaze on her was so earnest and vulnerable, but she looked away. She hadn't expected him to open up to her, and now that he had she almost wished he hadn't. Because he'd also made it clear that they would never be more than just friends with benefits, and she didn't want to fall for him any more than she already was. Not when she wanted someone to love her in return.

22

DASH

Dash waited for Sophie to say something. He'd just revealed his feelings—a thing he never did—but she'd helped him to get to this place where he could be honest. Now he just had to see how she would respond.

But not knowing how someone would react was a special kind of torture. And as Sophie blew out a massive breath and brought her knees to her chest, he realized with a sinking weight in the pit of his stomach that he'd miscalculated.

"I don't even know how to say this." She avoided meeting his eyes. "But I think I fucked up. Like, I know you don't want a relationship, or anything, but I do. In the past, I have this problem with not speaking up about what I need. And what I need right now is someone who wants to be with me."

"Right," Dash said. Of course she deserved an actual relationship. And while he'd expressed that she made him happy, that wasn't the same thing she needed. If he was a stronger person who wasn't terrified of losing their sobriety, he would commit to her. But he couldn't, not when he knew that committing to someone could mean a relapse. Yes, he wanted to be with Sophie. And maybe someday he'd be ready for that, but not today.

His tongue was leaden as he searched for the right words to say, but in very Sophie fashion, she filled the silence. "And I, uh, just started seeing someone. We're not exclusive, or anything, yet."

"That's great, Soph," he forced himself to say. And he *should* be happy for her, but he absolutely wasn't.

"Yeah." She looked down at the bed and brushed a piece of lint from the duvet. "Yeah, um, it's great. But what happened today just has to be it, you know? Like, I know we said it was a onetime thing before, but then we…"

He hesitated, but of course what happened today wouldn't happen again. If she was starting to date someone, then she couldn't keep being with him. He gave her what he hoped was an understanding smile. "Of course."

"Okay. I'm sorry. I feel so ridiculous that I'm even bringing this up, but I promised myself to be more honest about what I need. I just really want to try to give this new thing a chance. I can't do that if we're…" She rapidly blinked, as if to fill in the blanks.

"Who are you seeing?" He sounded defensive and, he supposed, he was. He aggressively tugged his T-shirt back on and was grateful that it covered his face as she answered.

"Carla."

Dash cracked his neck as he adjusted the shirt. "And you're happy with her?"

He nearly shook his head for asking the question because, again, her choices were truly none of his business. But he liked Sophie as a person, and she deserved to find someone who appreciated all the cracks that made her so perfectly unique. Was Carla the right one? He had no idea, but he wanted to make sure Sophie was certain, if only because the *friend* part of their relationship was still important.

"I am." Sophie rubbed her elbow with her free hand. Then she stood from the bed, grabbed her clothes from the floor, and slipped into her dress. "I think we could make it work. The last time we dated, I wasn't true to myself. I just hope she likes what she sees this time around."

"Of course she will." His chest tightened. *Of course* Carla would like Sophie, more than like—she'd love her. And she'd find her happily-ever-after without him in it. He knew he needed to let her go, but he couldn't help but feel like part of him would be hollow when she left.

"You're a really good guy, Dash." Her eyes finally met his, and he stopped himself from moving to hold her. She wasn't his to hold.

"I want you to hear me when I say this, okay?" She waited for him to acknowledge her, but all he could do was swallow down his panic at losing her. "You deserve to be loved, deeply. Please remember that."

Eventually, she walked over to him, grabbed his shoulder, and softly kissed his cheek. He closed his eyes. The kiss was friendly. Sweet. He shouldn't have been bothered, but he also didn't know how to think of her as someone else's girlfriend. They fit together as naturally as his own hands forming clay. But what she wanted was so far from what he was able to offer, and he wasn't about to make her think otherwise. She deserved a relationship, and he would let her have one. Even if it was with someone else.

Without lingering—because, really, what more was there to say?—she walked out of his room and, he worried, maybe out of his life for good. He barely remembered trailing her as she left his house, but what he did recall was the sight of her turning back to look at him one last time before she walked across their lawn without him.

As Dash sat across from his mom at a booth in the Polo Lounge at the Beverly Hills Hotel, he was distracted, not by the green-and-white-striped ceiling overhead, or the table of influencers creating a photo shoot with their caviar and oysters, but by his phone. More specifically, by the lack of any texts from Sophie on the screen.

"I didn't know you could write."

Dash looked up at his mom's voice.

Kitty took off her reading glasses and leaned across the table. "You wrote this?"

Yes, he was going to tell his mom he wrote the speech, because if she knew that he had hired an outsider and told them private details about his dad, then she might actually have him killed. Or inundated with parking tickets, or whatever a powerhouse Hollywood agent was capable of. And he knew the speech might be the distraction he needed to keep her from asking questions about the reporter at Reece's premiere.

"I did," he said.

"This is good. I got a little emotional just reading it." She wiped something away from the corners of her eyes, though there were no actual tears there. "Since you don't want to be in front of the camera anymore, have you considered being behind it? Your brother is making his directorial debut. You could pivot to screenplays."

"Mom." Dash rubbed a spot on his forehead. His mom really had no way of turning her professional side off. Her time was valuable, and the way her brain worked meant that there was always an opportunity for a potential new deal.

She exhaled sharply as she leaned back into the booth's leather seat. "Okay, you don't want to talk about work. Do you want to talk about what happened at the premiere?"

No, he did *not* want to talk about that either, not at all. But he leaned forward and exhaled a rattling breath, because there was no more running from the fact that his mother probably already knew all the details. "What do you want to know?"

"I know about your rehab stay. I know it was booze..." Her voice was low as she crossed her arms. "Is there still a problem?"

"Not anymore." And that was his truth. He'd had a problem, but now he was sober. His mom knew his secret, and he should feel relieved…but he sensed this wouldn't be the end of the conversation.

"I'm your mother, and half of you is me, and even though you don't talk to me about these things, I know something is going on. It's fine if you want to keep whatever that is to yourself, but you're my child, and believe it or not, I do care about you." Her expression visibly softened and turned to something akin to concern.

Dash scratched at his neck and looked off as he weighed his options. "I don't want to do the speech. I can't. I'm trying to stay focused on my sobriety, and the speech—"

"Are you telling me the speech would cause you to *not* be sober? Dash, do you have a problem or not?"

He clenched then unclenched his jaw. The answer to her question was complicated. Sobriety was complicated. But he sensed that trying to explain those things to her wouldn't be well received. So he simply replied, "No, I don't have a problem."

"Then, can't you do this one thing for your father? The press release has gone out, and the event is in two weeks. Sitting around and doing nothing with your life is not an option. And now that someone out there knows about your…past problem, getting back to work will be the easiest way to stop any further questions from popping up. If you're working, they won't wonder whether or not you're on the wagon."

"Working on set is what led me down this path in the first place." He sat back and let his fingers nervously tap the sides of his thighs underneath the table. He'd never stood up to his mom in any kind of way. She'd always known best and made it clear that he wasn't invited to disagree when it came to what she wanted for him.

"Being an actor is a gift. Millions of people want the kind

of career you could have. Do you think if you worked a nine-to-five job like your sister that you'd be happy? Everything your father and I have worked for is so that you and Reece and Poppy will be taken care of. That doesn't mean you get to just retire at thirty-six. And if you're having a problem staying sober then you need to tell me so we can get you the help—"

"I've been working since I was eight," Dash interrupted her. "You had me going to film commercials instead of going to school. Did you ever stop to think that I might just want some time to figure out what my life should be?"

But as his mother's eyes dug a hole through him, he knew that being vulnerable in front of her wouldn't achieve anything positive.

Dash stood from the table, even though his mother's jaw was so tight he could almost hear her teeth grinding. She did not like scenes, or anything that could make their family look bad, so he knew she wouldn't try to follow him. Especially not at the Beverly Hills Hotel, which was always a place where celebrities—and some of her clients—could be. She would sit and pay the bill, and if anyone asked, she'd say Dash had to go to an audition. She'd make up her own reality, the way she always did.

"This lunch is over," he said. "Unless you have any notes on the speech."

His mother refolded the napkin in her lap, as if calming herself, before answering. "Lose the bit about your father being afraid of sharks. That's not the image I've created for him. Unlike you, your father's career isn't done."

The part of the speech that was most personal to Dash, and revealed something he admired about his father was, of course, the one thing his mom wanted to remove from it entirely. Still, he wasn't going to fight. He didn't care if she watered it down to something more palatable. He wasn't doing this for himself. He'd do it because he had no other choice.

"And, Dash?" She dabbed the napkin at the corners of her

mouth, barely looking at him. "I need you to promise that nothing will go wrong at this event."

Of course his mother would say that to him—always assuming he'd be the cause of some kind of trouble. Dash wanted to leave, though, so he nodded as a kind of answer.

He was practically vibrating with anger as he turned and walked toward the doors that would take him out of the restaurant and back to the safety of his car. He didn't want his mother's words to affect him: *Unlike you, your father's career isn't done.* But his eyes burned as he lowered a pair of sunglasses onto his face to hide any potential tears spilling out as he handed his valet ticket to an attendant.

He knew he was the most disappointing of the Montrose children. Even without his mom explicitly saying so, he'd understood his place in the pecking order at every dinner and family function. Still, her words caused his chest to tighten as he got into the car.

Before pulling away to drive home, he took out his phone. There was only one thing that would potentially interfere with the speech for his dad.

He typed a new message to @craftycindy. Can we talk?

23

SOPHIE

Sophie had never been good at puzzles. She didn't have strategies—like, corner pieces first—to finish them. But still, she'd taken out her notecards and done her best to piece together all the information she'd received.

Across her kitchen table was a makeshift puzzle of neon-green cards for Carla, neon-pink for Ned, and neon-blue for Jewel. She'd written down all the reasons the relationships hadn't worked out, along with what her obvious issues were (the word *trust* was circled on several of the notecards). But maybe because she didn't have all the pieces, she just wasn't seeing how they fit into a solution.

The last and final piece of her ex-periment was Kyle—an ex she truly did not want to see based solely on the fact that he was an absolute nightmare person. He'd catcalled a woman (terrible enough) *while* on a date with Sophie, for example.

Sophie would need to see Kyle before she could draw any final conclusions. So she scooped the cards up and tucked them into her desk drawer. Then she opened a text and typed in Kyle's name, which is when she saw what she'd saved him as:

Unfunny Kyle. She cringed at the accuracy because he was the least funny comedian she'd ever met.

Sophie: Hey, it's Sophie. Would you be open to catching up soon?

She didn't have to wait long for a response.

Unfunny Kyle: Sophie who?

She glared at the text. It was possible he had multiple Sophies in his life, she was just a little dubious that he didn't have her name saved.

Sophie: Lyon

Unfunny Kyle: Roar ☺

She put her face in her hands and instantly regretted texting him. Maybe she could just forget she'd messaged him at all. Almost as quickly, another winner of a text came through.

Unfunny Kyle: Sure thing, little miss lion, get ready to purrr.

Sophie didn't have long to wallow in the unfortunate wake of texting Kyle, though, as there was a knock at the door. She checked the time, and it was already past seven, which meant Carla had arrived for their date night.

When Sophie opened the door, the sun had set, which should've cooled the air, but outside still felt warm and stagnant. Carla stood in her hospital scrubs with a headband holding her hair back from her face. Sophie felt an intense rush of déjà vu at the familiar sight. There had been so many nights where

Carla would come to her place after a long day of surgeries and making rounds, and Sophie would massage her shoulders while Carla picked a show for them to watch. They'd had the kind of effortless domesticity that Sophie had always wanted and that she hoped to find again. Maybe that could be with Carla.

Sophie stood on her tiptoes, wrapped her arms around Carla's neck, and brought her in for a kiss. The kiss was a kiss—not fireworks, but still intimate—and Sophie tried to focus on Carla's thick hair between her fingers and the way her soft lips curled up with pleasure as they stood locked together.

"Hey," Sophie said as she pulled away.

"Hey." Carla grabbed Sophie's hands and held her there.

"Are you hungry?" Sophie pulled her hands back as she took out her phone. "We could order something."

"No worries, I got us tacos." Carla picked up the paper bag at her feet and walked through the door and into the house. "I remember that you don't cook."

Sophie could do this. She could refocus her energy on Carla, the same way she'd been zeroed in on Dash. Carla had wanted a future for them, and Sophie wanted one, too. Or, rather, she wanted to want one.

So when Sophie closed the door behind them, she also gathered her courage. She didn't wait for Carla to settle in. If she was going to say the things she'd always been afraid to, she would just have to do it.

"Carla, I need to tell you something." Sophie wrung her hands as she spoke. "I realized that I have this…pattern with people I date where I just kind of let them decide everything for me, like, what we do, where we go, what we eat. Don't get me wrong, sometimes I like when those decisions are taken off my plate, so to speak, but if this is going to work, I want you to get to know me."

"Okay." Carla crossed her arms and studied her. "Do you not want the tacos?"

"No, no, I very much want the tacos. Tacos are delicious. But I'm just saying, like, moving forward." Sophie gestured in front of her, as if to the future.

Carla gave an affectionate smile and placed the take-out bag on the kitchen table. "I can do that."

"So you're okay with everything I said?" Sophie's hand had instinctively gone to her pacemaker, and she held a finger against the scar there.

Carla opened the bag of food and began to take tacos out one at a time. "I want you to be yourself. If ordering food does that, then you will order food."

Sophie waited for the familiar swirl of tension that came whenever she was in a situation that might make her unlikable. Confrontation made her skin crawl. She'd spent so much time making sure everyone else was happy that she hadn't spent much time being clear about what made her happy. But relief swept through her like a balm.

"So how do we do this?" Carla's hands were on her hips, her stance was wide, and she looked like she was analyzing next steps in a surgical case. "Do you want to talk about what happened between us?"

"Maybe it's better if we just start over." Sophie approached Carla and rubbed her hands across her shoulders. "I held back a lot when I was with you, but I want to make this work. I don't need to hash out everything that went wrong."

"Okay." Carla finally relaxed, and her hands fell to her sides. "I just want to be here with you."

Those words were so sweet and earnest that Sophie wanted them to punch her in the gut with flutters, but none came. Still, Sophie wrapped her in a hug, and Carla embraced her back, and they stayed like that for a few long moments. Sophie breathed in the soapy scent of her and tried not to think about how Dash smelled like the earth and freshly cut wood.

Because the thing was, she could see a life with Carla. They could be good together if Sophie stayed away from Dash.

But when Carla's fingers wove through Sophie's hair and pulled her bun loose, Sophie tensed. Carla gently grabbed a handful of her hair and tilted Sophie's head back so they locked eyes as she searched for permission, but Sophie wanted to take things slow, especially as she learned to set boundaries and speak about her own needs.

As Carla leaned in, Sophie stopped her with a finger. "Could we just hang out tonight? I want to get to know you again before we…"

Carla's full lips parted, then closed. She straightened and loosened her hold on Sophie, but not unkindly. Finally, she said, "Yeah, let's just…be together."

Sophie knew there had been a moment between them, and she'd not ruined it, exactly, but she hadn't played along either. To her surprise, though, Carla wasn't upset. She was just trying to recover from the small rebuff. Sophie gave her space by grabbing plates from the kitchen. As her back was turned, she took a deep breath and reminded herself that she'd be lucky to be with Carla—a successful doctor who'd already proven herself to be relationship-ready. Still, as they arranged themselves in front of the TV, none of what they were doing felt quite right. Because what Sophie wanted was to be seated next to Dash, with all those annoying fluttery feelings between them.

24

DASH

Dash wished he was sharing a table with Sophie. But instead, he was seated across from Cindy—or, as he'd known her best, @craftycindy. Cindy was tall and thin and wore her straight brown hair down and around her face. But her curtain of hair couldn't hide the intense way that her eyes had locked onto his.

Dash regretted agreeing to this meeting. But at the time, he hadn't seen a way around it. Cindy was only willing to talk if they met face-to-face, and Dash hoped that in doing so he could convince her to stay quiet and leave him and his family alone.

The Sunset Tower had seemed like the best meeting spot option, because celebs loved to frequent the hotel's restaurant and bar, which meant there was a heavy security presence, so there was backup in case he needed to call over a bodyguard or two. And based on the fact that Cindy's foot had snaked its way to his ankle, Dash planned to call one over very soon.

Dash moved his foot away from her and wiped at his forehead with the back of his hand. Their table was outside by the pool; being in the open felt safer than a cozy indoor booth, but the summer sun beating down on him only added to the stress sweating.

"I know that you told a journalist about my…recovery," he said in a hushed tone. He waited for Cindy's reaction, but she frowned and sat back in her chair, as if confused.

"What? No, I didn't." She reached her hand across the table toward his, and he had to lean fully back in his chair to avoid the contact. She slid her sunglasses off and a sincere expression crossed her face. "I would never do anything to hurt you."

"You're the only person who knows this very specific fact about me." His jaw clenched. How could he have been so naive as to tell her? Sure, he needed people to talk to, but that's what Chris was for. "If you didn't tell, then who did?"

"I don't know." She raised her hands up, as if in surrender. "But you have to believe me when I say that there's no one I've told."

Of course he didn't believe her. He'd hidden his identity from her, sure, but she'd hidden the fact that she knew who he'd been the whole time. Maybe the only reason she was friendly with him in the first place was to take advantage of his celebrity status. Dash hated feeling used. He had no idea what else she might know, or who she planned to tell. What he did know, however, was that he needed the situation contained. He didn't want to loop in the authorities, because he had secrets to keep that they would surely spill. And if his mom found out that not only had Dash told a random online person about his problems but that he had an anonymous social-media account for crafting, she might actually explode. He had to handle this on his own.

"You knew who I was this whole time, somehow, but you never told me," he said. "Why would I trust you?"

"The tattoo on your arm," she quickly said.

He rubbed at the wave that started at his wrist and worked its way up his forearm.

"I saw it in one of your videos, and I'd only ever seen that on one person. You." Her eyes turned soft as she spoke. "And I thought, what are the odds? The person I've had a crush on since I was a little girl is secretly a crafter, just like me? And then I realized it was fate intervening, showing me the way to you."

More like bad luck, Dash thought, but he didn't dare say that out loud.

Cindy leaned forward again, her elbows on the table, her voice eager and hopeful. "I messaged you, and you messaged back, and it was so easy to talk, just as I knew it would be. I was going to tell you, eventually, after we'd met. But you kept shutting me down, and then you said you had a girlfriend."

The disgusted way she said *girlfriend* hung in the air like a bad smell. Cindy's nose even twitched, and she wiped at it with the back of her hand. "I had to say something, otherwise I'd miss my chance."

"Your chance for what?" Dash was equally terrified and riveted by what she was saying. He'd had online stalkers over the years, plenty of them. But he'd never interacted with one for this long. Did they all think this way, or was it just her?

"My chance to be with you."

In that moment, he knew that she'd created a fantasy of who he was and what they could be. And that by agreeing to meet with her, he'd fed that fantasy and given her some kind of false hope. She'd built him up to a point of thinking they might actually be together. He didn't want to hurt her but understood she had the power to hurt him, if she wanted.

"Then, why would you tell someone about this part of my life that you know is so personal?" he pressed.

"Dash, I didn't. I would never betray you."

"I can't have anything more come out about me so, please, just don't go to the press again." His voice had become shaky at the mere thought that more secrets of his would be revealed. "Believe me."

Something about the way she said that made him wonder if he might.

She reached her hand out again, but this time she held a doll out toward him. Cindy was a knitter, and apparently she'd done a new craft.

"It's you." She turned the thing over to reveal a little Dash doll with a white T-shirt, detailed tattoos, and the brooding glare he'd perfected for so many of his indie films. He wouldn't admit it in front of her, but the resemblance *was* uncanny. She had talent. "I love you," she added.

As Cindy pushed the doll closer to him, Dash exhaled sharply and forced his features to remain neutral. He'd agreed to meet his stalker, and he'd gotten unique gifts from fans in the past, so while a handmade doll of himself was odd, it could've been worse: the doll didn't appear to be made out of human hair, for example. He just wasn't sure what the best next step was here. He was not about to hold a doll version of himself...or play with it? What did people do with something like this?

"You're very talented," he eventually offered.

"I could make you so happy. I already know everything about you, Dash. Where you get take-out food, your favorite candy store, the type of clay you work with. We could be together." The hopeful expression on her face almost made him want to hug her. Then she pointedly tapped the doll's chest. "All three of us."

As much as he didn't want Cindy in his life—and now she was really starting to freak him out—he also didn't want her to suffer. Unrequited love could burn a hole through your core and not stop until you were ash. He didn't want that for this person, and he could see what looked like real loneliness, not malice, in Cindy's eyes.

"Cindy, if you know all of this, then it's clear you've been following me around in real life, which I'm not okay with. If I find out you're continuing to track my movements, I'll need to get the authorities involved, which I don't want to do. And more importantly, I want to be clear when I say this: I will never love you. My heart is with someone else." He looked directly at her then, so she'd know he was serious. And, he realized with some dread, he *was*. His feelings were only for Sophie, and that fact was almost as scary as the reality in front of him. "And I know that might hurt to hear, but it's the truth. I hope you find everything you're looking for, but it will never be with me."

He didn't want to wait for her reaction as there was nothing more to say. She'd denied going to the press, and she was sticking to that version of reality. He'd said his piece and asked her not to continue to feed them stories, which was all he could do. But she wasn't going to apologize or tell the truth, so the sooner he left the better it would be for her and him. He quickly stood and placed enough money on the table to cover their orders, tip, and extra if she needed some for the ride home.

"Wait, Dash." Cindy pushed herself up from the table, her phone pointed at him and the Dash doll clutched to her chest. "Can we all take a selfie? Just for my own memories?"

His brows must have gone all the way up his forehead. He was *not* about to take a selfie with his stalker and her stuffed doll. The thought of that was not only unsettling, but borderline absurd. He had to leave. Without saying another word, he turned and walked back toward the entrance to where Chris waited with a getaway car.

"How did it go?" Chris asked as Dash opened the car door. He locked it behind him.

"Drive before she runs out here and writes down your plate." He buckled his seat belt and checked for her in the side mirror.

"Oh, shit. That well, huh?"

Dash finally looked at him. "I'm not kidding. She knit a doll version of me."

Chris's eyes widened. "Was it at least a good replica?"

"Yes. The thing *was* me. Now can we please go?" Dash waved at the road in front of them.

"You should've at least taken a picture."

"She would've loved that." Dash glanced behind them again as Chris pulled out of the driveway of the hotel and turned right onto Sunset Boulevard. They drove past a billboard for Reece's movie, *Final Judgment Day*. There was Reece in a leather jacket, with buzzed hair, and a cut on his lip. He gave Dash a look that suggested a final judgment had come, and it was that Dash had totally fucked up.

"She said she didn't tell anyone about my sobriety." The thought that maybe she was telling the truth kept worming its way around his head and made him question coming in the first place.

"Yikes, so she didn't own up to it?"

"That's just it, I kind of believed her." Dash shook his head at how hurt she'd seemed at the very suggestion that she'd betrayed him.

"I'm sure you've had stalkers do worse. Hell, even I had some rando send me panties in the mail when I played for the Dodgers." Chris scratched his eyebrow. "They're stalkers for a reason. Have you thought any more about telling the police?"

"She won't come looking for me, not after what I said to her." And he believed that to be true.

But if Cindy hadn't told his secret, then who had? Dash gave a quick glance at Chris, who drove them back to Dash's house. Chris wouldn't tell someone about his sobriety, would he? Unless Chris had taken the whole idea of Dash telling his story to help other people get sober one step too far...

"You know I wouldn't ask this normally, but you didn't... tell anyone about me, did you?" Dash had gotten used to people he loved betraying him, and while he didn't think Chris would, he still had to ask.

Chris looked over at him, like Dash had just asked if they

could go grab raw vegan burgers for lunch. "Dude, I'm going to pretend you didn't just ask me that."

"Fair enough," Dash quickly replied. The tension in the car was thick, and Dash wondered if he'd once again pushed someone away, like he always did.

SOPHIE'S TIKTOK
Ex number four
Name: The "Comedian"
Occupation: Stand-up comedy
Length of relationship: Seven months
Reason for breakup: Some bullsh*t
Weeks until book is due: Less than 3

Britney Spears's "Toxic" plays in the background.

"My next ex, who I'm seeing tonight is…"

Sophie pointed a finger up to the corner of the screen and the words *passive-aggressive* appeared. She pointed slightly lower, and the words *always complains* popped up. Then to the bottom corner of the screen where the words *doesn't read books* materialized. Sophie's brows rose, then she leaned close to the camera and said, "Wish me luck."

COMMENTS:

@destinedtobee has there ever been a romance book about a stand-up comedian?? I smell an enemies-to-lovers idea…!

    @nobullallsheets Hello, she said he's toxic.

      @destinedtobee classic start to an E2L book, honestly

@jamesthetang to quote John Waters, "If you go home with somebody, and they don't have books, don't fuck 'em."

@tokcrafty2me Just be yourself, Soph

25

SOPHIE

O'Gradys was not a bar Sophie was familiar with, but when she entered, she had to allow her eyes to adjust because…damn, the place was dark. Like, they had not paid their electric bills and just decided the glow from people's phones would have to suffice. Still, she managed to walk forward with her hands outstretched, feeling around to make sure she didn't bump into anything.

She spotted an open two-top table and made her way toward it. She had no idea if Kyle was even there yet. But with her luck, if she tried searching the restaurant, she'd trip and knock herself unconscious on a plate of hot wings. She sat down, took out her phone, and sent a text.

Here! At a table.

She drummed her fingers along the wooden tabletop. She wasn't nervous to see Kyle, exactly, but she'd been a very different person when they were together. She'd allowed their relationship to be unbalanced, like how she'd gone to every one of his stand-up shows, but he'd never even offered to read the book pages she worked on.

To distract herself, she swiped open her phone and went into her messages. There was Dash's name, but nothing new. She shouldn't even be looking at his texts. He wasn't an option. But then she couldn't help wondering what dry joke he'd make about a bar like this one.

Sophie exhaled as she typed a message, but to Carla—the person she needed to focus on. Miss you, she typed, then deleted because those words didn't feel right. How's your night going? she wrote instead, then hit Send. Her phone pinged, and she was surprised to hear from Carla so quickly but was soon disappointed.

Unfunny Kyle: Coming.

Sophie looked up and saw his long, lanky arms first—Kyle was duck-under-doors tall. She needed to get their meeting over with, so she stood and stretched out her arms to go in for the hug.

"Hey." She wrapped him in a tight, meaningful hug and held him there for a few seconds. He froze, but eventually softened and gave her a *There, there* kind of hug back. Which... fine, she would take whatever meant that he was willing to have a conversation. When they broke apart, she added, "It's good to see you."

She lied. She had to, otherwise her memories would force her to flee the restaurant.

"You, too," he answered hesitantly.

"This is a really interesting spot." She tried to make small talk and rocked back on her heels, wishing she could speed up to the part of the night where she got to leave.

"Yeah, I've been here for about three years now," he dryly said.

Oh, great. He was leading with sarcasm, trying to make her feel bad because, apparently, he'd been waiting for her to show up. She took a deep breath in and braced for more.

"What can I get you?" he asked.

"Oh, you don't have to get me anything. Let's just sit and catch up." She sat down at the table and waited for him to do the same, but he just stood there.

"I have other tables." He looked at her then, holding a pad of paper and a pen, which is when she realized that this person was *not* in fact Kyle but the waiter.

Which was made even more apparent when an equally tall man with slicker hair and a ratty T-shirt came up and sat down at the table across from Sophie.

"Ordering without me?"

She looked at the waiter, then at Kyle. "God, I'm so sorry," she told the waiter.

But Kyle, in very Kyle fashion, assumed she was talking to him. "Appreciate the apology. I'll have a double vodka, please."

"I'll have a soda water, thanks." Sophie was deeply grateful that the low lighting concealed the embarrassed flush that ran hot across her cheeks.

Their waiter nodded, then walked away quickly, not that she could blame him.

Kyle scratched at his patchy beard. "You're not drinking? On one of those weird cleanses again?"

Sophie sucked in her top lip, then said, "I'm just not drinking tonight." Even though she kind of needed a drink to get through this chat with Kyle, she hadn't had a drink in almost a week. And, to be honest, not drinking helped her feel way more in control of her life than she had in a while. She might just keep it up, but that was none of Kyle's business.

He readjusted the collar of his shirt and looked at her. "So what's this all about? You know I'm kind of seeing someone, right?"

"No, I didn't know that."

"We're not exclusive. So if you wanted to say, you know, get in a little something-something now." He made a clicking noise with his tongue, as if to sweeten the proposition.

"What?" Sophie shook her head. "What are you talking about?"

"What are *you* talking about?" Kyle crossed his arms, as if offended.

"I asked you here to find out why we didn't work out. Geez, Kyle." She sat back in her chair and crossed her arms, too. She *was* offended.

Kyle performed at open mics, acted in an improv troupe, and was, in general, the absolute worst, most self-centered human being alive. He'd implied throughout their relationship that Sophie was very lucky to be with him, and for a time, she'd believed him.

"Uh." He ran a hand through his hair and looked off. "You're asking me for closure? *You* broke up with *me*. Which was honestly kind of a shock because I've never been broken up with before. We had a fight, and then you stopped returning my texts." Kyle put his elbows on the table and leaned forward. "I even called, but you never picked up. And you *always* picked up my calls, even that one time when you were at the lady doctor. If anyone needs closure, it's me."

Sophie didn't immediately respond, as she was still processing everything Kyle had just said. He wasn't wrong—Sophie had always put him first in their relationship, and she was sure her silence *was* a shock to him. But she couldn't believe he was trying to put the blame on her—classic Kyle. "I didn't see the point in returning your calls since you were a massive asshole when I ended our relationship."

"Whoa, whoa, whoa." He put his hands up, as if to shield himself from her. "When did you get so angry?"

"I'm not angry. I'm just being honest. You were a jerk!" Her voice was absolutely getting louder, but she found she couldn't just sit back and let Kyle be Kyle. She'd done plenty of that when they were together.

The waiter dropped off their drinks, and Kyle immediately took a swig from his glass. Sophie wrapped her hands around the cold tumbler, willing herself to calm down. Because while talking to Kyle had never exactly been easy, she found this whole interaction infuriating. Even if he wasn't totally wrong.

Sophie exhaled and steeled herself to do the thing she'd never done when they dated: confront him. "You know what, Kyle? The truth is that you wanted me to be the easygoing type and ignore that you were always hitting on girls after shows. I saw you do it all the time. But that got really old. And yes, I should've just confronted you about it. But I didn't feel like I could, because then I wouldn't be that perfect cool girl you needed me to be."

She thought of Poppy and how she'd be fist-pumping the air for her. She decided to press on, just to make Imaginary Poppy proud. "And what about when I told you that you were addicted to your phone, and you told me I was the one who was a tech addict because I needed a pacemaker to live?" She touched the scar on her chest for emphasis, not that he could even see her doing that in the darkness of the restaurant, but still, it was the principle of the thing.

"Well, uh, you *do*." He chewed on a piece of ice as he spoke, and vodka-water dribbled down his chin. "It was just a joke. You laughed at it back then."

"I always had to laugh at your jokes because of your fragile ego!" Okay, yes, she was shouting now, and it felt really good, too. "That's why I broke up with you!"

"No, Sophie, *you* have trust issues. Period. *That* is why we broke up. Not because I made some clever joke about your pacemaker or because I had adoring fans."

Sophie rolled her eyes at the fan comment. She already had more fans on social than he'd likely had at any of his shows.

"Kyle Slannis?" Someone tapped on the end of a microphone. "Kyle to the stage, you're up."

Sophie's mouth dropped open. "Did you seriously ask me to meet you at a bar where you're doing a stand-up set?"

"What? You always loved coming to my shows." He raised his hands in a what-can-you-do kind of gesture.

"You clearly haven't been following the fact that most of our relationship was one big lie, on my part." Sophie stood up, eager to flee. "I think I got all the closure I'll ever get."

"Whatever. Can you make sure to close out our tab?"

Sophie ran a hand through her hair and grabbed the end of her messy bun. "Our tab? I ordered a water."

"Yeah, but I have to go onstage, and you always used to get the tab." He leaned down to give her a ridiculous peck on the cheek, which she didn't even have time to swat away.

But when he pulled away, she *did* have time to grab his vodka and toss the remaining icy water all over his shirt. "This time, the tab is on you."

"Are you serious right now?" Kyle jumped back from the spot where he stood and desperately tried to wipe the wetness off his shirt.

"That's something I should've done a long time ago." Sophie's fists balled at her sides. She turned and walked away from Kyle and the table.

As she exited the bar, adrenaline rushed through her. She knew that she wouldn't be learning much from this experience with him. He accused her of having trust issues, but what he *really* meant was jealousy. She supposed she was a little jealous, at times: not wanting to share Jewel with an open relationship, and spying on Kyle to see if he was cheating. Maybe jealousy could be holding her back from falling in love, but it also felt like she'd just picked the wrong people.

Sophie checked her phone while walking to the bus stop, and there was a message waiting from Carla.

Seriously long night. Can we hang soon?

Sophie should've been thrilled, but all she felt was empty.

26

DASH

Dash had been in recovery long enough to know that there were good days and bad days. On the good days, he only had brief thoughts about drinking that flickered like a failing light bulb. On the bad ones, drinking became more of a daydream he couldn't wake from.

More specifically, he'd fantasized about how easy it would be to just head out his front door, cross the lawn, open the gate, and walk the two blocks to the liquor store. He'd buy a dark brown bourbon, bring the bottle to the register, and have his first long pull right there in the store before carrying it back home to fill a tall tumbler. He ached to have the burn across his throat as he swallowed down the one thing that could numb all his thoughts.

He never should've agreed to meet Cindy or to help his parents with the speech. *Or help Sophie.* That last thought crossed his mind, but then he pushed it away. Sophie was the one change that hadn't been a mistake. While the others had brought self-doubt and anxiety, she was light and air and one of the few people who accepted him for exactly who he was.

But he couldn't dwell on her for long. He had to stay busy to keep his mind from wandering to how nice it would be to just give in to the inevitable and drink. So he'd decided to take on a bigger-scale project because he needed an outlet to pour all of his feelings into.

As he was about to head toward his work studio, he glanced out the window next to his front door. Not because he was hoping to see Sophie, necessarily, but he couldn't deny he'd been checking out that window multiple times already just to see if she was around.

And, as it turned out, this time she was. Sophie was in the Adirondack chair on her porch, her laptop open and resting on her knees. She scowled at the screen, and he wondered if a coffee might help.

"Hey." He carried a mug filled to the brim with a fresh cup from his French press.

Sophie looked up, and her expression softened at the sight of him. Something about being able to put her in a better mood made his heart thud a little faster than normal. Or maybe it was the quick walk across their shared lawn.

"You're home." Her loose marigold-yellow caftan with a deep V-neck whooshed and clung to her curves as a breeze fluttered through.

"I'm always home," Dash said in an attempt at humor and shielded his eyes from the sun with his free hand. "You look like you could use some fuel. Coffee?"

"Sure, thanks." She licked her lips before catching his eye again. "I don't know if I've ever thanked you for…supporting me, I guess. But I think it's really nice that you helped me write at the spa, and you're bringing me coffee while I try to work. Not everyone does that."

"Well, you looked a few seconds away from throwing the laptop." His brows rose. "Can't have that."

"I'd like to say I've made some progress on my old book, but

I'm just...stuck." Her determined little canine tooth crested her lip, as if threatening to bite him. What the tooth didn't know was that Dash would very much like that. "I met up with the last ex I needed to see, and it went terribly."

"Do you want to talk about it?" Dash would talk about anything with Sophie, even her exes.

"I thought that when I saw him, everything I'm trying to figure out would click into place. But he just made me so angry about the fact that I tolerated dating him for as long as I did. I made a lot of bad choices in my twenties." She blew across the top of the hot coffee.

"I don't know." Dash rocked back on his heels. "Those choices all led you here, didn't they?"

She stopped blowing and looked up at him. There was a moment between them that he couldn't quite place, and instead of Sophie filling the silence, he did. "Maybe you just need a few days to process your meeting with him, then you can revisit."

Sophie blinked, then sipped the coffee. A low sound of satisfaction escaped her, then she asked, "Where are you off to now?"

"I've got plans for a new plate. Something structured and with tiny detailing. I need a distraction."

"So do I." She closed her laptop and stood up, placing the computer on the chair. "Show me?"

An easy smile passed between them, and he thought that maybe he *could* keep Sophie as a friend and forget the undeniable chemistry that still simmered between them. Because having her in his life was better than not having her at all.

Dash led them through his house and opened the interior door to his garage. The smell of baked clay and wet paint wafted out as he flipped on the overhead light. That smell promised potential and an afternoon of focus. His whole garage studio felt like a space that was entirely his. But now, with Sophie in it, he was revealing an intimate part of himself she hadn't yet seen.

"Seize the Clay?" Sophie smirked as she pointed to the wooden sign he'd commissioned and hung against one wall. The name had come to him after visiting Ojai's idyllic main street, which was cluttered with cutesy, pun-filled names.

"It was that, or License to Kiln," he said, chuckling.

She walked the perimeter of the garage, inspecting the countertops with her fingertips. "I always wondered what you had in here, since it's clearly not your car. I just assumed bins of gummy bears."

"That's not a bad idea." He leaned against a worktable. "Most of my videos are about how to make ceramics using a kitchen oven or microwave. I get a lot of engagement on those because it's an easy point of entry for newbies. But when I need a bigger project, I use the kiln and the pottery wheel."

He pointed to the kiln in one corner, then the pottery wheel in the center of the room. Dash led her to a worktable next to a line of lockers where he stored materials. She picked up a now-dry dish that sat on top of a clean tarp. The fresh glaze made it sparkle and she rotated it from side to side, turned it over, and ran her fingers along the top and bottom.

Her mouth quirked up. "This is the most beautiful thing, like art."

He was glad she thought so. The dish was inspired by Sophie: the shape was the curve of her hips, the dots were her freckles, and the center looked like the pixie tangerine he now associated her with. "Have you ever worked with clay?" Dash asked.

She shook her head no.

"Want to try?"

She seemed surprised by the question but quickly smiled as she said, "I'll try anything with you."

Her words echoed through him, bouncing around in his head until he felt dizzy. *I'll try anything for you*, he thought to himself. And he realized, in that moment, that he *would* do anything for her. Which scared him because he didn't know if he could ever be what she needed him to be.

She sat on a stool next to the pottery wheel as he removed clay and filled a measuring cup with water. He placed the materials on the throwing surface and showed her the handle to make the wheel spin, then put her hands on the lump of clay. Of course, as the wheel began to rotate, along with the clay, Sophie lost grip of the wet mixture and shaped it into, well, something quite lopsided.

"This is the worst vibrator I've ever seen." She frowned at the poor thing.

Dash laughed as he released the lever, and the wheel came to a slow stop. "I would never suggest you need help because you don't."

"Of course not." She rested her hands on the wheel and gave him a crooked smile.

"But do you *want* some help?" Dash pulled up a small stool behind Sophie's chair and situated himself as near as he could. When he wrapped his arms around the outside of hers, his chest touched her back.

"Are we about to have a *Ghost* pottery-scene moment?" She turned to look back at him.

"Minus the ghost part." But plus the erection part, because with his mouth so close to her neck, breathing in the citrus scent of her, Dash grew hard. He moved the wheel's lever to try to stay focused, and the table began to spin. He guided her hands up and around the clay, then helped her fingers form a hole in the center.

As the wheel spun and their bodies formed a kind of unit, he was aware of the rise and fall of her chest as she breathed, and how his chin grazed the side of her cheek. Eventually, he stopped the spinning wheel. His hands lingered on top of hers, both of their fingers damp and caked with clay. She turned her head, and their mouths were just inches apart.

"Dash." Sophie's voice was sweet and smooth and went down easy.

"Yeah?" He swallowed a sliver of longing. He needed to kiss her.

"You think I can't feel you against me?" She moved her ass back against him, and a shallow moan escaped his lips as an answer. "When I kiss Carla, it's not the same as when I kiss you," she said quietly. "You're like electricity. That's how a kiss should feel, isn't it?"

He didn't say a word. He didn't want to think about her kissing Carla, but he couldn't deny the truth to her words. They just sat there, breathing with each other, waiting to see what the other did.

Dash knew that he should stand up and walk away and let whatever moment they were having pass. After all, Sophie wanted a real relationship, and he couldn't give her that. But then she swiveled her stool so she faced him and closed the small distance between by pressing her lips to his.

He pulled her onto his lap, and she wrapped her clay-covered hands behind his neck and wove her fingers through his hair. She ground her softness against his hardness and another deeper moan passed through him.

She took his bottom lip in her teeth and gave him a nip. "Why can't I stop kissing you, like, ever?"

"I guess you want to get electrocuted. Get it? Because you called me electricity?"

"You are so corny." But she laughed against his mouth, and her forehead fell to his shoulder. He took the opportunity to slip her earlobe between his teeth and gently bite. She looked up and placed her hands on either side of his face. When she licked her lips, her eyes searched his. "I know you don't want a relationship, but I can't stop touching you. Does that make me a bad person?"

What did Dash really know about what a bad person was? He'd been a bad person plenty of times, especially when he'd been drinking. "I don't want you to feel bad about what I'm about to do to you. I want you to want it. And if you don't, then we need to stop."

"I want it. This is what I've been missing. This *thing* that lights up my whole body." Her thumb stroked along the edge of his jaw, and then she pressed her lips hard against his.

He understood exactly what she'd meant. He hadn't been able to get her out of his head either. And ever since she'd come into his life a few weeks ago, he'd finally felt like he was waking up—like all of him was alive for the first time in years.

"I made that dish for you," he said.

"I know." She bit across his neck. He placed his hands under her ass, wrapped her legs around him, and began to carry her back toward the door.

"We're very dirty." She trailed a clay-covered finger down the front of her chest and in between her breasts.

Dash took in Sophie's hands, which were covered in dry clay, and the little bits of gray speckling her cheeks. "You're filthy."

"You have no idea," she whispered against his ear.

He undressed her as they tumbled through the door, setting her down so he could lift her dress over her head, unclasping her bra, and letting her breasts come free. She lifted the corner of his T-shirt, and he helped her peel it off. When they got to his room, she was only wearing panties and he was unbuckling his jeans.

"Sophie." He swallowed a lump in his throat, nervous she wouldn't want all of him. "We don't have to, but I want to…"

Sophie was busy bringing her panties down her legs but stopped and looked up. "Are you, um, ready?"

"I'm ready," Dash said.

"Oh, thank God." Sophie's mouth turned into a grateful smile, and he licked his lips.

He was going to make sure she was grateful every single second, and he was going to take his time.

27

SOPHIE

Sophie vividly remembered being on submission for her first book with her agent. A terrible time when her manuscript was sent out to publishers for consideration. She'd waited two months before they got a nibble from the publisher who eventually bought her book.

But that wait seemed like nothing compared to the few weeks Sophie had spent waiting for Dash.

"I'm STI-free and on birth control." She hopped on one foot as she took her underwear all the way off. "Do you have condoms?"

She threw the panties at him, and he nodded. "I do. And I was tested six months ago. No STIs."

Sophie clasped her hands together, looked up to the ceiling and said, "Thank you, whoever is up there." What was this, her birthday?

Dash pulled a condom out of his bedside-table drawer and rolled it on. Then he pulled her to him. "You're sure?" He stroked a little circle across the apple of her cheek.

She would end things with Carla because she wasn't willing

to say goodbye to Dash. She'd tried to force a spark with her, but the way she felt for Carla was so drastically different from the passion she had for Dash, and that couldn't be ignored.

Even if what she had with Dash wouldn't be forever, all she needed was to be tangled up with him for as long as they could be. He didn't want a relationship, but she would take what he could give and then figure out the rest once they'd ended. Like Dash's tattoo—*You Chose*—that would be her choice.

Dash grabbed Sophie's ass, lifted her, and wrapped her legs around his hips. He pinned her against the wall, and his erection pressed against the opening of her lips.

"I must've been really good in a past life," she said. How else to explain this situation where she was about to have sex with the man she'd had a crush on since she was a teenager?

He brushed hair behind her ears and held on to her thigh with his free hand. Then he pulled her chin up slightly with the tip of his finger. "Tell me if any of this is too much, okay?"

She laughed. "For the record, I've had sex before, like, a lot, so you don't need to be gentle."

He gave enough of a smile that the dimple in his cheek showed, even through the dried clay that dotted his face. "Good girl. Then put me inside you and go slow. I want to feel every inch."

Sophie opened her mouth to say something, but there were no words. She made a kind of strangled noise that was satisfaction because, really, if her knees weren't already locked tightly around him, they would've melted into a puddle on the floor. She reached her hand to meet him, and his cock throbbed against her palm.

"I just want you to know that I'm really going to enjoy this," she said.

Dash bit his lower lip as she pushed back against the wall, giving herself room to accept him. She rubbed his tip in a circle against her clit, then lowered him down, down, until his head met her entrance. She was already so wet from his words that when she began to slide onto him, there was no resistance.

She sighed as his cock inched inside her, and he moaned as her hand guided him all the way in. Eventually he pressed the full length into her, and they both grunted as he settled there. She was so deliciously filled by him but ground her hips to try to get more.

"Oh, my God, Soph, you feel so fucking good. And you tightened that pussy for me, didn't you?"

She had.

He pushed into her again, and her arms wrapped firmly around his neck.

"Just fuck me already, please," she practically begged.

He placed a hand on one of her knees and pushed it up against the wall, so she had one leg wrapped around his waist, and the other hiked up. And then he pinned her in place while he drove his cock in, then out. He circled his hips as he entered, and she moaned loudly. So then he did it again, and again, bouncing her up and down as he drove into her.

"You are fucking me so good," Sophie breathed into his ear.

"Say my name. Say it." He ground faster and harder, demanding the words.

"Dash," she breathed into his ear, and he drove harder. "Oh. My. Dash." She took every single bit of him. She wrapped her leg tighter around his waist and bit the top of his shoulder. "You're going to make me come."

At those words, he pulled them both back from the wall, and carried her to the bed. "I want you to look at me as you come," he said.

He laid her down on the bed and spread her legs wide. He settled in between them and dipped his cock into her, again and again. His index finger found her clit, and he rubbed light circles around her bud as he thrust. His other hand rested next to her hip, and she clung to the crashing-wave tattoo inked there.

"Dash, Dash," she repeated as the pressure began to build. "I'm going to come on you."

"Look at me," he ordered. His mouth met her nipple, and he sucked her in sharply.

Sophie did not have a problem looking at Dash as her body tightened around him and wave after wave of pleasure rolled through her. Only when she twitched from the aftershocks did Dash say, "I'm coming." She grabbed his ass, and he pushed himself farther inside as he came.

They stilled there, and the only sound in the room was their deep breaths. Eventually, Dash kissed her forehead, then each of her eyes, and moved away from her before rolling the condom off. He lay on one side of the bed, and she was on the other. She reached her hand out toward Dash and their fingertips met. They lay side by side and held each other's hands. This could be enough, just the feel of him next to her.

Though, perhaps the fact that they could never be in a relationship should've worried her more. Because, really, what Sophie felt for Dash went beyond friendship. When they were apart, the nudging reminder that she was missing something rose up. And when she was around him, she wanted to touch him, or hold his hand, or feel the press of his lips against hers. She'd started to daydream about the simple act of exploring his tattoos with her fingertips.

"What does this tattoo mean, Dash?" She turned on her side and traced the ink that wrapped around his forearm with her middle finger. "Why is there a little seagull flying above the waves?"

"That birdie is called a tern, actually." Then Dash sat up and extended his right arm to give her a closer look. There was one enormous swell of inky black and dark blue with sea spray all around. She rubbed her thumb across the lone bird just above the tip of the wave. "I got this one after being sober for a year. One of the people I met in AA was an ornithologist. She was always talking about birds she'd seen. She told us that whenever terns are threatened by high water, they furiously collect objects and vegetation to raise their nests and protect themselves. And I liked the idea of that. These small but mighty birds who will just adapt and do whatever it takes to build a wall of protection from the chaos around them. So the waves, for me, symbolize the chaos, and the tern is a reminder that I can stay above it."

Sophie admired Dash, her little tern, all the more then. She'd wanted to get a tattoo but had never been able to settle on what design would be meaningful. She'd had a hard time landing on something that would always bring joy when she looked at it. Plus, she hadn't thought as deeply about a tattoo as he clearly had.

She propped herself up on her elbow. "If I got a tattoo, I'm pretty sure I'd get something really ridiculous that I'd be embarrassed about."

"Oh, you mean like this?" Dash brought his leg up, grabbed his foot, and lifted his big toe to reveal a little smiley face inked on the underside. The face had one winking eye and a floppy tongue hanging out playfully from the side of its thin mouth.

She bit her lip as she inspected the sweet drawing. "Oh, Dash, I want to laugh so much, but I honestly think the winking eye makes it very endearing."

"I don't really remember getting that one. All I know is I woke up the next morning with saran wrap on my foot and couldn't put any pressure on it for a good twenty-four hours. Which the director of the movie I was working on loved, obviously." He looked down at the bedspread, maybe embarrassed by the memory. "But at least I didn't get it on my ass?"

"That's the spirit." She rubbed his back, which was still damp with sweat.

"What about this?" The tip of his finger ran across the scar on her chest. "What's the story there?"

She ran her own finger across the faded pink scar. "I was

born with a congenital heart defect. This thing called aortic stenosis, which basically means I had a valve that was too small."

"The valve couldn't handle your big heart," he said jokingly.

She rolled her eyes but also appreciated that he wasn't scared by her condition. "They did a surgery to try to replace it when I was a kid, but the valve wasn't growing the way it needed to. We decided the pacemaker would be the best option after I passed out when I was driving one time. That's why I still don't drive, actually."

He brushed hair behind her ear and placed a soft kiss on her cheek. "You're one tough lady, Soph."

"That's what makes me part robot, as Nina likes to say." Sophie shrugged because she barely noticed the pacemaker anymore.

"If you're telling me I just slept with an AI, then that makes me weirdly more excited."

She giggled because anything that made him happy made her happy, too. "You have a scar, too, you know." She ran her thumb across the little line in his eyebrow.

"Mine doesn't come with technology that makes me superhuman, though." He purposefully raised his brow. "I was five, and Poppy was chasing me through the house. I tripped on the marble stairs, and my face landed at the edge. Apparently I almost ruined my mom's antique Persian rug with all the blood."

Sophie imagined his mom emphasized that point when she retold the story. "Kitty always knows what's important in life."

"Always." His jaw tightened slightly. But then Dash's doorbell rang, and they both turned. "It's probably a delivery."

But then it rang again.

They eyed each other. "Maybe it's your friend Chris?" Sophie wanted to at least be wearing a bra if it was someone who wasn't a delivery. She stood, found her bra, and quickly put it on.

"Chris knows I hate surprises." Dash stood and slipped into

his boxers. His phone on the bedside table vibrated, and he frowned as he picked it up. "It's Poppy."

Sophie checked her phone, but there was nothing from her.

"Poopy Pants?" Dash answered. His tone changed to something more akin to panic. "You're here?" He moved to his bedroom window to glance out, but as he did, Poppy's face appeared.

Sophie dropped down to the ground and hid herself behind the bed. Poppy was there, at Dash's place, and Sophie was inside, and they'd just...

"Shit," she muttered to herself. Had Poppy just seen Sophie in her brother's room in nothing but a bra?

28

DASH

When Dash opened the door and saw Poppy holding a Tupperware container, he felt a few things. First, annoyance that she'd shown up at the absolute worst possible time, and then an overwhelming sense of guilt. Because Sophie was Poppy's best friend, and he'd wedged himself between them.

"Bone broth!" She smiled brightly as she held up the container. "I had extra in my fridge and just figured that since we're doing the random stopovers I would bring you some. It does wonders for the digestive system."

Poppy breezed past him in oversize jeans and a plain white T-shirt, her long blond hair swishing as she walked. She'd been thinking of him, and he hadn't so much as considered how his actions were about to change her life.

She went into the kitchen and put the broth on the countertop, then she opened his cabinets until she found a mug. "Oh, this is so cute. Who knew you had taste?" She rotated the mug—his design—and appraised it with an appreciative look. It would be the perfect time to tell her he'd made it, if he didn't need her to leave. "The broth makes an excellent snack.

I'll heat some for you. There should be enough here to last the next two days."

He could not think of anything less appealing than a cup of hot bone broth as a snack, but he would keep those thoughts to himself. Especially because he wanted to get her out of his house before she realized Sophie was there.

"I can heat that up." He quickly moved to take the mug from her, and she let him. Maybe if he just drank the damn thing she'd leave.

"Ew, Dash, what's that on your hands?" She eyed the clay still dotting his hands. "Were you gardening?"

"Uh, yeah," he lied, the same way he always did whenever his family got close to learning something real about him.

"Well, wash them before you get your sod, or whatever, all over the place." She took the mug back from him.

He was about to make an excuse for why she had to leave, but then there was a crash from his bedroom. He winced, and Poppy turned toward the noise.

"Oh, no, don't tell me you have someone here? Gross." Poppy's nose wrinkled, but she walked toward his bedroom because she couldn't help but be her nosy self.

"It's probably just the wind."

"It's as hot as a sauna outside. There's no wind…" Poppy trailed off as her eyes caught on something. He followed her line of sight as she bent down and picked up one of Sophie's sandals, then her dress. She held them at eye level and her face shifted from curious to confused. "Aren't these Sophie's?"

He didn't answer. He couldn't. He was frozen in place from fear that he'd just completely destroyed his sister's trust, and he had no words that would make the situation okay. In his silence, though, Poppy advanced toward his bedroom.

He took a step to try to stop her, but then his door creaked open. Sophie held on to the frame and looked over at Poppy. She wore a long T-shirt of his that just skimmed above her knee, and he wasn't quite sure, but he thought he saw a tremble in Sophie's hands.

"Sophie?" Poppy's voice went up in surprise, and then she turned to Dash. Her expression went from dazed to hurt as she began to understand exactly what was going on.

"Hey." Sophie cleared her throat, then tried again. "Hi there."

Poppy's shoulders shrunk in on themselves. "Sophie, please, please, please tell me I'm jumping to conclusions about seeing you in my brother's clothes and walking out of his bedroom."

Sophie shot Dash a look, but her expression was unreadable, which made Poppy glance over, too. He knew he should say something to smooth the situation, but all he could come up with was "You should've texted before coming."

Well, he knew *that* wasn't the right thing.

"You mean so that you could both put the correct clothes on?" Poppy's eyes narrowed, her hand was in a fist on her hip, and she leaned forward like one wrong move and she'd lunge for his throat.

"Poppy, this just kind of happened." Sophie's hands gestured between herself and Dash. "We didn't plan for this."

"You're with my best friend, and you're with my brother?" She pointed between them. "And neither of you thought to tell me? How long has this been going on?"

Dash was about to open his mouth to say something, but Poppy continued, "What, you thought I just wouldn't find out?"

"We didn't do this to hurt you," Dash added. "It's not Sophie's fault. I started—"

But Poppy wheeled toward him with a raised and accusatory finger. "Do you realize how fucked up this is that you were both keeping the fact that you're…" Poppy seemed to dry heave but then course-corrected.

"I know this looks bad," Dash began to say, but Poppy stopped him with her hand.

"Just so you know, I stole ginger from your garden the last time I was here and didn't tell you. I added it to the bone broth because I felt guilty. So I hope you enjoy that super-healing, yummy broth, because it's the last time I'll be making it for you!"

She turned to Sophie and shook her head. "And you. I've always given you free samples from the spa when your skin is looking sad. You don't deserve them!"

Then she stormed toward the front door and brushed past Dash's shoulder with such force that he stumbled backward. She slammed the door shut behind her.

"I should go after her." Sophie made for the door.

"She needs time, Soph."

"Poppy's my best friend!" Sophie gestured toward the door. "First I destroy my relationship with Nina, and now Poppy. I can't believe I did this to her. I'm a bad person."

"You didn't do anything wrong." Dash wrapped her in a hug. She hesitated, then wrapped her arms around him, and he squeezed her tight. He couldn't say the words that immediately came to mind—that he'd never felt as close to someone as he did to her. And that, even though he wasn't ready, he saw a future for them.

"I have to go." Sophie loosened herself from his grip and quickly collected her clothes from the floor.

"You don't have to." He followed her, like she was the sun, and he was the earth helplessly pulled to her. "We can talk about this."

"I can't talk right now, Dash. I—" she shook her head "—I have been spiraling, like, trying to figure out what's wrong with me, and attempting to make things work with Carla. And now I just totally messed up with Poppy. I need to clear my head. I'm sorry." She finally looked up, all her clothes bundled in her hands, still wearing his shirt and barefoot. She was upset, he knew that, but what he didn't know was how to fix it. All he could do was listen to what she needed, and she'd said that was space.

"Okay." His fingers nervously tapped at his sides, as she walked past him and toward the door. Before she left, he grabbed her elbow and placed a kiss on her forehead. Something to let her know he was there and ready for her, whenever she was. But she didn't reciprocate the gesture. Instead, she turned and walked out without so much as looking back.

29

SOPHIE

Sophie: can we talk?

Sophie: I'm so sorry, I never wanted to hurt you

Sophie: please just talk to me

Sophie: I totally GET why you're mad, and I will give you space, but please let me explain

Poppy: You've been secretly seeing my brother and didn't plan to tell me. There's nothing to explain

Sophie had read and reread Poppy's text and, well, she was right. Sophie had intentionally kept her relationship with Dash a secret from her best friend. There were multiple moments where she could've come clean and worked this out, but she'd actively chosen not to.

And the only conclusion Sophie could come to was that she

was deeply selfish, like, probably one-of-the-worst-humans-on-the-planet-level selfish.

"So you don't think I should respond?" Sophie asked.

Nina, who was shoving a tortilla chip loaded with guacamole into her mouth, turned to look at her. "I know I asked you to stop being a flake, but no—I think you should wait, like I told you the last few times you asked."

Sophie grabbed a chip and bit it more aggressively than necessary. They sat at the counter of Pink Metal, a restaurant that was impossible to get a table at but was owned by Nina's best friend, Jasmine. The restaurant was, as the name described, decked out in splashes of pink and chrome, giving the interior an edge while the food served was a warm and cozy contrast. Jasmine stood behind the counter and fixed all three of them margaritas.

"I agree with Nina. There's nothing more annoying than when you need space but someone won't give it to you." Jasmine slid a pink margarita across the counter, the rim dusted with bright pink sugar. "Don't be that person."

"But I can't stand that she's mad at me. I mean, we usually text every day. This isn't normal for us." Sophie sipped from her drink and was surprised by the kick of jalapeño. She wrapped her hair up into a bun and secured it with the hair tie from her wrist. "Okay, I'm already sweating."

"Do you really want to do this now? In the middle of this restaurant with other people around?" Nina crossed her arms, clearly annoyed.

"There are no other people here." Sophie looked around at the empty restaurant, which Jas had opened early for them specifically so they could have a vent sesh.

"I know that, but I didn't want to have to yell at you." Nina sipped from her drink.

"Just tell me what I need to do." She held her hands out, as if Nina would place the answer into them.

Nina exhaled and swiveled in her seat to face Sophie. She placed her hands on Sophie's knees and leaned forward. "You are sleeping with your best friend's brother. Yes, Poppy is *your* best friend, but you also need to understand where she's coming from. Two of the most important people in her world have a relationship outside of her. If you want to make things better, then you need to stop fixating on how uncomfortable *you* feel and start thinking about how Poppy is doing."

"So I'm selfish is what you're saying." Sophie sat back and pursed her lips, secure in the knowledge that she'd been right about herself.

"I didn't say that." Nina leaned back.

"Why didn't you just tell Poppy sooner?" Jasmine waved a tortilla chip in front of her, like the obvious thing would've been to confess.

Sophie absentmindedly brushed sugar off the front of her dress. "Dash and I hadn't figured out what we were doing, or what we even meant to each other. I mean, not until yesterday."

"Mmm, the sex day." Jasmine sipped her drink, but Nina whacked her arm. "Ow!"

"And you didn't think she'd find out at some point?" Nina asked.

"I didn't want her to find out, because then we'd have to stop seeing each other."

"Maybe she would've been cool with it." Jasmine shrugged. "You never know."

"Sounds like you didn't trust her," Nina said.

"No, I—" Sophie stopped herself, though, because she realized that Nina was right: she hadn't trusted Poppy. She'd convinced herself that if she told her, then Poppy would react negatively. But would her best friend have reacted as badly if she'd told her sooner? There was no way to know.

"Well, fuck, I think I'm having one of those self-realization moments." Not only had she not trusted Poppy, but she hadn't trusted any of her exes with her heart. *Trust* really was the issue holding her back.

"My margaritas tend to do that." Jasmine raised her glass in a cheers. "You sure you don't want some tequila in yours?" She nodded to Sophie's glass.

Sophie shook her head no, because her whole body already felt unsteady, even without the tequila. She'd lost trust that love could happen after her dad left their family and from her mother's reinforcements that she should never rely on another person for her happiness. And she'd carried that fear that if she ever trusted someone with her heart, they'd break it. So she'd chosen to never trust anyone with it.

Until Dash. Because the truth was that he'd gained her trust, and she'd given him her all. The person she couldn't be with, and her best friend's brother, was the first person she'd actually trusted. Well, that was just perfect.

Sophie grabbed her glass and downed the rest of the margarita for courage, because the next stop she had to make was to go and see Carla.

Carla sat behind her midcentury-modern office desk. Her space was like something from a catalog: impossibly chic and impeccably designed, with one wall of the room covered in floor-to-ceiling floating bookshelves and another lined with abstract art that Sophie knew to be original.

"So just to be clear, you're breaking up with me on my lunch break?" Carla had pierced some salad with her fork but hadn't yet taken a bite.

"I had to make this appointment with your assistant, and she said this was your earliest avail." In hindsight, maybe Sophie could've waited a few days until Carla was off from work and they could sit down. But pretending to continue things with Carla for even a moment longer felt wrong.

Carla stood from her desk and walked around to the luxe

swivel chair Sophie sat on. "I'm not going to beg you to be in a relationship with me. I'm a catch."

"Trust me, I know." She shifted slightly in her chair and swallowed down a little lump. She'd be lying if she said there was nothing between them—they had history—but she knew the difference between what she had with Carla and how Dash made her feel. Sophie wanted to chase what she had with Dash.

"Not that it matters, because we're *definitely* not getting back together again, but relationships should make you a better version of yourself." Carla sat on the edge of her desk and glared at Sophie. "And it sounds like you're running from what we have and going for someone who may or may not be there for you."

Sophie frowned. Carla had always been able to see to the depths of what she was insecure about and poke there with a little stick. Was she running from Carla toward an unavailable person? She knew she was, but staying with Carla didn't feel like an option either.

"You don't have anything to say?" Carla's hands flew up in frustration.

And Sophie stood so they could be eye-level—well, she was shorter than Carla, but still. "Carla, I really hope you find what you're looking for, because it can't be me."

"And I hope you don't regret what you're doing right now, because I won't be here the next time you realize you've fucked up." Carla gestured toward her office door with a flourish.

Sophie hesitated, unsure if they should hug or…

"That hand motion was for you to get out, please," Carla said with emphasis.

"Yes, okay." Sophie began to walk out the door, then turned back. "Do you want it closed or…"

Carla's salad bowl unexpectedly flew toward the door, and Sophie ducked out of the way to avoid being hit.

"Out!" Carla shouted after her.

As Sophie walked down the narrow hallway toward the

exit, past the waiting room, and toward the elevator, a tremor of dread went through her. She shouldn't be worried about what Carla thought of her. If anything, there was a sense of relief at the truth being out there. She was no longer hiding in the shadows.

But still, there was something Carla had said that gave her pause. *I won't be here the next time you realize you've fucked up.* Sophie had fucked up plenty of times in her life, multiple within the last twenty-four hours, and she didn't have a great track record when it came to making the right choices.

While she knew in her core that being with Dash was where she was supposed to be, she also knew that what Carla told her had a grain of truth. She was, more than likely, going to get her heart broken.

She took out her phone to distract herself as she rode the elevator down to the lobby. There were no new texts, but when she opened her TikTok app, she had a new message from a user called @craftycindy.

@craftycindy your boyfriend has been naughty...

There were screenshots of conversations between @craftycindy and another user called @tokcrafty2me. There was clearly a lot of flirtation and innuendo happening, but Sophie wasn't sure what any of this had to do with her. Who was @tokcrafty2me or @craftycindy, for that matter?

@sophiewrites I'm so sorry, but I think you have the wrong person

Sophie was about to put her phone away, when she noticed the user she'd just messaged was typing back. She stared at the screen and waited for the response, which didn't take long.

@craftycindy no, I don't. ☺ You're Dash's girlfriend.

"Uhh," Sophie said, nearly dropping the phone. There was a woman messaging her who knew Dash and knew they were kind of together (sometimes). What was happening here? Sophie's fingers started to tremble, and she brought them to her pacemaker to steady herself. She stepped out of the elevator, then typed.

@sophiewrites Dash?

@craftycindy omg please. He comments on all your videos, you're one of twenty accounts he follows—and you're his most recent add, you both uploaded vids from Ojai on the same day, and I recognized his yard from your posts. I know about Dash's secret TikTok account. You can stop playing innocent.

@craftycindy Look, we even had lunch together last week.

There was a blurry photo of Dash standing next to a table and a wad of money in front of him. He wasn't looking at the camera because his sunglasses were on, but it was definitely Dash.

@craftycindy he tried to give me hush money to cover our relationship up. But I didn't want to mess with girl code. Sorry to be the one to tell you he's cheating, but you deserve to know...

Sophie was still wrapping her head around everything this woman was telling her—that Dash was in a secret relationship and that he'd paid the woman hush money. What did all this mean? She looked at the username @tokcrafty2me and clicked into the profile. The avatar was of an oddly familiar vase.

As she stared at the vase, she realized she'd seen the same one in Dash's room. She clicked into a video that had a thumbnail of a ceramic dish, and as she watched she covered her mouth with her own hand at the realization that this was Dash's secret account.

She went back to her own feed and clicked into each video. He'd left a comment on every single one.

@tokcrafty2me good vibes only

@tokcrafty2me Nothing changes if nothing changes

@tokcrafty2me I'm Team Sophie

@tokcrafty2me be kind to yourself, change is hard

@tokcrafty2me you are perfect.

@tokcrafty2me just be yourself, Soph

Sophie felt sick to her stomach. She'd just been thinking that Dash was the only person she could ever really trust, but here was the other life he'd never let her into. And the other woman she'd never heard about. She'd been okay with the fact that Dash had a secret account, but she was definitely *not* okay with him keeping some other relationship from her.

Still, she had a gut feeling that everything she'd just seen wasn't quite right. There was a missing piece that only Dash could put into place, and she just hoped that whatever explanation he had would prove that he hadn't been lying to her this whole time.

30

DASH

Maybe it was the late-July heat or the fact that Dash hadn't heard from Sophie since his sister walked in on them, but something inside him must've snapped.

How else to explain why he'd printed out a dozen shirtless pics of Richard Gere from *American Gigolo*? Perhaps more concerning was that he was squatting in the grass and gluing the photos to a metal collar around the base of the tree.

"What are you doing?"

He heard Sophie's voice, then looked up to see her, but lost his footing completely and landed in the grass with a hell of a thump.

"Ahh," he managed to say as a photo of Richard Gere's abs landed on his face.

Sophie pulled the photo off and stared at it, then him. "I guess I have a few questions. For starters, why are you covering the tree with this handsome man? And why not cover my windows with him instead?"

Dash rolled his eyes as he pushed himself up to sitting. "You're the one who got me associating the damn squirrel with Richard Gere. I put a metal collar around the base of the tree, which apparently stops them from being able to climb, but I thought if anyone can intimidate Dick the squirrel, it's a shirtless Richard Gere. It's like a scarecrow, but a scare-Dick, if that makes sense."

"Sure, sure." Sophie held out her hand, and Dash took it, pulling himself up to stand. He brushed dirt and grass off his jeans. But Sophie wasn't smiling at him, the way she normally did. Her mouth formed a thin line as she swallowed.

She licked her lips and blew out a long breath. "Did you... Are you @tokcrafty2me?"

Dash frowned and shifted his weight from one leg to the other, the way he always did when he wasn't sure what to do. He had not expected her to say that, and the fact that she knew his secret-account name gave him pause. "How did you..." He started to look around the lawn, as if an answer might be there.

"A woman named @craftycindy messaged me." She held up her phone for him, and he saw the avatar of Cindy, along with a stream of messages. But Sophie pulled the phone back before he had time to read them. "Is that you? Are you @tokcrafty2me?"

He weighed his options, which weren't many: tell Sophie the truth, or lie. "Yes, that's me."

Sophie cleared her throat and held the phone to her chest. Her gaze fell to the pavers at their feet, cracked from the overhead sun. Her lashes were thick and heavy against her cheek. Dash wanted so desperately to pull her to him, but he sensed she wouldn't be open to that.

"What did she tell you?" Now he was starting to get worried.

"She told me that you're in a relationship with her and paid her hush money not to talk about it."

Dash guffawed and took a step closer to her, but she held up a warning hand. "She's lying."

"But *you* lied to me. You were playing me. You have this whole other life I didn't even know about. I know you and I

aren't a thing, really. We're just fooling around, or whatever."
She swallowed and tucked the photo of Richard Gere closer to
her chest. How very unfair that *he* got to be pressed up against
her, and not Dash. "But this makes me feel like garbage, like
you don't even care about me."

"What? Soph, no, please. I care about you. I *do* care about
you, very deeply." He was about to reach for her, but a sud-
den jolt caused him to trip backward. Sophie took a step back,
too, nearly falling.

"Was that…" She glanced around but, as she did, another
ripple from the ground caused Dash to lose his balance. Then
the ground began to sway. Sophie balanced from one foot,
then to the next, as she crouched low and tried to stay upright.

"Earthquake!" Her voice was almost a piercing shriek.

He reached for her, and they both toppled to the grass. The
earth beneath them shook, and the soil rippled like a wave. He
brought her in as tightly as he could, then curled himself around
her until he was a protective shield. Dash held Sophie for what
felt like several minutes until the earth stopped moving.

Car alarms blared from the nearby street, and there was the
distant sound of dogs barking. A siren screamed, and Sophie
shook in his arms. He wrapped her up tighter against him.

"I don't think I've ever felt one that big," she said. "And don't
you dare make a dirty joke out of that right now."

He let out a chuckle. "I usually sleep through them."

"I spent the walk home watching your videos. Dash…"

He clenched his jaw, unable to control the fact that the way
she said his name still affected him.

"You used to make some truly terrible pieces. That giraffe
mug, specifically."

And he laughed, so loudly that it hurt his chest. "I had to
start somewhere, didn't I?"

"Yes, at the bottom, apparently." Sophie softly smiled at her own joke, which made a flutter of relief fill him. "You've been commenting on all of my posts."

"I have," he quietly said.

"And saying these very insightful, helpful, and sweet things." He smirked in acknowledgment. "Yes."

"I thought it was just some very random but wise TikTok teenager living in their parents' house," she quickly said.

"I'm thirty-six." Dash stood and extended a hand to her, which she took and pulled herself up. "Can we go talk?"

Sophie smoothed her dress down and looked toward her place. "I need to check on Rain Boots. He hates earthquakes."

Dash knew when Sophie was avoiding something, and she clearly wanted to avoid this conversation. "I need to tell you about Cindy. She's not who you think she is."

"I'll give you five minutes." She put her hands on her hips and eyed him, then beckoned for Dash to follow her. He tried to fight back the urge to reach for her hand.

Rain Boots was, as Sophie had promised, a bit of a hard-ass. The fish stared indignantly back as Dash waved to him with a warm smile.

"He's really playing hardball today." Sophie held her hand up to the fish's bowl, and Rain Boots seemed to touch his nose to the glass. "Or maybe he can sense my unease."

Dash turned to face Sophie and reached for her hand. She reluctantly let him take it. He knew she was mad, but he just had to explain the situation. "I don't know exactly what Cindy told you, but she's got a warped perception of me, to say the least. She's been stalking me and figured out who I was just by watching my videos."

Sophie's hand dropped from his, and he instantly burned to reach for her again. "She had all these screenshots of flirty messages back and forth. I don't want to sound jealous, but you told me you hadn't been with anyone else."

"I haven't." Dash suddenly felt like the tables had completely turned, and he now understood the fervor from Cindy as she tried to explain that she hadn't sold him out to the press. How could he make Sophie believe him? "I did flirt with her online for a long time before you and I got together. But as soon as you and I kissed, I stopped. I told her I was with someone."

"Why does she have a photo of you?" Sophie turned her phone screen to him, and he saw a shot from the restaurant where he'd met Cindy. He bit his lip and looked up to the ceiling. He hadn't known she'd taken a photo at all, but here it was.

"I met up with her a few days ago for the first time," he admitted. "But it's only because I needed to confront her. I think she told the press that I was in recovery."

Sophie frowned, and she rubbed a spot at her temple. "The press knows about...about the drinking?"

Dash exhaled as he realized just how much he *hadn't* told Sophie. "When I went to my brother's premiere the other day, a journalist asked if I'd been seeking treatment for drug abuse."

"Oh, my God, Dash." Sophie stepped toward him and took his hand. "I'm so sorry. Are you okay?"

"I'm okay." He squeezed her hand back. "I had to confront Cindy and make sure she doesn't leak anything else before my dad's big event. But I don't know that I'll ever fully recover from the handmade doll of me that she'd crafted—that was a real surprise to see."

He nodded toward Sophie's phone, and she zoomed in on the object on the table. "She even got the eyebrow scar." Sophie cocked her head. "She's talented."

"Yes, she is." Dash dug his heel into Sophie's plush rug.

"I think you need to get a restraining order." A little shiver ran through Sophie, and she shook it off. "She said part of how she found me was because she recognized our yard from my videos."

His jaw clenched. Yes, he would absolutely need to file a restraining order. He couldn't have Cindy anywhere near Sophie.

He waited for Sophie to say more, but all she did was lick her lips as she stared down at their joined hands.

"Soph?" His pulse pounded in his ears. What was going through her thoughts right now? Had he completely ruined everything once again?

"I believe you. I do. But…" She scratched at her forehead, then looked up at him. "I don't know why I feel so hurt. I know you didn't mean to, but it just feels like I don't even know you. You kept all these big secrets from me and…"

He waited to see if she'd say more, but when she didn't, he quickly jumped in. "I didn't tell you about her, because having a stalker is scary, and Cindy seemed harmless enough at first. I didn't want you to freak out."

"I'm more freaked out that I didn't know any of this was going on. Like, you were probably so terrified, and I didn't even realize it." Sophie exhaled and rolled out her shoulders. "I don't want to sound mean or make you feel bad. But, like, what else don't I know about? Why didn't you just tell me about her?"

Because I'm a coward.

Because I didn't want you to leave me.

Because I ruin everything.

Dash sat on the edge of her bed and let his head fall into his hands. He felt sure that he was about to lose Sophie, and he deserved to: he wasn't good enough for her in the first place. But that didn't matter. What mattered was that he'd hurt her, and all he wanted to do was make sure she was okay. "I'm so used to handling things on my own and keeping my life private." He looked up at her, and she watched him, but there was still hurt lingering behind her eyes. "This just seemed like something I needed to take care of myself. And I didn't want to drag you into any of it because then you might not want anything to do with me or my messy life. You deserve someone who doesn't have all these problems."

Sophie knelt next to the bed. She put a hand on his knee and he covered her hand with his. "It just makes me so sad that you didn't trust me with any of this."

And then his heart completely cracked open at the realization that he was losing something he knew he couldn't give up.

"Dash." Her voice was so gentle and kind. "I just need a little time to process all this. We're friends, and we'll always be friends no matter what. But I think everything has gotten muddled. Like, what are we even doing, really? You don't want anything serious, but I do. I need to fix things with Poppy, and you need to focus on the speech tomorrow."

The speech. The absolute last thing he wanted to do was stand in front of a crowd and pretend like he was part of one big happy family. But Sophie was right. He didn't want to lead her on when he wasn't ready to get into a real commitment. If he was actually ready to date again, he wouldn't have hidden all these secrets from her.

"You probably should go home and rest." She wiped her thumb across his cheek. "Your mom would kill me if she found out I'm the reason you have puffy eyes before a red carpet."

He laughed, and she cracked a small smile, too. "Are you still coming tomorrow? I'd like you to." His voice was low because he already knew the answer would be no.

"Let me think about it, okay?" Sophie stood, and so did Dash. But as he walked through her place and toward her front door, his heart raced at the idea that because he'd hidden so much from her, he'd completely lost her trust.

31

SOPHIE

Sophie was in a swing-a-baseball-bat-and-blow-car-windows-out kind of mood, so she'd picked a fiery-red dress with a plunging neckline and gold kitten heels. Her outfit had to match her thoughts, which were vengeful and a bit angry.

Mostly, she was angry at herself for trusting Dash. And then angry at him for keeping so many secrets. But also angry about the fact that she might never fall in love. She was close to falling with Dash, but she'd also been close to falling with Carla, and look how that had turned out. She'd always be the romance author who'd never fall in love.

She couldn't wait to film *that* TikTok video.

"Not that Dash was ever even a real option, seeing as how he doesn't want a relationship!" She shouted the words to the shirtless photo of Richard Gere that she'd taped to her bedroom wall, just above Rain Boots's bowl. They both needed a pick-me-up after the earthquake from the day before. "Why did I do this to myself? Why did I pursue something with an unavailable person?"

She still wasn't sure if she was going to the Walk of Fame

ceremony, even though she'd already dressed the part. She just didn't know if seeing Dash was a good idea. Maybe having her in the audience would be a distraction, in a bad way. Still, he'd told her he wanted her there, and even though they were in a kind of fight, or whatever, he'd shown up for her—getting her to write again—and she needed to return the favor.

"Wish me luck," she said to Rain Boots, then blew Richard Gere a kiss.

The security guard in front of the white tent pursed his lips as he scanned his tablet for Sophie's name. The event took place at the corner of Hollywood Boulevard and Vine—a notoriously touristy and swamped intersection that the city had shut down specifically for the ceremony.

"My name is Sophie Lyon." She cleared her throat. "I should be on the list."

Unless Dash had changed his mind and taken her off the list, of course...

"Right this way." He opened the velvet rope—an actual velvet rope, with red fabric and gold metal poles—and she walked through it. A second guard attached a blue bracelet that would give her greenroom access.

The ceremony was set to start in twenty, and Sophie was sure the greenroom was where Dash would be. So she would just walk through quickly, avoid Dash, and find her seat. Sophie ducked in through the canvas door and entered the backstage tent. The makeshift holding area was crowded with men in suits, which Sophie assumed were industry insiders like agents, managers, and publicists.

There was also, of course, the Montrose family. If this was any other circumstance, Sophie would be thrilled to see Poppy, but as she clocked her best friend deep in conversation with William, an ache rose in her chest. Now they were both in the same room, and if she and Poppy were ever going to speak again, she'd have to be the one to try. She needed to find her seat, but maybe a quick amends-making pit stop wouldn't hurt. She shook out her shoulders, walked up, and tapped Poppy on the arm.

"Hey, Poppy," Sophie said. She tried to channel the confidence of the celebrity impersonators just outside the tent asking for tips as they walked Hollywood Boulevard. But she was sweating behind her knees, so how confident could she really look?

Poppy turned with a bright smile on her face, but as she noticed Sophie she pursed her lips. "Oh, no. This isn't happening." Poppy's index finger waggled between them. "We're not talking."

Sophie glanced to William, who didn't say a word, but his eyes noticeably widened. *Okay*, she would try a different approach. After all, she wasn't afraid of confrontation the way she used to be. And maybe Poppy just needed to be reminded of the fact that they were *best* friends, and no one would change that.

"I totally get that you're still upset. I will respect that. But I just wanted to say that I'm happy to see you, and I really love your dress." Sophie waved a hand at the crisp, white sheath with gold cuffs that hit Poppy's midthigh and left her tanned, golden legs on full display.

"It's vintage." Poppy crossed her arms. "I upcycled. But don't think that compliment makes everything better."

"Poppy, are you seriously going to be this petty?" Dash's voice simmered with anger. He came to stand next to Sophie, and she had to stop herself from reaching for him. He was handsome in a white button-up shirt and a navy jacket. Sweat ran across his hairline, but she was sure that was just from the lack of strong AC in the tent. Apparently, he'd seen or heard their exchange. But Sophie cringed as she realized that she'd unintentionally dragged him into their fight.

"Is it petty to be mad about my best friend and my brother lying to me for weeks?"

Sophie had to admit that Poppy had a point there. Still, she wanted to nix this line of conversation. Sophie put a hand on Dash's arm. "I'm fine. You have the speech to focus on, okay?"

His eyes finally met hers, and something in his gaze softened. The familiar spark that crackled between them returned. If she didn't smother it, she'd catch fire and never be able to extinguish the need she had for him. So she quickly stepped back, but too quickly, apparently, as she tripped and fell with a thump to the ground.

"Ouch." Her ass had, naturally, fallen on what was undoubtedly the hardest part of the concrete.

As Dash moved to help Sophie up, Kitty materialized from nowhere, like she'd sensed drama and teleported over. She leaned down and said in a hushed and serious tone, "There are no human speed bumps allowed in this tent." Kitty glanced from Dash to Sophie. Eventually her lips formed a thin line as she glared at Sophie. "That was my way of telling you to get up, love."

And so Sophie did.

"Dash, it's showtime." His mom went to work straightening his suit jacket and brushing invisible dust from his shoulders.

Dash glanced over to her. "I'll see you out there?"

"I'll be in the audience. Good luck." Her body didn't want to leave the room, even though her brain was screaming to. She took the seat assigned by a placard printed with *Montrose Guest, Lyon.* The first row was reserved for the Montrose family, whereas hers was five rows back. Not ideal, but at least Dash already knew she was there.

As she waited, her curtain bangs wilted from the heat, and

she dabbed at the sweat that started to bead there. The rows ahead of her were crammed with older actors who'd clearly come to support William, and she vaguely recognized some as costars from his early films. On either side of the chairs were two barricades—one for paparazzi and press, and another for fans. Eventually, the Montroses—sans Kitty—took their seats as well.

Sophie sat as still and warm as a roast chicken while she waited for the event to begin. She looked at the time on her phone, and it was ten minutes past when they were meant to start.

Sophie couldn't help it. She texted Dash. Everything okay?

But when she didn't hear back and a minute turned into five, she stood and began to make her way toward the front. When she got to the first row, though, Poppy blocked her path.

"My mom is handling Dash," she said to Sophie.

Sophie exhaled. She had to stand up for herself in order to keep fighting for Dash. So even though she was terrified of saying something less than nice to her best friend, she was going to do what she had to. "Dash needs someone who is looking out for *him*."

"What's that supposed to mean?" Poppy said as her tall-as-hell frame loomed over Sophie.

But then, like the phantom she was, Kitty appeared and stepped between them. "Dash will be out momentarily. Poppy, there are *cameras*. Do sit down. And, Sophie? Get to your row."

"Yeah, get to your row," Poppy echoed. Sophie looked between the two women. She knew Poppy was coming from a place of hurt, but what was Kitty's excuse? Other than being the consummate Mommy Dearest.

Still, Dash was on his way out, which was all she needed to hear. She snuck a glance at Poppy, who stared back at her defiantly. Sophie was absolutely outnumbered in this situation, and she wasn't about to cause another scene.

As she made her way back to her seat, though, she had a sinking feeling that she was missing something. Because the Dash she knew would've texted her back, and that made her worry.

32

DASH

Dash wasn't someone who normally kept people waiting, but after seeing Sophie and interacting with her as if they were just friends—nothing more—he had a lot of nauseating, overwhelming, and panic-inducing feelings.

Because as Dash had watched Sophie walk away from him—again—he'd realized, with some dread, that he *did* love her. Even if she didn't love him, he absolutely was filled with nothing but pure love for her. But love wasn't always enough. Not when his love came with caveats. And Sophie didn't deserve love with warning labels, though Dash was covered in them.

Warning: Substance abuse issues.

Warning: Deeply dysfunctional family members.

Warning: Former child actor who suffers from massive insecurities.

Sophie deserved perfectly bold love from someone who lit up a room just as easily as she did. But when Dash thought about being with Sophie, it was clear that he was an eclipse of issues threatening to swallow her sunny warmth.

So he would keep his mouth shut. Stay strong. And not let his own feelings derail Sophie's future. That's all he could think about when Kitty barged into the room and began to tersely discuss their agreement of a drama-free event. He barely heard her but eventually followed her out the door to meet his handler.

He wanted to get the speech over with. He'd practiced his lines for a week straight, the first time he'd had to memorize a script in years, and he had them down. All he needed to do was step out of his dressing room, make his way to the stage, find Sophie in the crowd, and speak the words to her.

A representative from the Hollywood Chamber of Commerce asked for William to come onstage, which was Dash's cue that he'd be called up shortly. If he could just get through the next twenty minutes, then he'd be okay.

His dad stood next to the podium, and the man at the microphone called on Dash. He took the steps up to the erected stage, and William gave what appeared to be a proud nod, which Dash locked onto. He returned the nod with a practiced hug.

"You all right?" William said into his ear.

Dash frowned at his concern, surprised, but quietly replied, "Yes."

He was all right. He would be strong. Just as he always had to be.

When Dash got up to the mic, he lowered it to meet his mouth and cracked a joke. "People always think Reece and I are the same height."

The light chuckles from the audience eased the tension in his shoulders as he settled in behind the podium.

"Where's Reece?" a voice from the crowd shouted.

"Reece is filming a movie, but he wishes he could be here, because today is a truly important one for our family." Dash smiled over at his dad, who gave him an encouraging nod. Then he searched the crowd for Sophie, who he knew would be a few rows back, until he landed on her. He sighed in relief as she gave an enthusiastic smile back. He could get through the speech as long as he saw her there. The jittery taps of his fingers stilled as he looked down at his notes, then took in a big breath and began.

"For those of you who don't know, my name is Dash Montrose, and I am honored to be here today to tell you about how special my dad is. I'm told that the day I was born, he was filming a rock-climbing scene for an action movie called *The Devil's Tongue*. Have any of you seen it?" He waited for applause, and some came. "While he was on the edge of a cliff, quite literally, a crew member had my mom on speakerphone as she told him that I was a boy, and she wanted to know what to name me. My dad told her he'd get to the hospital in a dash. But the reception wasn't great, and all my mom heard was 'Dash.' I guess it could've been worse—Crag or Rappel could be giving this speech today."

As laughter trickled up, more of the tension he'd felt began to ease. The speech was going well. He'd been worried for nothing. He glanced back to his notes, which is when he heard a voice from the crowd.

"When did you get out of rehab?"

He kept his eyes on the paper and breathed in, then out, even though his heart pounded in his ears. He wouldn't let that person, whoever they were, derail him. He just had to find Sophie again and deliver the speech and then he could go home. He searched for her spot, but his gaze landed on his mother instead, whose lips had turned into a thin and seething line. Then he caught Poppy next to her, who looked more confused than anything. Dash's palms turned clammy, and he glanced down to his notes again.

"I've never worked with my dad on a film, but I felt like he brought our family with him to every project. Sometimes, we would travel to set in order to spend time together." He wiped the back of his hand across his forehead without thinking, then winced as he realized just how nervous he was. As he peered up at the crowd, desperate to see Sophie's face, he heard another question.

"Dash, are you drunk right now?" the same voice shouted.

Dash's hands gripped the sides of the podium as the tip of his tongue trailed across his teeth. He felt the heat from the overhead sun so intensely that he wondered if he might pass out. He'd lost his place in the speech but decided to skip ahead. He needed to get this over with. "My dad has always been deeply committed not only to his job as an actor but to being a wonderful father to us. Hollywood is part of him now, despite the British accent you may hear. My father loves this industry, and in awarding him this star, he will continue to be the legend he already is. I cannot think of anyone more deserving of this recognition than him." Dash turned to face his dad, and realized his voice had a tremor to it. He steadied himself as he took a deep breath and said, "Dad, congratulations."

Then Dash began to clap so hard that his hands ached from pounding them together. There was a ringing in his ears as his father brought him in for a hug and mumbled something. Then he released him and stepped up to the microphone. Dash's whole body was numb, and a white noise filled him as he walked offstage. He was meant to take a seat next to his mom but walked to the greenroom tent instead. He needed to stop the blaring hum that grew ever louder and get out of the space as quickly as possible.

But as he moved toward the exit, a hand gripped his bicep to stop him. He turned, and there was Kitty, her brows knit tightly together as she said, "Where are you going?"

"I need…" His whole body shook as the words bubbled up within him. "I can't do this. I told you I couldn't do this."

"You are *my* son. You can do anything. Montroses don't quit." His mom stomped her foot, as if calling him to action.

But he had nothing left. "I gave the speech. I did what you asked."

"How do you think it will look if you just leave in the middle of your father's speech?" Her voice was hushed but still terse.

But he didn't care how Kitty felt because he was feeling so much that he couldn't keep his emotions in any longer. "I don't care how it will look, Mom. A reporter just asked if I was drunk. A stalker leaked my story—"

"I leaked the story," Kitty said.

He frowned, and the silence around them was almost as strange as the words she'd just said.

"What?" Dash's voice was so loud it filled the tent. "You did what?"

Kitty didn't so much as flinch but kept her gaze trained on Dash as she said, "You needed a push. I'd hoped that the pressure of a story leaking would get you back to work. You think I didn't know about your stay at a rehab center as soon as it happened? I was hoping you'd tell me in your own time. But then months went by, and nothing. And you have been doing nothing except for passing up perfectly good jobs. You know how secrets are in this town. They always come out. The best thing I could do was get the story out there before someone else did. And then you'd get back to work. Back to filming. And everyone would be able to see that you'd moved past this *problem*."

All the air seemed to leave Dash's body as he realized what his mother was saying: she was the person who'd tipped off a reporter about his rehab stay. And of course she'd known about his addiction struggles, the way she always knew everything about her children. And over lunch, she'd encouraged him to take a role to bury the gossip.

But Dash was done acting, on camera and off.

"How could you do this to me?" Tears stung his eyes, and he didn't bother to wipe them away. "I'm not one of your clients who you can just fix with some good press. I'm your son. This is my life. You don't get to decide how I live it."

"Your life is *our* life, too, Dash," Kitty said in a voice so measured it was unsettling. "Don't pretend like we're not all connected. And for what it's worth, I didn't think the reporters would have to continue asking you this question. I thought you'd have said yes to a role by now. Problem solved. I told you at lunch to take a script, didn't I? Or write one? You not working is the problem, not whether a reporter knows."

And there was the inevitable, sinking feeling he had whenever he was reminded that he wasn't just a person but a *Montrose*.

"Dash." Sophie's voice cut through the loud hum, and he turned to see her rush into the tent with Poppy in tow. "Are you okay?"

She reached for his hand, and he reached for hers, and her cool skin felt soothing against the burn that coursed through him.

"What the hell was that reporter talking about?" Poppy asked. "We should sue! Now they're just making shit up about Dash."

"Poppy." Kitty turned to her. "Don't say another word. There are people—"

The rage that Dash had felt for so long about not being able to tell his family for fear of what they'd think evaporated. As Sophie tightened her grip on him, he was reminded once again of the power that words could hold. He had the power to tell them the truth, and he was finally going to. He cut his mother off midsentence. "They're not making shit up." His voice shook. "I've been sober for nineteen months now. I went to rehab for alcoholism."

"You what?" Poppy looked so shocked—even more so than when she'd discovered Sophie at his house—that he almost felt bad for keeping this secret.

"I was going to tell you eventually. When I was ready." He ran a hand through his hair and felt a tremor in his fingers. "But then, Mom leaked the story to the press."

Sophie's hand slipped out of Dash's, and she began to gesture as she spoke. "That was his story to share or not to share. You don't have permission to just tell people."

"And you don't have permission to yell at me when you're a guest at my husband's event," Kitty hissed out at Sophie.

"Then, allow me to do the yelling." Dash stepped in front of Sophie and faced his mom. His hands balled at his sides, and he straightened. Even though Kitty was undeniably taller, in that moment he felt her shrink. "*Kitty*, consider this the last time we're ever connected. Because I can't be around you anymore, not when you've made it so clear every single time I see you that the only thing I'm good for is an IMDb credit. From now on, I'm not a Montrose. You're not my mother. I don't want to see you ever again. I don't want you to call me. I don't want you to even think about me. I am *done* being Kitty Montrose's son."

He stared her down, and her eyes widened as if, for the first time, she was truly seeing him and what she'd done. But, then again, this was Kitty, and he highly doubted she was self-aware enough to even understand that he was cutting her out of his life.

"Dash, let me fix this." Kitty stepped toward him, but he took a step back.

"Mom, you didn't do this to Dash." Poppy's hand grabbed Kitty's shoulder and forced their mom to turn toward her. "Oh, my God... Wait, did you?"

Before Kitty had time to notice, Dash turned away from her and everyone else and walked through the tent toward the exit.

When he got to his car, he slammed the door and turned the key in the ignition. He didn't look back as he drove down the street. His thoughts felt like a bowl of murky water that was impossible to see through clearly. He drove and drove without much thought as to where he was headed. When he stopped at a red light, he turned to look out the window, and there was a neon sign lit for a local bar. *His* old local bar, The Viper Pit. He'd driven there without even realizing it. And he remembered the feel of the leather stools, the faint lull of the jukebox, the dark lighting, and corner booths that made it easy for him to disappear for hours behind drink after drink.

He could do that again now. Going home wasn't an option as Sophie would be there, maybe even his family, and he wasn't ready to face them or their questions. But he could park his car, walk inside the bar, and order a drink. Just one. Just to have that old familiar comfort of placing an order. Then, later, he could go home and not think about this awful day ever again. He just needed something to take the edge off the throbbing pain that coursed through him and wouldn't go away.

When he slipped into the cracked red-leather booth, a bartender in jeans and a T-shirt immediately approached for his order.

"Vodka neat and a soda water," Dash said.

He would just hold the vodka, smell it, raise it to his lips, and then put it back down without taking a sip. The very act of being in the bar would be enough to get him through this day. His phone buzzed and buzzed and buzzed, and eventually he took it out and saw Sophie's name on the screen. Sweet Sophie, who had done so much to save him but couldn't. What would she think if she saw him in a bar? He didn't deserve Sophie. He'd never been good enough for her and never would be.

So when the bartender brought him two glasses, one with vodka and one with soda water, Dash took the one with vodka, brought it to his lips, and inhaled it. He wasn't going to drink. He wasn't. But then his phone buzzed again, and this time it was his mom calling.

His old instincts kicked in, and without too much thought, he threw back the vodka like he'd never *not* been drinking. The burn of the liquid flooded his mouth and warmed him completely. He wanted more.

"Another," he called out to the bartender.

33

SOPHIE

Sophie was a fucking mess, to put it lightly. She'd anxiously tapped her foot so hard that the heel broke off, and she'd nearly thrown her phone when the Lyft app told her it would be a twenty-minute wait for a ride.

Poppy and Kitty were tensely arguing with each other. But no one other than her seemed to be concerned about the fact that Dash had disappeared and wasn't returning anyone's calls.

Sophie sharply exhaled, steeled herself, and approached Poppy.

"Do you happen to have Chris's phone number?" Sophie asked.

"Chris?" Poppy said, maybe annoyed. "Who are you talking about?"

"Dash's best friend, Chris." Sophie was also getting annoyed. She understood Poppy was still mad with her, but did they really have to play these games, especially when Dash was MIA?

"Never heard him mention a Chris before," Poppy finally said as she eyed Sophie.

Sophie sucked in her bottom lip. Dash had kept so many secrets from everyone around him, so she wasn't surprised he'd kept Chris from Poppy, too.

She just needed to find Dash to let him know she would be there for him, no matter what.

Her Lyft was ten minutes away, which felt like a lifetime. She scratched the side of her head as she went into her texts and tried Dash again.

Dash, please, just tell me you're okay.

I'm coming home and we can talk about this.

Text me back.

She spotted Kitty out of the corner of her eye—smiling and making small talk with people in the room. William, however, didn't seem to be able to plaster on a smile, the way his wife had.

"This day is so messed up. First my mom intentionally hurting Dash, and then you not only keeping the fact that you're dating my brother a secret from me, but also that he has a drinking problem." Poppy crossed her arms.

"Could you not make this about me and you right now?" Sophie's nerves were wrapped as tight as a rubber band, and she was about to snap. "Your brother, who is a recovering alcoholic, just experienced a traumatic event. He's sensitive about his sobriety, and I'm worried that this whole thing pushed him too far. He's just trying to stay sober."

Poppy frowned. "Too far?"

"I don't know, but he's not answering my calls or texts. I'm worried about him, and you should be, too."

Poppy licked her lips and studied her. "Okay, I'll drive you to his place, but you have to tell me everything," she eventually said.

"Dash is the only one who gets to tell his story. I'm sorry." Sophie hoped that Poppy could put aside her feelings and see the bigger picture before it was too late. "But, please, let's go. I want to make sure he's okay."

Without another word, Poppy tucked her purse under her arm, grabbed Sophie, and led the way to the exit.

When they got to the house, Dash's car wasn't there, and Sophie's concern mounted when she spotted Chris sitting outside the gate.

"I saw the livestream," Chris said by way of greeting, and a worried line worked its way between his brows. "He's not with you, then?"

"No," Sophie said. "Do you know where he'd be?"

"We can check the AA meeting we used to go to, but I want to go to his old spot first." Chris dug the toe of his shoe into the dirt, exhaled, and waved for them to follow.

The Viper Pit was a bar that smelled exactly as Sophie imagined, stale and smoky. Dash was hard to miss as he relaxed against the seat of a booth with his rumpled blond hair and button-down shirt. He had a drink in one hand and looked up when they came in.

His eyes were glassy and red, as if he'd been crying. And when he caught sight of them, his jaw clenched. He wouldn't look at her, but Sophie kept her eyes locked on him, because she needed him to know she was there.

"Let me get him," Chris said.

But Sophie wanted to help, too. "Is it okay if I talk to him first? If you think it will make things worse, I won't."

"Sure," Chris said. "But, Sophie, you've never seen him intoxicated. He might say or do things he wouldn't normally. Don't take anything personally."

"I won't," Sophie assured him.

"I can't believe I didn't know any of this," Poppy said quietly.

"It's not your fault," Chris said. "All we can do is help him through it."

Poppy nodded, then looked to Sophie. "Let us know if you need backup."

Dash didn't say a word as Sophie slid into the booth next to him. She could no longer smell his clean, earthy scent, only vodka and something spoiled. His body was loose in a way she wasn't used to, and she held a steady palm on his back.

She wasn't often at a loss for words, but here was Dash, the man she so deeply cared for, and he was in pain. So much pain that he'd had to numb all of it with the one thing he'd worked so hard to remove from his life. She stroked the side of his face with her fingertips and brushed the hair from his eyes.

"Let's get you home" was all she said.

"I don't deserve a home. Or you." His voice was soft and his words slurred together.

Sophie wanted to cry but stopped herself. She ached for what he was going through and how badly he must hurt to have come to this bar. She needed to bring him back to his place and hold him until he knew he was safe.

She tilted his chin up so he could look at her. "Dash, I hope you can hear what I'm about to say. I am not leaving. I am here. We are here for you. Okay?"

She tried to get him to meet her eyes, but he wouldn't.

"You must think I'm disgusting," he eventually said. "You should go."

"No," she emphatically replied. And then she wrapped her arms around his neck and hugged him so tightly he coughed. But she didn't know what else she could do or say in that moment, because she'd never been in a situation quite like this. All she knew was that she didn't want Dash to lose hope, and she wanted so desperately to be able to care for him the way he deserved.

34

DASH

When Dash woke up, he was alone, and he was grateful for that. He didn't want Sophie to be part of his life anymore, not when he couldn't control himself. For a few weeks, he'd fantasized about being able to stay sober and good enough for her. But he'd known all along that was a lie.

He pushed himself up to sit on the edge of the bed and the old, familiar pulse of a hangover throbbed just behind his eyes. He'd had so many in his life, but this one felt raw and sharp. He'd fucked up so badly he couldn't see a way back. What the hell was wrong with him? He fisted a clump of his hair and pulled in frustration.

Dash put on jeans and a shirt, brushed his teeth, and combed out his hair. He may not have been emotionally ready, but nevertheless he opened his bedroom door to face whatever judgment awaited him.

What awaited him was the smell of maple syrup and bacon. His stomach lurched from the lack of food and overabundance of vodka, and his throat felt dry even after drinking the full glass of water that had been left at his bedside.

Chris stood from the couch in the living room and moved to hug Dash. He let him. And Luna was there, too, wiggling on a soft blanket on the floor.

"She's doing her tummy time, which she hates." Chris picked Luna up and held her against his chest. "Are you feeling sick? Because you look like you're in need of soup, or a trash bin, or both."

"Thanks." Dash wiped a hand across his face. "Chris, I should've called you. I don't know what I was thinking."

"What happened is done, and you're safe, which is all I care about." His friend shrugged so nonchalantly that it felt like they'd just talked about something that wasn't a massive relapse.

"Here." Poppy handed Dash a plate—one he'd crafted—loaded with bacon, two waffles smothered in syrup, and a piece of toast with butter and jam. She didn't look happy about any of it. "Enjoy your heart disease."

"I will." He took the plate but grabbed Poppy's hand. "I'm so sorry I didn't tell you."

She squeezed his hand back. "It's okay. I will make you feel bad about it during strategic moments where I need to manipulate you. Don't worry."

His sister smiled widely at him, and a little sense of relief came. Not the same relief he'd felt from initially telling Sophie, but it made him feel lighter all the same.

"Hey," Sophie said as she entered the room. She held a mug of coffee and was in one of her loose dresses with her hair up in a messy bun. She'd showered, and the makeup from the day before had been washed off. The freckles on her cheeks popped as she attempted to smile at him. She was so gorgeous that he had to look away.

But she handed him the mug, which he took. The coffee aroma made his temples twitch with longing. He sipped.

Dash took his coffee and plate of food to the kitchen table, where Chris and Poppy had already sat down. Sophie came next to him and rubbed her palm across his back before taking a seat. He'd worked so hard to keep all these parts of his life separate—family, friends, and relationships—but now they were here and expecting…what, from him, exactly?

"Am I the only one eating?" he asked.

"Bro, it's noon," Chris said. "Believe it or not, some of us wake up early and have already had a second lunch. Thank you, Poppy."

"No problem." Poppy waved a breezy hand at Chris. "And I made myself an energizing smoothie with goji and chia and saved you a glass for later."

She winked at him, knowing how much he'd dislike all those words in one sentence. He played along and winked back.

But he knew they couldn't dance around reality forever. He'd relapsed, and now he had to find a way back to sobriety. "Is it too late for me to ask for help?" Dash stared at his food and waited for a reply.

"We're kind of already on it," Sophie quickly said.

Chris bounced Luna on his knee as he answered. "Let's do one thing at a time. Have breakfast, drink coffee, start to feel like a human again, then we can talk about the options. Okay?"

Dash nodded, and when he looked up, Sophie watched him warmly. There was no judgment or fear from her, just kindness, and he knew he wanted to do everything he could to never hurt her again.

As Dash packed a bag that he'd take with him to the rehab center, the door to his room creaked open, and he turned to see Sophie.

"How are you feeling?" she gently asked.

How was he feeling? Oh, about three million shades of shitty. He was ashamed that Sophie had seen him drunk in a bar and still in total shock that his mom had sold him out in an attempt to get him back into acting. Where to even start, really?

"I can't believe..." He let out a shaky breath and looked at his feet planted firmly against the creamy shag rug. "I threw everything away."

To his surprise, she wrapped an arm around his waist and rested her head on his shoulder. He released a relieved breath at the feel of her fitted perfectly against him.

"You didn't throw anything away," she said. "I'm here. Poppy's here. Chris is here. We're all here for you."

When he didn't say anything, she pressed him. "Do you want to talk about it?"

He rubbed at one of his eyes, willing himself to not be hungover. But he knew that was useless. And yes, he did want to talk about it. All of it. So long as it was with *her*. He was done keeping things from Sophie.

"My mom..." he said despairingly.

Sophie filled in after an extended silence, "I'm so sorry she did that to you." She wrapped her fingers through his and held him steady.

"In her own twisted way, she thought she was helping me. That's the fucked-up part." His lips twitched, and he blew out a breath. "I guess, looking back, I always had a kind of tendency to try to handle everything on my own. I didn't like to ask for help, so people never really knew when I was in trouble. And I started to drink a lot because I was convinced that drinking made me a more interesting person. I was so sure that no one liked me when I was sober and that drinking brought out this fun, charming part of me. The part that my mom always wanted me to have, and that Reece and my dad have naturally. When I drank, I felt like I'd become the Montrose she and everyone else expected me to be. I was loud and cracked jokes and stayed out all night partying. It became this sort of crutch, like, I needed to drink to be worthy of my own last name. And without a drink, I was just Dash."

He had never fully told this part of his story to anyone—just snippets so he didn't reveal too much of himself. Now that Sophie knew, though, he felt like a poison had been drained from him. He was lighter.

"*Just Dash* is who I like best." She gave him a soft smile and scratched his back with her nails. "What made you get sober?"

He took in a deep breath. He never had liked thinking about this moment. "For movies, you have to get a physical so they can take out insurance and make sure that if anything happens on set, you're in tip-top health. And I was about to start this movie that I was really excited for. It was another indie film and a role I really felt like I understood. My mom hated it, of course—she always thinks indies aren't worth anyone's time. But when I was with the doctor doing the exam, they ran some bloodwork and did a physical. At my follow-up, she told me that my liver was starting to fail, and if I didn't stop drinking, I would die by the time I was fifty."

"Oh, my God," Sophie breathed out.

"I just... That really sobered me up, for lack of a better phrase." He reached for the now-cool mug of coffee on his nightstand and took a needed sip. "I didn't want to die. I don't know, I just had this massive wake-up call, and I went to an AA meeting later that day. I was drunk when I showed up, but it's where I met Chris."

Sophie tightly gripped his hand, which reminded him that she shouldn't even be there with him. She should stay as far away as possible from his chaos. He loosened his grip on her.

"You don't have to do this," he said. "You can leave. I'll be okay."

But would he be okay? He wasn't totally sure. He just forced himself to say the words so she'd have an easy out.

"I'm not leaving." She was a little more forceful with her tone than usual.

"Why are you being nice to me?" He shook his head as he looked at her. "I left you and drove to a bar and got drunk yesterday. That should scare you. You should want to run from me."

He hadn't been mad at her, not until that moment when she was making the dumbest mistake of her life by trusting him. Again. He had to talk her out of wanting to be by his side.

But she brushed the hair from his face and grabbed his shoulder, squeezing so hard that he started to say *ouch*.

"Listen to me, Dash Montrose." Sophie's eyes went wide. "I've been waiting my whole life for you, just as you are. And if you think I'm going to walk away because of one mistake, then you're wrong. Despite everything, I trust you. I always have. And I trust that if you make more mistakes, we'll figure them out *together*." Then she released his shoulder and smoothed a hand over her bun. "Now, hurry up and pack so you can say a proper goodbye to Rain Boots and Richard."

Sophie walked toward his bedroom door, but he hated watching her go.

"Soph?" She turned, and her expression changed from steadfast to open. He knew this was the moment when he had to tell her his feelings, whether either of them were ready or not. He stood and moved to her, so they were just a few inches apart as he began to talk.

"This is going to be hard. It's an everyday, every minute kind of thing for me. And now that I've relapsed, I..." He shook his head, so deeply regretting his choice but not being able to do anything about it either. *You chose to drink*, he thought, but now he'd choose to do better *for her*. "I didn't think I would ever drink again, but I did. And I don't know how to promise you that it won't happen. I really hope I don't relapse again. And I will try every day not to drink, but I have no idea how I'll be in a week, or a month, or a few years. This won't be easy. Staying sober has been the hardest thing I've ever done in my life. But

I want to work at it with you, because I want to be with you forever. And I know you aren't ready to say those words back yet, but I love you, Soph. I fell in love with you unexpectedly, but I plan to keep loving you fiercely."

"You…" Her mouth opened, and he waited for her response. "What did you say?"

He swallowed and ran a hand through his hair, then met her gaze. "I love you."

35

SOPHIE

Sophie's mouth hung open long enough that it had fully dried out. And when she went to swallow, she coughed from the lack of moisture. She knew he was waiting for a response. She'd been in this situation before—with Carla—but this time, she didn't feel the overwhelming urge to flee. She felt rooted to the spot where his gaze pinned her.

She should say *I love you* back in big capital letters and with multiple exclamation points. She willed the words to pour out of her. She knew she wanted to continue a relationship with Dash. She'd chosen Dash over Carla. So what was the problem?

Say it.

Say it, you absolute and complete turd.

Just. Three. Words.

But she couldn't tell Dash she loved him. She was absolutely terrified, and her whole body felt leaden from the expectation that she needed to. Sophie reached a hand toward his shoulder, hoping that touching him again would spark the words out of her, but nothing came. His eyes searched hers, and she saw something like defeat. But she didn't want him to feel defeated. Sophie really, really liked Dash. She knew she could love him someday. Maybe she still just had to work out her issues or something.

Eventually, she shook her head and said, "That is so fucking romantic." She pressed her lips to his, and he pressed back. She just hoped that the feel of her against him was enough for now.

When she pulled away from him, she leaned her forehead against his and closed her eyes. "I will get there, Dash. I'll trust you, if you trust me."

"Deal," he breathed out. And she really hoped, for her sake, that he meant it.

Sophie needed to feed Rain Boots a late lunch, so she stepped out of Dash's place and started toward hers. Which is when she saw Poppy on her porch, leaning against the front door.

"I just spent ten minutes watching a squirrel attack a photo of Richard Gere." Poppy crossed her arms. "It was violent."

"Dash won't be thrilled to hear that." Sophie gave a soft smile as she came up the porch steps.

"I wanted to thank you for helping with my brother." Poppy's expression didn't warm, but Sophie knew how weird this must be for her—to discover so much about her brother and feel like even more of an outsider than she already had. "Dash needed someone on his side yesterday, like you said. And you were the only one who knew what to do."

"Of course. I care about him, Poppy. As a friend, and even…" Sophie knew this maybe wasn't the best time to bring up her relationship with Dash, but she wasn't sure when a good time would be. So she just went for it. "Can I officially apologize now?"

Poppy cracked her neck. "Okay, let's get this over with."

Sophie steeled herself for the very real possibility that all would *not* be forgiven, but she had to try. "Poppy, I've been inexcusably horrible. I should've told you about Dash as soon as it happened, but I was just scared. I love you so much, and our friendship is the most important thing to me, but I was having all these confusing feelings."

"For my brother," Poppy quickly fired back.

Sophie looked down to regather her thoughts. "Yes, for Dash, and I didn't know how to tell you. And he and I hadn't really figured out what was happening either."

"But you still kept hooking up with him."

"He's more than just a hookup to me." Then Sophie looked up and locked eyes with her. "What can I do to make this right? I will do anything. I can work for free at the spa for the rest of my life, or be your personal assistant, or—I don't know— walk around wearing one of those giant sandwich signs with the words *Terrible Friend* in big letters."

Poppy thought for a moment, inspected her nails, and pursed her lips before she answered. "You can tell me what the hell you were thinking, for starters. I got you this spot at Dash's because I knew you needed the discounted rent. I've had you at our family's house. You've never told me you had a crush on Dash."

"Everyone had a crush on Dash growing up. It didn't seem helpful for me to tell you that I liked him as a teenager." Sophie sat in the Adirondack chair on her porch, ready to settle in for however long this would take. "And when I moved into his place, there were no feelings. I didn't feel any kind of way for him. It just sort of happened, all at once, and I couldn't stop. Trust me, I tried."

"Dash is one of the most important people in my life," Poppy said.

"I know."

"No, I don't think you do." Poppy started to pace the length of the porch. "If you hurt him, especially after everything he's been through and is going through now, I will be in the very awkward position of having to kill you. And I don't want to be a murderess. Though, I think we both know my mug shot would be fierce."

"It would," Sophie quickly acknowledged. "But I won't hurt him. I just want to be his person."

"But you're my person." Poppy's voice had gone soft, and her eyes met Sophie's.

Sophie stood. "And you're my person, too. But, like, my *friend* person."

"In this life, but what about the next one?"

"Fingers crossed." Sophie crossed her fingers and held them up, and then Poppy wrapped her in the biggest and warmest of Poppy hugs. Sophie hugged her back, enjoying her head resting in between her friend's cleavage. "I really missed the boob hugs."

"They missed you, too."

36

DASH

Chris drove the DADG ERS station wagon to Dash's house and helped load up luggage into the back. There was no waiting a day or two to let life settle back to normal. The rehabilitation center options were ones that could take Dash immediately, so he could start recovery again as soon as possible.

There was the one in Santa Barbara that focused on healing through meditation and spirituality, another in Austin with an emphasis on equine therapy, and one in the hills of LA that operated as a working farm with combined group and individual therapy. Dash had always been someone who needed to keep busy as part of recovery, so he'd chosen to be a farmer.

When the car was loaded, Dash hugged Poppy, who assured him of her plans to disown Kitty, despite his protests that his problems weren't hers. Then he turned to Sophie and held her close. Sophie slipped a piece of paper into his hands and whispered into his ear, "Open that when you need some company." She gently pecked him on the cheek, and he closed his eyes to savor the feel of her against him.

He slipped the paper into the pocket of his jeans as he got

into the car with Chris. In a way, he was relieved to be in a safe place: he couldn't have another drink if he was with his sponsor or at rehab. And he didn't trust himself not to drink now that he'd slipped.

"Did you and Sophie get a chance to talk about visitation at the rehab center?" Chris asked as he pulled out of the driveway.

"We didn't exactly have a lot of time." Dash shot Chris a look. He wanted to glance back to see Sophie, but watching her fade into the distance would be too painful. "I'm not sure what's going to happen. I told her I loved her. But I'm not sure she feels the same way."

"I once got hit in the eye with a foul ball, but even I can see that she's in love with you." Chris smirked.

"She didn't say it back." He knew, logically, that Sophie had a problem with saying those three words, but it didn't stop the pain he'd felt when she hadn't returned the sentiment.

"You know that annoying saying, *actions speak louder than words*?" As they hit a red light, Chris turned in his seat to look at Dash. "Sophie stayed with you in your room all last night to watch you sleep and make sure you didn't get sick. Did you know that? If that's not love, then what do you call that?"

Dash had *not* known that she'd stayed up with him the night before, but of course she had. She was Sophie. "She said she needs time."

"Then, be a good listener and give her time." Chris shook his head. "You think Mira was just convinced to spend the rest of her life with me because I have The Rock's pecs and Christopher Meloni's ass? No. I had to work every day to convince her that life with me would be fun. Hell, I learned how to make latte art so I can surprise her every morning with a new drawing. And you know I'm not artistic!"

"Well, I'm pretty sure that by relapsing, I did the opposite of showing her how fun I can be." Dash landed back against the seat with a thud.

"Okay, I'm about to pull some action-movie shit." Chris dramatically turned the wheel of the car and pulled over to the side of the road.

"What are you doing?" Dash asked as Chris killed the car engine.

Chris clapped a hand on Dash's shoulder with a grip firm enough to remind him he'd once played major league baseball. "You are not your drinking. You don't have to live the rest of your life alone just because you made a choice to drink yesterday. You're always going on about choosing. And guess what, you can choose to allow yourself happiness or to be miserable. That is *your* choice. But don't say Sophie doesn't love you. She does. Love is a word, but more importantly, love is action. She has shown you over and over again that she loves you. What she did these last twenty-four hours? That is love."

Dash's mouth pinched closed as he held back all the reasons why he wasn't good enough for Sophie and never would be. Instead, he deflected. "You and Mira are different. *You* are a better person than I am."

"If you want to tell yourself that so you can feel good about shutting Sophie out, then be my guest." Chris held his hands up in surrender. "But you forget that I didn't retire from the Dodgers, I got fired. And not just for drinking—for being so drunk that I pissed in the mascot's uniform."

"Sort of funny," Dash admitted.

"And then shit in the umpire's hat."

Dash held back a laugh. "Still funny."

"We are not different, Dash. I've just worked to forgive myself, while you're not there yet. You continue to punish, but don't be like Kitty. Be your own best friend. You have to be, otherwise you're going to lose the woman you love."

Dash stared at Chris and knew his friend wasn't just saying these things to try to make him feel better. Chris genuinely believed in Dash. But Dash couldn't yet see a world where he'd believe in himself.

When they arrived at the rehab center, a valet placed all of Dash's luggage on a cart. Dash and Chris hugged goodbye and made promises to see each other at the first open visitation. As his friend's car drove off, Dash reached into his pocket and pulled out the folded piece of paper Sophie had given him.

When he unfolded it, a shirtless Richard Gere stared back.

37

SOPHIE

It had been over a week since Dash had left for rehab, and Sophie hadn't been able to communicate with him during that time. Not because she hadn't wanted to, but the center required a tech detox for the first half of the stay.

So she'd buckled down on writing and poured every single feeling she'd had for Dash into the book she'd started at the spa with him, when they'd first begun to like each other. She was almost to the end, just past the all-is-lost moment, and should've been able to see her way to the happily-ever-after finish line...

But she'd gotten stuck, again, and couldn't seem to write her way out of it. Instead of wallowing in the self-pity she'd grown used to whenever the writer's block hit, though, she got out of the house and took herself on the bookish date of her dreams to try to clear the debris.

Sophie got off the subway at the Culver City stop and made her way down the stairs to the street, where she'd take a short walk to the bookstore she loved most. The Ripped Bodice was just off the main downtown street, with a pink storefront and an enormous glass window with rotating and impressive displays. Their current summer window was no exception, with the bottom covered in sand and book-sized beach chairs holding copies of recent summer releases. A glittery rainbow sun hung over the top and twinkled in the afternoon light.

The door of the bookshop dinged as she walked through, and the familiar warmth of the place made her smile. A few shoppers browsed the aisles as Sophie walked through the store. She allowed her fingers to skim the spines of the fantasy-romance section and stopped at a copy of a new Regency romp she'd seen a lot of chatter about on Instagram. She decided to take the book home with her and brought it to the register.

"Sophie?" The woman behind the register recognized her, and Sophie instantly brightened as she set the book on the counter. "It's been a while!"

"The window display is fantastic," Sophie said.

"I'd love to have your next book up there." She waved to the window as she rung up Sophie's purchase. "When can we expect another from you?"

"Hopefully soon." Sophie nodded, and she felt those words so deeply that it sent a rush through her. Her book was technically due the next day, but she'd already prepped her agent that the book she'd agreed to write—the meteorologist who falls for the storm chaser—wouldn't be what she was turning in. If she was lucky, she'd find a way to finish the new book and cross her fingers that her editor would like this unexpected surprise.

"Good to hear." The bookseller shrugged happily and smiled as she handed a bag with the book to Sophie.

As Sophie turned and walked toward the exit, she felt a new energy ripple through her. A kind of motivation to have another book on the shelves of this store that had meant so much to her. She'd dreamed of being the kind of author a store like The Ripped Bodice would carry. And here they were, encouraging her to write more. She wasn't going to let this be the end of her story. She had a book nearly finished, and she planned to get to the end this time.

She made her way to the boba tea store down the block, ordered an oat milk boba for fuel, and sat at a cozy booth to write.

There was no hesitation when she cracked open her laptop. She had a fully charged battery, enough caffeine to fuel a jet plane, and fingers that were anxious to type. She was going to finish her new book, the one that was, more or less, about her and Dash.

A grumpy-sunshine, best-friend's-brother story, all set in a spa. And the hero had tattoos and piercing blue eyes. And the main character was a wavy-haired health nut who had a Cinderella-esque charm over animals. She'd already written the loose framework—a humiliating meet cute, being forced to help each other, only one bed, and outside circumstances that took them apart. And as she sat, she started in on the ending she wanted her characters to have.

She found herself exploring the issues she'd faced through her TikTok experiment while she wrote. Her main character, like Sophie, was a people pleaser to her core and wanted everyone to like her. When things got hard, she bailed instead of dealing with the issues. But she was also a hopeless romantic with grand, sweeping dreams of what love could look like. And the hero of the book was able to make those dreams a reality. With him by her side, she was finally able to acknowledge what *she* wanted because he encouraged her to be exactly who she was.

She wrote until her fingers hurt and drank three bobas, shaking from the caffeine. But she felt wildly invigorated and knew that she could complete the book. She was going to finish this one, and her characters would get to live happily-ever-after, even if she and Dash didn't.

It's not that she'd lost all hope of them ever being together, but she also planned to respect whatever Dash wanted for himself once he got through his treatment plan. As she stood from the booth and packed up her things, she took out her phone, too. There was a text from Nina: a selfie of her, with Leo in the background as he assembled what looked to be a crib.

I'm going to have to hire someone to redo this so the thing doesn't collapse, but it's cute that he's trying, right???

Sophie sent a thumbs-up back.

On her walk back to the subway, Sophie felt sure of herself, which was something she hadn't experienced in a long time. She was going to publish this new book—she just knew it— and she would write more books.

She stopped outside the window of a tattoo parlor. There were sample designs hanging from a board and, when she looked in, an artist gave her a smile. Sophie decided to just duck her head in to check the space out.

"Hey, we're closing in thirty, but what can I do for you?" The woman wiped down a chair with a clean cloth as she spoke.

"I was thinking I might, uh, get my first tattoo?" Sophie's voice went up a bit higher as she said the words because, she realized, she actually *did* want one.

Sophie felt one hundred percent sure that the tattoo she planned to get would be one she would never regret. It would have meaning, and importance, and she trusted herself to do this. For the first time in her life, she trusted everything she was doing.

And it was then that she realized something else: she loved Dash. She was in love with Dash.

"Oh, well, for something this momentous, I think I can stay open a bit longer." The woman stood up with the rag at her side and took Sophie in. "What did you have in mind?"

Now that she knew she loved Dash, she couldn't wait to tell him. She just hoped his feelings hadn't changed. "One sec," she told the artist.

Sophie took out her phone and typed in Dash's name. She'd sent him a photo of Richard the Squirrel every day since he'd been gone. She knew he wouldn't see anything from her until after his tech detox was complete, but still, she sent him one more.

Can I come visit you?

38

DASH

Dash had never been a morning person, but that didn't seem to matter at The Well Center, because every morning at six he was woken by soothing bells and a light in his room that grew brighter over the course of ten minutes until he was finally surrounded by enough illumination to rival the Vegas Strip.

He'd also never collected chicken eggs, but there he was, standing in a henhouse with a basket gently gathering them up.

"Pardon me, Shirley," he said to a red-speckled hen. He'd come to know the ladies over the course of the last two weeks, visiting them every morning as part of his daily tasks, and bringing the eggs to the center's chef who would then use them as part of the breakfast-omelet selections.

And, he had to admit, there was a certain joy in getting to know his ten chicken friends—their names, their different markings, and their attitudes. Tia always seemed pleased to see him and even allowed a few gentle pets across her feathers, whereas Heather actively tried to chase him out with a series of pecks to his hands.

Still, he enjoyed the work, if only to keep his mind away from how completely and utterly he'd messed up his life.

"Now, Heather, we do this same dance every morning. I come in, you scowl, I reach for an egg, and you make an attempt on my life. Do you think we could try something new? Maybe you look away, I reach in, and we just pretend I was never here?" The hen only seemed to burrow deeper into the nest and on top of her egg.

Still, Dash reached under her and, as predicted, she viciously pecked at his hand. When he didn't flee the coop, the chicken took his inaction as a sign to move on to phase two, which involved flying out of her nest directly at him. Dash ran for the door of the henhouse and escaped before Heather was able to follow.

"No offense, but you take way too long with those eggs, and I'm starving." Geon was one of the program's directors and, more immediately, made sure Dash did his job.

He wasn't Dash's babysitter, exactly, but he wasn't *not* watching over Dash. And he was a big guy—well over six feet and built like a former football player, because he had been a pro baller before having an addiction problem and cofounding the program—so Dash wasn't about to mess with him.

"Heather doesn't like me," Dash said as he brushed a rogue feather from his shirt. "I don't know what to say about it."

"Have you tried giving her a blueberry?"

Dash sighed. Blueberries, for some reason, reminded him of Richard the Squirrel. And Sophie. But, then again, everything reminded him of Sophie. "No. Why would I have tried that?"

"I mean, I did leave a pamphlet in your welcome packet with fun facts about the animals here, but clearly not everyone is as voracious a reader as I'd hoped." Geon gave him a side smile as they walked. "Chickens have their little treats, like how you love cookies, and she loves a nice blueberry every now and then."

"I'll try the blueberry thing," he eventually said.

Dash shook his head as they approached the center and wondered what Sophie would think of this whole situation. She'd probably love knowing that a chicken was keeping him on his toes. He wished he could tell her about it, but he'd been on a tech freeze for the last two weeks. Today was the day, though, when he'd finally get to check his phone and talk to her.

But first, he had therapy.

"Is there anything specific you want to work on this morning?" his therapist, Jerome, asked.

Since Dash had entered rehab, he and Jerome had worked on the painful memories that had triggered him to want to drink again. Along with forgiving himself for all of the damage he'd caused while drunk. But part of his therapy involved reliving those memories so that the pain and trauma from them lessened each time he brought them up.

Of course, most of his memories involved situations with his parents, being on set, and some very specific instances with Reece. But today, he wanted to talk about what life outside of rehab would look like and, more specifically, what a life with Sophie could be.

"I brought in my Looking Forward worksheet." Dash reached into the pocket of his jeans and pulled out the piece of paper he'd been given a few days into recovery. It asked him to imagine what he wanted to accomplish upon leaving and how the center could help prepare him to meet those goals.

Jerome took the paper and began to read. "You'd like to sell your ceramics."

"I would." Dash looked down at his hands in his lap, which clenched and unclenched. Sophie had told him that he could sell what he made, and those words had stuck with him and become a fantasy all their own.

"You want to forgive yourself for relapsing."

"That would be nice."

"And you want to try to have a relationship?"

"Yes." Dash exhaled sharply. "I don't know if I'm ready to be the person Sophie needs me to be, but I want to be who she thinks I am."

"Who does she think you are?"

"A good person."

"And you're not a good person?"

Dash didn't love these chats, where he made a statement and then it was, essentially, repeated back to him, but they were effective. "She made me feel like I could be a better person."

"Did she ever ask you to change who you were?"

Dash thought about that, but she never had. Not once. "No."

"Maybe, then, you're putting unrealistic expectations on yourself. It sounds like Sophie has accepted you as you are, but you've decided that she's wrong to love you. Remember what we've been talking about. You need to forgive yourself. You're not defined by your mistakes."

Dash exhaled as he took those words in and knew they were true. He needed to allow Sophie to love him if he ever had any chance of having her in his life.

When Dash got back to his room, which was more like a suite at the Four Seasons—complete with California king bed, a soaker tub, and floor-to-ceiling views of the mountains— he thought about whether he could be the man he needed to be for Sophie. Sophie, who'd never specifically asked him to change any part of himself. Sophie, who'd seen him at an incredibly low point, and was still there for him. Sophie, who never judged him.

But that was then, and now that they'd been apart for two weeks, maybe she'd had time to reevaluate whether Dash was worth all the effort she put in. Maybe she'd reconsidered her time with Carla, or just decided to be on her own and give up Dash completely. Whatever her decision, he wanted to hear what she had to say, and he was ready to open himself up fully to her.

A knock on his door made him stand. He went and found Geon holding out a bag. "Cell phone time. You've got thirty minutes to make calls and text. We restrict emails and browsing, so this will just be to connect with your people. And, uh, sorry, there's no porn either, but if you need something for that, we can arrange."

Dash chuckled as he took the bag. "I'm all good. Thanks for looking out, though."

"My job is so weird sometimes." Geon shrugged his big shoulders and turned to walk to the next door of the center's residential wing.

Dash closed the door behind him, took out his phone, and swiped it open. There were lots of text messages and voice mails. He looked through the call list and didn't see anything from Sophie, then went into his texts and saw her name there with a string of Richard the Squirrel photos and a new message waiting.

Sophie: Can I come visit you?

He let out a shuddering breath and braced his hand against the wall. Yes, he wanted to see her desperately, but what kind of a visit was this going to be? Was she mad at him? Would she be happy to see him? He needed to be truthful with her—that much he knew—but he didn't want to put her in an awkward position either. He treaded carefully.

Yes, please come. I miss you. Are you doing okay? Are we okay?

He hit Send and waited for a reply.
As he waited, he went through the other messages he had. There was a voice mail from Poppy.

I really miss you, you dumb asshat. I know I'm supposed to be supporting you right now and, for the record, I am. I went in on

Kitty and Reece and Dad so aggressively that I lost my voice. But I wish you were here and not at some unreachable place. Can you please get better and come back and never do this to me again? Please?

A voice mail from his dad. *Dash, I just want you to know that I love you. I…I didn't know your mother leaked the story to the press. If I'd known…it wouldn't have happened. I am so sorry, my boy.*

Something about his dad's voice made Dash believe he was telling the truth, though that didn't necessarily make him feel any better.

There were voice mails, plural, from his mother. He almost deleted them before listening, but some sick curiosity got the better of him.

Voice mail 1: I know you told me not to call. But your sister tells me you've checked into a facility. I'll make sure to keep this out of the press. And…well, I'm sorry.

Voice mail 2: As an update—I've set up family therapy sessions for myself, your father, Poppy, and Reece. They're replacing our weekly dinners and will hopefully allow us to better support you when you return. I do hope you'll forgive me.

Voice mail 3: We had our first family therapy session which, as expected, did not go well. Your father is not keen on opening up, and I'm not particularly used to it either. Poppy seems to be enjoying herself, and Reece is doing his share, too. Dad and I will continue to work on this.

Dash hesitated, but then deleted her voice mails. He was glad she was getting therapy—long overdue—but ultimately, he wasn't ready to give her another chance, and he wasn't sure if he'd ever be.

And then there were many, many texts from Chris.

I'm helping your family transition into support mode. Set them up with an Al-Anon counselor. They seem open to the suggestions.

Just so you know, your family is sort of...wild.

Poppy offered to give me Reiki?

I know this will probably not help, but Reece is very dreamy. Did you know that?

Your mom has intense momager energy.

Your dad is very quiet, which I was not expecting!

I checked the mail and, well, Dash the Doll was waiting for me! I told the police that Cindy violated her restraining order, and they're going to file a report. But, honestly, this thing is adorable. She's a very talented crafter and stalker!

Dash liked all the texts except the Dash doll one, to which he gave a thumbs-down. He then texted Poppy a middle finger emoji with no other context, and also texted Reece to wish him luck on the film he'd started to shoot. Yes, Dash had some unresolved tension with his brother, but that simmering anger was something his mom had stoked for years. And maybe now that Dash had cut her out, he and Reece could find a way back to just being brothers, rather than competitors.

But there was still no response back from Sophie. Not even a read-receipt confirmation. A knock sounded at the door, and when he answered, Geon was there waiting. "Can I make one quick call? It will only take a minute."

"Sure." Geon glanced down the hall. "I'll go collect some-one else's phone, then circle back. I hate that phrase, *circle back*, but it really gets the job done."

Dash closed the door, then hit the Call icon next to Sophie's name. He waited for a ring, but the call went straight to voice mail. All he left on the message was "Richard Gere and I miss you," then hung up. Geon came back and Dash handed his phone over.

The next day was Visitor's Day. If Sophie came, he'd know they were okay, but if she didn't? Well, he'd have more things to talk about in therapy.

39

SOPHIE

Sophie had never really done a grand, romantic gesture before. She'd read plenty of them and seen loads more in rom-coms. But for Dash, the man she was in love with, she wanted the first time to be special.

"This is not all going to fit into my car." Nina stood in the driveway, with the trunk of her luxury sedan popped. "Balloons take up a lot of space."

"You should've gone for the biodegradable confetti, like I suggested." Poppy twirled a piece of her long, blond hair and gave an I-told-you-so look back.

But nothing, not even balloon shame, was going to get Sophie down. Not today, because it was Visitor's Day with Dash, and she'd finally be able to say the words she'd never told a partner before. She'd missed his phone call, but she was going to give them both the happily-ever-after they deserved, whether he knew it or not.

"You both know this is the most important day of my life, right?" Sophie walked down the porch steps and made her way to the car, carrying a giant cake box.

"Well, you once told me that getting Rain Boots at the state fair was the most important day of your life, so forgive me for being a little dubious." Poppy hip-checked Sophie, and Sophie stumbled before righting herself. "But I think it's really sweet that you're doing all this for Dash. He's probably going to shit himself."

"Now, there's an image I didn't want." Nina grimaced and sipped from the to-go coffee cup in her hands.

Sophie managed to fit the cake box between a container of tea lights and a giant bag of sour gummy worms. "Okay!" She clapped her hands. "I'm ready."

The grin that crossed her face was almost as big as the balloon banner she'd have to close into the trunk.

"You're forgetting something." Poppy waved Sophie's phone at her.

Sophie grabbed the phone with a knowing look. "I just need five minutes."

Poppy and Nina settled themselves into the front and passenger seats of the car as Sophie made her way to the avocado tree. She was going to record a final TikTok video to close out her *romance author who'd never been in love* series. Because, as her audience was about to find out, she had fallen in love...

SOPHIE'S TIKTOK
Relationship status: Complicated
Times I've fallen in love: 1
Happily-ever-afters written: 1

Sophie stood in front of the bare avocado tree, a bitten and shirtless Richard Gere dangling by a thread next to her. She smiled to the camera as she began to talk.

"It's been a little while since I've posted an update video. Two weeks, if we're counting. And if you've been following along, then you know my book was due a few days ago. And I did turn a book in to my agent! Yay!"

Sophie bit her lip as she shrugged to the camera. "It's just not the one I was under contract for. So, yeah, I finished a book. And I'm really excited for you to hopefully get to read it someday. It was inspired by my first time falling in love. All of which never would've happened if I hadn't started making these videos in the first place.

"So you might be wondering about why I put my relationship status in the corner there as *complicated*." Sophie pointed to the text on the screen. "The truth is that I am in love, but the person I love is dealing with a lot of personal things they have to work out. And as much as I'd like to be with them, I'm giving them the space they need. I don't know if we'll be together at the end. But I do know that I have my happily-ever-after, because I love them, and that's all I need."

40

DASH

Dash woke up early, as the chiming bells and bright light demanded. He went through the motions and made coffee, drank a cup as he waited for the hot water in the shower to kick in, put on fresh clothes, brushed his teeth, and combed his hair, then finished a final sip of coffee while he stared out the window and watched the sun rise.

He made his way down to the communal snack room and grabbed a handful of blueberries, then walked to the animal pens. He took his basket into the henhouse, fed Heather a blueberry—though she had no new eggs for him—then collected eggs from the others. He had breakfast. He went to individual therapy, then group. But mostly, he was waiting for four o'clock to roll around—visiting hours.

In the late afternoon, Dash typically hit the gym and the occasional art class. They even had a state-of-the-art kiln on site.

But he was really, really hoping to see Sophie. He wanted to know if anything had changed, regardless of what it meant for them as a couple. Not being able to be near her for two weeks had left a dull ache in his core. Reminders of her came in bits and pieces: the sound of her infectious laugh, or the thick strands of wavy hair that fell across her eyes and the black lashes that hid underneath them. When he was struck with a memory, he felt consumed by the need to go see her. But he couldn't, because he hadn't been able to control himself and his emotions, and now he was starting over again.

"Dash, there's a package for you. I left it in your room." Geon shuffled through a stack of letters and didn't look up as Dash nodded and headed for the stairs.

When Dash got back to his room, the world's smallest gift bag was on his bed, matte black and the size of his palm. When he peered inside, there was a single neon gummy worm. He picked up the worm and studied it. Was this a joke? There was a small card next to the bag and, when he opened it, a message.

Want more? Follow the clues. Your first one: karaoke.

Dash looked up. There *was* a karaoke machine in the game room. He took the stairs down and headed there. When he reached the game room, he walked past two members who were deep in a game of Scrabble and jogged directly to the machine, which had another, but larger, gift bag resting on top. There were two gummy worms this time, and he read the next clue as he chewed one.

I never would've gotten to know you had it not been for my sad night out. And you impressed me with your ability to lift...

He raised his eyebrow. He *had* carried Sophie into her place... The work-out room! He popped the second gummy worm into his mouth and headed to the work-out center. He raced past the row of treadmills and ellipticals, past the Pilates machines, and straight to the free weights, where he spotted another gift bag, slightly larger, along with a note.

You aren't perfect, and neither am I, but I adore every imperfect part of you just as much as the perfect ones. I've even begun to watch your favorite show, Dating Roulette, *despite how much time they spend by...*

The pool. Lord, the singles were always by the pool. Dash plucked out three gummy worms, ate them all at once, and ran out of the work-out room and toward the pool. When he got outside, he ran past benches and tables where other people in the program were already meeting and spending time with their loved ones. He couldn't waste another moment without seeing her. He ran as fast as he could toward the pool, which was perched on top of a hill that overlooked the mountainsides. When he got there, bags of candy were scattered around the deck like roses. A giant balloon arch curved over the top of a table, and on the table were bowls of various kinds of gummy candies. But the most important thing was missing: Sophie.

"Soph?" he called out as he walked the perimeter of the pool. "Sophie?"

"I'm coming!" she called back to him.

He frowned as he looked over the hedges surrounding the pool. He searched and eventually saw her climbing up the hill, carrying a large box. She smiled up to him and his eyes began to sting with the threat of tears.

He hadn't known how much his body had missed her until he saw her there. She was radiant, in a deep emerald sundress with a plunging neckline. And he was grateful they were up so high, because the wind coming off the mountains sent a breeze that blew her dress tightly around her so he could see the gorgeous lines of her curves. He saw nothing but her as he sprinted. When he reached her, he took the box out of her hands, set it down beside them, then lifted her up. She wrapped her legs around his waist and pressed her mouth to his. He tasted salt and lemons and the sweetest kiss he'd ever known.

They eventually pulled apart, and she looked into his eyes and said, "I didn't realize you'd figure out the clues so quickly. I had to run in these wedges just to catch up. I'm exhausted!"

"I couldn't help but run. I'll always run toward you from now on."

"I'll make sure not to scale any mountains from now on, then." She beamed at him.

He laughed.

"I saw your text." She ran a hand through his hair, mussing it up and curling her fingertips against his scalp. "And we're okay, since you asked."

"Good." He smiled widely at her. "What's this?" He pulled her arm away and gawked at the ink he saw on her wrist—what looked to be a deep black line and a small turquoise heart just above it.

"I got a tattoo." She shrugged, like it was no big deal that he'd been gone for two weeks and she suddenly had a tat.

"What, uh, what is it of?" He twisted her arm slightly to examine the design.

"It's an em-dash, which is my favorite kind of punctuation to use. But the em-dash is also misunderstood and some people kind of hate it. I think it's a bit of a rebel without a clause, though."

"Oh, my God, talk grammar to me." He hugged her in tighter. "And the heart?"

"Well, whenever I use an em-dash now, I can't help but think of how you helped bring me back to my writing. And, you know, your name. I added the little blue heart, because it's the color of your eyes, and I do love those eyes. But to me, this tattoo symbolizes how much I love you."

He looked at her then, and she smiled back at him. "I love you, Dash Montrose."

They both stilled, but he placed his hand on her cheek and rubbed his thumb in slow circles, as he realized that Sophie was saying these words for the first time...and to him.

"This is..." He was at a loss. He hadn't known that *I love you* would be a massive turn-on, but he was definitely hard.

"Dash, no, not yet." She pointed an accusatory finger at his pants. "I have a speech I memorized to whisk you off your feet! And you know how great I am with speeches."

"Well, who am I to deny an award-winning speechwriter?" He set Sophie down on the ground, and she took his hands in hers as she looked into his eyes.

"Okay." She shook out her shoulders before she finally looked up at him. The world slowed as he saw himself reflected in her eyes, and there was nothing but love. "Dash, in the places where we've both been broken, being together makes me feel whole. As soon as I fell in love with you, I knew I couldn't be without you. I've never been in love before, but I know what love is because of you. I write about people falling in love. I fantasize about what that feels like for my job. But I did not realize how much sweeter the reality of loving someone else would be. It will be impossible to fully capture what loving you feels like for a book, but I tried."

Then she turned to pick up the box, which was wrapped in a matte black bow, and handed it to him. He untied the bow and opened the box to discover a stack of pages—a new manuscript. *Her* new manuscript. The title across the top page read *Second Chance Summer*.

"This is our story?" he asked.

"It's *inspired* by our story," Sophie clarified. "Though, I think our happily-ever-after will be much better."

"I love you," Dash said without thinking. "I will love you for the rest of our lives, and I will do everything I can to make you happy."

He brought her into him and held her face in his hands. She looked to him as she said, "And I will never leave you, Dash. Even when things get hard, I will be here."

He wove his fingers through her hair, and she wrapped her arms around his back. She tilted her chin up to meet his mouth, but he said, "I don't want to crack a joke."

"Then, don't." Her voice was throaty, and her nails dug into his shoulder blades.

"But you said *even when things get hard...*" He pressed his hardness against her, and she rolled her eyes, but a smile crossed her lips.

"I love you, despite that joke." She laughed.

And then he kissed her, and she kissed him back. And he knew that all the roads he'd been down, the broken and bruised ones, had all led him to her, and he would never regret that.

EPILOGUE

ONE YEAR LATER

Sophie stood outside the entrance to Seize the Clay, the pottery studio slash showroom Dash had opened a month prior. The windows were lined with matte bowls, etched flowerpots, ornate wall art, and dishes so flawless they resembled a layered cake when stacked together. Each piece was a work of art and handcrafted by her *boyfriend*.

Today was the pub day of her book, *Second Chance Summer*, which her editor had, thankfully, agreed to read and liked enough to publish. So while Sophie had a busy day of visiting local indie bookstores to sign copies of her book, she wanted to make a stop to see Dash first.

A horn beeped, and she looked over to see Poppy at the driver's seat of her electric sports car. "Come on, go smooch my brother, and let's get this book tour on the road!" Poppy slid her aviators down her nose and gave Sophie a warm smirk.

Poppy had offered to drive Sophie from bookstore to bookstore for her release day. And they planned to have dinner with their family—Dash, Jasmine, Nina, Leo, Baby Olive, Sophie, and Poppy—at Pink Metal that night to celebrate. Dash was still working through issues with his parents and Reece, but they'd formed their own little found family, which was more than enough.

"Sorry!" Sophie made a show of cringing. "I got distracted by all of the shiny new mugs in the window."

"If you see something good in there, tell Dash I need it for the spa!" Poppy had started selling Dash's jewelry dishes before his store ever opened. When they'd sold out within a week, he had the motivation he needed to finally open his own place. But he still gave Poppy exclusive items that only Glow could sell.

"On it." Sophie saluted her. Then she took her phone out of the pocket of her dress and started to record.

SOPHIE'S TIKTOK
Relationship Status: Taken
Occupation: HEA Author
Days until book publishes: 0

Sophie opened the door to Seize the Clay, and as she walked in, she inhaled deeply. "Ah, gotta love that fresh scent of clay, and mud, and whatever else it is that makes a pottery studio smell so good. It's *almost* as good as the smell of a new book."

Sophie held up a copy of *her* book, which had an illustrated cover of a man and woman in spa robes. She smelled it to emphasize her point. "Happy pub day to my latest book baby, *Second Chance Summer*. I hope you all grab a copy from your local bookstore or library. I'm just dropping one off here to my favorite person in the world."

She panned the camera slightly, and there was Dash, waving a clay-covered hand while he smiled back. "Happy pub day!" He made an effort to jump excitedly, though he was in the middle of working on something.

"What's that in your hand, Dash?" she asked.

"This old thing?" He held up a wet piece of clay. "I'm pulling a handle for a jug." Dash pointed to the clay jug just behind him. He went back to stretching the line of clay the way you might some dough, pulling down on the end until it was long. The way that he had his hand at the top of the clay, then pulled down over and over again reminded her of, well, a different kind of hand job.

"This is like craft porn, right?" she said softly to the camera.

"I heard that!" he called out to her. "And yes, there's a fetish for this. Which I get."

"Well, that's a perfect segue for me to announce that my next book will be about a potter! They say you should write what you know, and what I know is that pottery is wildly sexy. And so is my next book. You can preorder it now at the link in my bio."

"I've read it. Twice. It's awesome." Dash nodded a warm and genuinely proud smile to the camera.

"Isn't he the best?" Sophie's eyes stung with happy tears, but she blinked them back. "And remember, you can follow

Dash on TikTok at @tokcrafty2me, and Seize the Clay studio @SeizetheClay on Instagram."

Then she ended the video, pocketed her phone, and moved toward her man. "How was that?" she asked.

He wiped his hands on a nearby towel, took off his apron, and closed the space between them. "I definitely liked when you told everyone I was the best." He pulled her into him. "You should keep doing that."

His lips met hers, and those jittery flutters she'd felt so many months ago for him were still there. He loved her, and he made sure she knew it every day.

She pulled back from him and said, "Keep on kissing me, and maybe I will."

"We can do more than kiss, you know." He raised a brow. "The stockroom in the back has a lock on the door. I can put up the Closed sign, lock the front, and then we could…"

A loud honk interrupted him, and they both turned to see Poppy glaring from her car window.

"My carriage is about to turn into a pumpkin." Sophie sighed.

"We can be quick." Dash walked to the front door, put the Closed sign up, and locked it, as he'd promised. "Come on, Soph, let me give you a proper celebratory kiss. It can be any-where you want."

Then he winked at her as he took her hand and led them to the back room, and she knew that no matter what they went through, he was the person who would make her happy for the rest of her life.

★ ★ ★ ★ ★

ACKNOWLEDGMENTS

I approached Dash and Sophie's journey with the utmost care and empathy, consulting with others to make sure this felt as authentic as possible. Thank you to the sensitivity and beta readers who helped me along the way. And if any of Dash's journey resonated with you and you feel you may need help, there are invaluable resources and support groups available.

Writing Dash and Sophie's love story has not only been a true joy, but also a personal journey for me. This book has helped me acknowledge so many parts of myself and explore my own identity. Thank you to everyone who came along with me on this ride and took the time to read my book!

And I wouldn't have this book without the support of those who read *For Butter or Worse*. If you read my debut, posted about it on social, wrote a review or reached out to tell me your thoughts—thank you so much. There are truly no words to describe how meaningful that launch was to me, and how much that support has meant.

I need to thank Brittany Lavery, who encouraged me to pursue writing this story in the first place. It was the book I was most terrified to write—the idea was kind of complicated!—but I'm so glad I did.

Lynn Raposo has been a truly fantastic editor and champion of my writing. Thank you so much for your continued encouragement, guidance and being an advocate for my work. I totally adore you!

Jessica Errera is, without a doubt, the absolute best agent. I am obsessed with her. Thank you for tirelessly working to help me make writing a career—please don't ever leave me!

I really also loved writing Richard ("Dick"), the squirrel, and must thank fellow romance author, Allison Ashley, for coming up with the name!

One of the best parts of publishing *For Butter or Worse* was the great excuse to meet fellow romance authors, and it's been so deeply helpful to talk about writing this book with Amy Spalding, Courtney Kae, Kate Spencer, Lacie Waldon, Taylor Hahn, Bridget Morrissey, and Noué Kirwan.

And finally, to my Eoghan: I love you very much and can't thank you enough for building a life with me that allows room for my creativity, our family, and dreams. I write books to try to impress you. Is it working?!